Sulu, Swordsman.

The bandit yelled in pain and Sulu slid his blade free. There was blood on the point. From somewhere to his left, another bandit screamed—Urmi's work. The prince was still busy with Lord Tayu.

Panting for breath, Sulu turned back to the other bandits. But they weren't nearly as enthusiastic as they had been before. Finally, a large man with a huge cutlass started toward Sulu. And Sulu tensed. The man's cutlass was large enough to break Sulu's own blade if he wasn't careful. But on the other hand, it ought to be a clumsier weapon. It would be a test of Sulu's own quickness—and perhaps his luck. . . .

Look for STAR TREK Fiction from Pocket Books

Star Trek: The Original Series

Star Trek: The Next Generation

SHADOW LORD

LAURENCE YEP

A STAR TREK® NOVEL

POCKET BOOKS

New York   London   Toronto   Sydney   Tokyo

An *Original* Publication of POCKET BOOKS

POCKET BOOKS, a division of Simon & Schuster Inc.
1230 Avenue of the Americas, New York, NY 10020

STAR TREK is a Registered Trademark of
Paramount Pictures Corporation.

This book is published by Pocket Books, a division of
Simon & Schuster Inc., under exclusive license from
Paramount Pictures Corporation.

ISBN:0-671-66087-X

First Pocket Books printing March 1985

10 9 8 7 6 5

POCKET and colophon are trademarks of
Simon & Schuster Inc.

Printed in the U.S.A.

To my brother,
Spike,
who went to all those
samurai and kung fu movies
with me

PROLOGUE

McCoy tugged at the collar of his dress tunic. "I don't think I'll ever get used to these blasted monkey suits, Jim. Why can't we just let Mr. Spock meet Prince Vikram? He enjoys being uncomfortable. Let him stand around all day in one of these things."

Mr. Spock coolly arched an eyebrow. "Comfort has nothing to do with diplomacy."

"You're always so conscientious about watching my weight." Captain Kirk self-consciously smoothed his own tunic over his stomach. "Maybe you ought to take your own advice and take off a few pounds, Bones."

"But I'm just here to fill out the crowd on the stage." McCoy swept his hand around the transporter room. "A mannequin would serve just as well."

"And provide just as much intelligent conversation," Mr. Spock added.

McCoy leaned back against the wall. "Tell me one thing, Spock. If normal human conversation bothers you so much, why don't you transfer to a ship with a

Vulcan crew? What little conversation they hold should be rarefied enough for you."

Mr. Spock's face was a rigid mask. "I'm also partly human, Doctor."

McCoy straightened. "Well, you'd never know it from the way you act." He wagged his index finger at Mr. Spock as if a new inspiration had come to him. "Or do you remain here because you hate yourself so much?" McCoy spread out his hands. "Is that it, Spock? Is this all some elaborate form of punishment?"

Kirk frowned at the doctor. Sometimes there was a fine line between McCoy's needling and actual brow-beating. "What does it matter as long as we've got the best science officer in the fleet?"

McCoy held out his left palm and then smacked the back of his right hand into it. "But it's the right of every sentient creature to be content. It's right there in the Fundamental Declaration of the Martian Colonies. And yet Spock can't be very happy here."

Mr. Spock looked away absently—the way he did when he was intrigued by an especially difficult problem. "I have never really considered the matter before this."

McCoy stared at Mr. Spock as if he suspected he was being set up for some sort of retort; but when Mr. Spock remained lost in thought, McCoy could only shake his head. "All that knowledge inside that computer brain of yours and you haven't ever considered the most obvious question?"

Kirk fiddled with his sleeve. "I'm less interested in philosophy at this moment than I am in fashion. I've got the feeling that we're all going to be underdressed compared to His Highness. Did you hear how many trunks he beamed over from the passenger liner? He's probably got enough clothes to outfit all of Angira."

"At least, it was enough to fill up an extra room," Scotty offered. "My back's still aching from helping to carry all of them."

"Why didn't you assign some yeomen to the duty?" Kirk demanded.

Scotty spread his arms helplessly. "But the trunks just kept coming and coming. I couldna have them cluttering up the transporter room."

"I'll examine you after the reception," McCoy promised. "Don't worry. I won't charge overtime."

"And in the meantime, Doctor?" Scotty pressed a hand to the small of his back.

"Take two double scotches," the doctor smiled.

"Just be glad it was trunks of clothes," Mr. Spock advised Scotty. "As the son of an absolute ruler of an entire planet, he's probably used to indulging every whim. You're lucky it wasn't a menagerie."

"Good Lord," McCoy said in alarm, "I just had a terrible thought. If he has that many outfits, is he going to expect formal dress every night?"

Kirk examined a plate of what looked like miniature candied trees but were actually sea worms still within their thin casings. "The Federation wants to make sure that the prince's return trip to Angira is as comfortable as possible. And if that means formal dress all the way, then that's what we'll do." He sampled one of the worms and, finding it tasty, took another. "Cheer up, Bones. You'll be dining out for years on how you entertained Prince Vikram."

"And I'll be able to show them the scars from this blasted collar."

"Put in for medical disability then," Kirk said and signed for them to be quiet as the door slid open.

"Greetings, ladies and gentlemen." Prince Vikram, ninth in line to the throne of Angira, wriggled his fingertips at them. Though his arms and pear-shaped torso were about the same proportions as a human's, most of his two and a half meters of height seemed to be taken up by his long, muscular legs.

His fur was soft and golden on his arms and legs, but the fur on his face had been raised in sharp hennaed spikes so that his large, mascaraed eyes seemed to be set within a rayed circle. With his head tapering to an angular chin, he gave the appearance of a rather dissipated lemur.

But his vest of black leather was scuffed and muddied and one leg of his orange and red checkered shorts was torn. And there was only one boot on his leg. "You must excuse my dress, but I came straight here from the most amusing little pub on the liner."

Though Kirk had seen stranger costumes, he hadn't been expecting the prince to be dressed this way, so it took him a moment to recover. "If . . . if Your Highness wishes to refresh yourself—"

"Nonsense, I live for temptation." Prince Vikram had to stoop to enter through the doorway and headed straight for the buffet table.

"Use a plate, Your Highness." A middle-aged Angiran with the ramrod posture of an old soldier stepped into the room. But in contrast to the prince, he wore no makeup and was dressed in a plain set of red coveralls.

"My hands are large enough, Bibil." The prince had already began to snatch things from the table with his right hand and set them on his left palm.

Bibil took the hors d'oeuvres from the prince's palm and set them on the plate. "You don't want to make these people think that Angirans are savages."

The prince stiffened as if he had just been lashed. Apparently it was an old argument between the prince and his servant. "But they *are* savage."

"We still know about plates." He thrust one toward the prince. "So take this."

The prince licked his fingertips and smiled tolerantly. He took the plate and turned to the officers of the *Enterprise*. "Please, let me introduce you to Bibil, who sometimes is my servant and sometimes my nursemaid and sometimes my keeper."

"And trainer," Bibil announced. "We will need facilities so the prince can practice his fencing." He fixed them with a stern eye as if he were prepared to convert the room at that moment into a gymnasium.

"Yes, you never know whom I might insult when I go home." The prince scooped several hors d'oeuvres into his mouth and began to munch happily.

McCoy folded his arms skeptically as if he did not expect anything nearly so serious from the outlandish prince. "Well, the closest thing we have to a cutlery expert is Sulu here."

"It's just foils mainly," Sulu said.

"Good enough," Bibil grunted. "We need to develop his eye and hand again and something quick like that is just the thing."

"Well"—Kirk clapped his hands together and continued to hold them that way—"we have all the facilities you might need; and what weapons we don't have, we can have made up to your specifications." He strolled over to the buffet table and picked up a plate. "Will that suffice?"

The prince scanned the table critically. "Personally, I would prefer political asylum."

The corners of Kirk's mouth turned up slightly as if he were trying to treat that as a joke; but the prince seemed quite serious. "I thought Your Highness would want to go home after all these years."

The prince gave Kirk a sad smile. "It is no kindness to take a boy from a limbo of ignorance and teach him to enjoy the pleasures of paradise only to exile him back to limbo again."

"But the opportunities are immense." Mr. Spock drifted over to the table. "What you can achieve—"

The prince kicked out one leg and left it there as if it stood upon a bar. His legs, at least, seemed well muscled. "Yes, perhaps they will enjoy the latest Terran dances. And then we shall all dance our way to political and ethical enlightenment." He lowered his foot. "No, my dear, that simply won't do."

Uhura was startled when he pointed to her. "Your Highness?"

"That hair fashion vanished—absolutely vanished two years ago." The prince strode over to her and, wiping his fingers on his vest, fussed with her hair. "There. That's the best I can do for now. But come to my cabin sometime and I'll do your hair so that you can go in any little Parisian club and be all the rage."

Uhura pulled away. "I don't want to be the rage of Paris—or any other place."

Kirk nibbled a small pastry. "You'll find, Your Highness, that fashions and hairstyles take a secondary place on a military ship. And what styles do reach us tend to be several years out of date. We generally don't worry about keeping up with the latest fads."

The prince lowered his hands, disappointed. "Yes, of course. I should have known." He stood there for an awkward moment as if he did not know what to do with his hands now. Most of the knowledge that had made friends for him on Earth was out of place on the *Enterprise*.

And there was something in his uneasy stance and posture that reminded Sulu of himself as a boy when his mother's work had taken him on to some new planet. The first few days—even months—there had been that terrible sense of standing out. "But you fence, Your Highness?"

The prince perked up and looked at Sulu almost gratefully. "Yes, I have a mild interest in any edged or pointed weapon. You have to realize that of the last nine emperors on Angira, eight have died from unnatural causes."

"But," Bibil was quick to add, "his father is in firm control of Angira now."

"Yes"—the prince returned his attention to the table—"they say the sun doesn't rise without my father's permission."

McCoy cleared his throat sympathetically. "That's quite a shadow to live in."

"No, no, I positively thrive within his shadow," the prince said. "Some men and women are like noble oaks that crave the sunshine, but I am like a fungus. Keep low and hidden and you'll always survive." He picked up a red stalk of some vegetable and whipped it through a bowl of dip. "And you are—?"

"Dr. McCoy. I'm what passes for a medical officer around here."

With a little deprecating nod of his head, the prince

jabbed the stalk at the doctor. "And I am what happens to pass for nobility." The prince turned the stalk toward the captain. "And you?"

"Captain James Kirk." Kirk twisted his head slightly as if puzzled by the prince. "You don't seem to take yourself very seriously."

There was something sad in the way the prince laughed. "Funguses rarely do, Captain." And he went on to introduce himself to the other officers until he came to Mr. Spock.

The Vulcan inclined his head slightly. "You went to Boca Tigris, I understand."

The prince brightened. "Yes, were you ever there?"

Mr. Spock shook his head slightly. "No, but I am acquainted with Professor Farsalia's work."

The prince smiled even more broadly. "Why, yes, dear old Farsie was my dissertation director."

"Indeed." Mr. Spock clasped his hands behind his back. "May I inquire on what?"

The prince took a napkin from Bibil and wiped his fingers. "It was a mouthful of a title: 'Rates of Change in Cultural Diffusion.'"

Mr. Spock lowered his eyelids as if he were hunting through his memory. "Then it would involve the Tokano coefficient on the role of the Outsider."

The prince pressed a hand beneath his throat. "Why do I feel as if I am in the midst of my orals?"

McCoy drifted over with two Cetian Coolers in hand. "That's just our science officer's form of cocktail chatter. You should feel complimented. He usually reserves it only for computers." With a slight bow, he presented one of the drinks to the prince. "Try one of these, Your Highness. I think you'll like it."

The prince took the glass in both hands, holding the

stem in his right hand and balancing the bottom of the glass on the fingertips of his left hand. "Such a delightful blue color. It reminds me of the sky over Boca Tigris."

The doctor sipped his drink. "And I've always thought of it as a southern sky. It's an insidious drink, isn't it?" He gestured with his Cooler. "It sets you to thinking of pleasanter places so you forget how many you drink."

In the meantime, though, Mr. Spock was looking past the prince as if he were getting ready to absent himself physically as well as mentally from the company of the charming, chatty doctor—as he had on so many other occasions.

But the prince merely nodded his head perfunctorily as if he no longer cared about mere amusement. "Yes, quite," he said to the doctor, but he was looking at Mr. Spock. "Tell me, Mr. Spock. Why does a science officer interest himself in the finer points of the social sciences?"

Mr. Spock glanced at the prince. "All the sciences interest me. True, the social sciences may not be as exact as the physical ones, but they are related."

"How?" McCoy asked skeptically.

"The Heisenberg Uncertainty Principle applies not only to physics but also to the social sciences," Mr. Spock explained. "The very act of observation changes the phenomenon being studied."

The prince bounced up and down on his toes. "But that's just it. Farsie's had to modify the coefficient."

Mr. Spock folded his arms. "In what way?"

The prince wagged a finger at Mr. Spock. "You have to take into account the technological level of the society being studied."

Intrigued, Mr. Spock pressed his thumb against his fingertips. "But in a primitive society—"

"Yes, of course, one has to assume a certain minimal level of sophistication and technology," the prince was quick to concede. "But there is a point in cultural development when the culture itself is ripe for change. A person has only to introduce exotic items like silk and tea and spices for medieval Europe to reach outward."

"And the Outsider?" Mr. Spock asked.

"She or he is only the catalyst." The prince set his drink down.

"I think you may be oversimplifying," Mr. Spock insisted.

The prince laughed much more easily this time. "That's the result of trying to condense a hundred pages of statistics and formulae into a few sentences."

McCoy's discomfort had been growing with each passing second. He wasn't used to having people prefer Mr. Spock to himself for conversation. But at the mention of statistics, he finally sighed. "You'll excuse me, Your Highness, Spock." But the pair were so deep into their conversation that they didn't seem to hear him. "Yes, of course, you will," the doctor muttered and retreated over to where Kirk was observing Mr. Spock and the prince.

"Did you learn a few things, Bones?" Kirk rattled a handful of candied worms in his hand.

"Just that my vocabulary is more inadequate than I thought." McCoy turned and scratched his cheek as if he were still puzzled by what he'd just seen.

Oblivious to everyone but the prince, Mr. Spock was nodding his head. "Fascinating."

McCoy nursed his drink in his hand. "I never thought Spock could get so intense when he was just talking about people. Usually he only gets that look in his eye when he's reprogramming the computer."

"Obviously you never found the right topic." Kirk popped another candied worm into his mouth.

McCoy rubbed an elbow. "But I didn't think Spock cared if he was an outsider or not. And now I suddenly hear him talking like a doctoral candidate. Do you think sociology is his secret vice? Does he read it the way other people would read porn?"

Kirk finished crunching the worm. "I've got another surprise for you. Spock put in for duty to escort the prince to Angira and help change the Angiran astronomical charts as the emperor requested."

McCoy looked down at his drink as if he thought the Cooler might be playing false with his hearing. "That can't be right."

"He asked for the mission himself," Kirk said. "Do you think he's branching out now from the physical sciences?"

"I gave up Vulcan-predicting long ago." McCoy edged in closer to Kirk and whispered, "But I do know this much. You can't let him go to Angira. It's the first time ever that Angira has asked for any outside technical assistance from the Federation. The people you send will have to be diplomats as well as competent astrogators."

"There's even more reason than you think." Kirk rubbed the ball of his thumb across his chin. "The Angiran court is supposed to have a ritual for everything. Do you know that they're not supposed to swallow their own saliva in the morning until they've performed the proper ceremony?" He studied the prince. "Except you'd never know it from Prince Vikram."

McCoy pursed his lips. "Do you think the Angirans will blame the Federation for the way he's changed?"

Kirk shoved himself away from the wall. "Who knows? But whoever goes on this mission had better be able to charm a bull right out of its hide."

"Well, that isn't Spock," McCoy said. "So he's out."

"Except for one thing." Empty plate in hand, Kirk returned to the buffet table.

McCoy kept pace. "What's that?"

Kirk studied his science officer, who was busy interrogating the prince about some abstruse point in statistics. "He insists on going."

"That's no reason to jeopardize your career and his," McCoy hissed.

"But look at how well he's getting along with the prince." Kirk nodded his head to the earnest pair.

"That's the prince, not the Angiran court," McCoy pointed out.

Kirk shrugged. "I still owe it to Spock to weigh all the factors before I decide on who goes on the mission."

"For a man who preaches the simplicity of logic," McCoy grumbled, "he certainly knows how to complicate what should be a routine mission."

Kirk pressed the rim of the plate against his stomach. "Routine missions have tripped up more than one starship captain."

"Touché, Captain!" Prince Vikram pressed the red bulb at the tip of his foil against Captain Kirk's chest.

Kirk stepped back and saluted the prince. It took a moment for him to catch his breath because the prince had given him quite a workout. "Mr. Sulu, I think His Highness needs a lesson in humility."

The prince clicked his tongue—a mannerism that he had picked up during his long stay on Earth. "This is supposed to be fun, Captain, not a time for schooling."

The captain raised his mask and strolled over to the side. "It stops being sport after you've been killed three times in a row. I'll let Mr. Sulu teach you about the feeling."

The prince whipped his foil back and forth through the air as if he had been fencing for only minutes instead of hours. "He's already taught me quite well."

Sulu lowered his mask. "You've won your share of matches."

"But only half as much as you." The prince saluted him. "Why should the chief helmsman of a starship want to master anything as archaic as a foil?"

"We can't always cart the *Enterprise* around in our back pocket." Sulu went on guard. "So fencing is handy to know."

"I can understand having rudimentary skills like the captain—" The prince raised his arm, angling his sword toward the floor in second guard.

"Thank you," Kirk said as he toweled the sweat from his face.

The prince wriggled the fingers of his left hand in deference to the captain. "I mean no disrespect, Captain, but you are hardly in the same league as Mr. Sulu or myself. Now in my savage little corner of the universe, fencing is a necessary survival skill so I learned it at an early age. But I gather that most of the crew regard it as a quaint if not amusing eccentricity in Mr. Sulu."

"Maybe I like the exercise," Sulu said. Suspecting that the prince was trying to distract him, Sulu watched the prince even more intently. The prince's lunges were quick and powerful. And it was only the prince's lack of familiarity with the foil and his own impatience that had let Sulu win most of their matches.

The prince's sword tip slowed. "But there are other forms of exercise that are just as strenuous and far less mirth provoking."

Sulu turned his head slightly to glance at Kirk; and it was as if Kirk saw the look and understood.

"We're equals within the gymnasium, Mr. Sulu," Kirk assured him. "What you say here won't go beyond these walls."

"And you can always puncture us if we repeat anything you say," the prince suggested.

Sulu would much rather have concentrated on fencing; but in the short time that the prince had been on the ship, Sulu had learned that the prince would not stop badgering him until he had an answer that satisfied him.

"I don't know. I guess I've loved fencing since I was a kid." Sulu paused, trying to analyze his immediate emotions. "I feel alive when I fence and . . . well, clean." Sulu raised his left shoulder in a slight shrug. "The whole world narrows down to less than a meter of steel, sometimes just to a centimeter."

"If that's true, why helm a starship cruiser? Why don't you transfer to some commando outfit?" The prince extended his arm, trying to bind Sulu's sword.

Sulu, however, was having none of the prince's tricks, so he skipped back a step. "That's too much like back-alley fighting."

The prince's sword point dipped toward Sulu's stomach. "I see. You wish for a certain style to your fighting as well—like French musketeers or English cavaliers. But isn't it hard for an efficient starship officer like yourself to keep that romantic streak hidden?" Sulu flicked his blade down to parry a lunge, but the prince's movement turned out only to be a feint. The prince seemed to be waiting for an answer, and that expectation annoyed Sulu. Few—if any—of the crew on the *Enterprise* ever tried to penetrate that surface of cheerful competence that the chief helmsman affected.

For one thing, it was considered bad manners for a space traveler to pry too much. As large as the *Enterprise* was, it could still seem very small during a five-year voyage. And, in general, Sulu was reluctant to discuss his own secret fantasies with anyone as chatty as the prince.

And yet, Sulu asked himself, how often did he have the opportunity of discussing things with someone from a society where fencing was not only more than an outmoded form of exercise but was actually necessary for survival? The prince was probably genuinely intrigued by Sulu.

"It's a funny kind of romanticism," Sulu finally admitted. "I think they knew their time was already up. Gunpowder was seeing to it that fighting was no longer a gentleman's game. So you had to live by your wits as well as your sword."

"But it's quite gentlemanly to fight by pushing the buttons on a panel." The prince bent his legs even more as if getting ready to spring. "You could kill thousands, millions, and never soil your hands."

"That's not it," Sulu said with a slight shake of his head. "The musketeers always seemed so sure of themselves. They just slid through situations so easily."

"Like their sword points through their opponents?" the prince asked.

"I guess that life was more exciting then than it is

now, and yet it was also simpler." Sulu was sorry that he had said so much and he waited for the prince to begin laughing.

But the prince pursed his lips together sympathetically as he began to swing his sword tip in a small circle once again. "It must be lonely when you're born six centuries too late."

To Sulu's surprise, there was more than a little truth to that statement. "Just four centuries would have done the trick. The emperor Meiji took control of Japan again by modernizing his armies."

"Well, you don't need a time machine. You simply must come with me. You'll find Angira similar to Meiji Japan." The prince seemed to rise up even higher on his toes.

Sulu got ready. "A closed society that's finally opening up to the rest of the galaxy. And you'll be right in the middle of things."

"Or right on the edge." Suddenly the prince's pear-shaped torso thrust itself forward at a sharp angle and his arm stretched out.

Sulu barely managed to skip a half step to the side and make his own time thrust. "Touché!" Sulu's tipped foil bent slightly as it pressed against the prince's padded jacket near his heart. With a laugh, Sulu straightened up and saluted the prince. "Care to try again?"

The prince returned the salute. "No, no, I've let the captain have his little vicarious revenge to put him in a good mood." He turned now to the captain. "You simply must assign Mr. Sulu to my escort when I return to Angira."

Kirk folded his arms across his chest. "I'll take it under advisement."

"Forgive me, Captain. I can see that commanders of starships are very much like emperors. You should never use the word *must* to them. Will you log it simply as a strong request?" The prince took off his protective mask and fluffed the curls about his face.

"I certainly will." Captain Kirk nodded politely to the prince and then looked at Mr. Sulu. "I'll have my yeoman return the fencing outfit later to the ship's armorer, but I don't want to have to carry this foil around the halls. Would you mind returning it for me when you check in your gear, Mr. Sulu?"

"Yes, sir," Sulu said.

"Please, Captain, must you leave so soon?" The prince placed a hand over his heart. "I was just going to propose we fence and recite poems at the same time."

"You'd find my poetry is even worse than my fencing." Kirk smiled and waved to the prince as he left the gymnasium.

Sulu lifted his mask and let it rest on top of his head. Perhaps it would have been kinder to let the prince win more often; but Sulu found it impossible to maintain his easygoing manner when he fenced. Once he had a foil in his hand, he was again a small boy with dreams of becoming a dashing musketeer. And though he had reached some compromises with those dreams as he had matured and entered Star Fleet Academy, he had never been able to suppress that younger self totally. "My watch is coming up pretty soon. I ought to shower and grab a quick bite to eat."

The prince cradled his mask in the crook of his left arm. "Actually, I was hoping you'd be a bit more sporting than that." He motioned to his grizzled old servant, Bibil. "I thought we might try Angiran swords."

Bibil bent down to lift the cloth cover from the long, flat box at his feet. Twisting a hand in a flourish, he proudly opened the case. There, resting on expensive flame silk, were a pair of swords in sheaths that curved slightly. The hilts, which continued the curving line, were clearly designed for two hands. "We call these *sena*."

Sulu knelt beside the case and set his foil down before he raised one of the ornate sheaths from the case and slid the blade out. The finely polished steel caught the light and Sulu caught his breath. "They're magnificent."

"My arthritis won't let me work out with the prince enough." Bibil held out his right hand to show the fingers arched like claws.

The prince switched his foil over to his bare left hand and flexed his right wrist. "It's not all that different from a Japanese *katana*. They're about the same length and weight and the blades are positioned in the sheaths with the cutting edge upward."

The prince seemed so confident of winning that for a second Sulu toyed with the idea of letting the prince have his own way. But Sulu found he could not. Though he was quite willing to give in on a good many other situations, this was one time he was not. Sword-fighting was too basic to Sulu's life to be compromised. And that younger, boyish self was drawn to the idea of a match and a trick he had seen once. It was not without a certain risk—if he failed, Sulu would look like the biggest fool on the ship; and yet that very danger made the attempt all the more attractive.

Sulu lowered his mask over his face. "I'm willing to try anything with an edge to it."

The prince could not be sure, but he thought he saw Sulu smiling slyly through the mesh of his mask. "At home on Angira, we used wooden sticks. They didn't have an edge, but it still hurt when you were hit. If you were slow, you could receive quite a beating." He pointed to a thin button attached to either pommel. "But we'll have to make do with these. I took the liberty of borrowing two guards from some sabers in the ship's armory."

Sulu picked up one sword. It seemed to balance well for his arm, though the hilt was made for the larger hands of an Angiran. "Has the magnetic field been adjusted?"

"Yes, I had the ship's armorer do that for me. They're quite safe. I'm not ready for mitosis and neither are you, I think."

Tugging off his glove, Sulu ran his finger along the edge of the blade and felt the slight tingling sensation of touching the thin magnetic field that covered the edge of the blade. "You've been planning." He glanced from the prince to Bibil.

Bibil handed the remaining sword to the prince and slammed the lid shut on the case. "He's gotten tired of losing."

"One's ego must live up to one's title." The prince lowered his own mask. Because they were both in fencing outfits, the prince had also brought along belts—though the sheaths were thrust through the belts rather than attached to them.

When they were both ready, the prince stepped back. "The draw itself is much like a samurai drawing his *katana*." The prince's right hand crossed over his stomach and grasped the upper half of the sword hilt, and he began to slide the sword from its sheath. As his sword point cleared the sheath, he brought his right arm down so that the blade itself began to swing upward. At the same time, his left hand clasped the lower part of the hilt, to add force to the arc of the blade so that it would swing down even faster and harder in a deadly slash.

The prince stopped the blade as it pointed at the ceiling. "Of course, you would do this as quickly as you could. And if you know some style of the *katana,* you should do all right."

"All the colonial worlds on which we lived only had teachers in European-style fencing." Sulu shoved his right hand back into his glove before he tried the several draws, one in which he raised the sword over his head as the prince had done and another in which he drew one-handed for a sideways slash. "So I never had any instruction in Japanese swordfighting until I got to the academy. I only know some of the rudiments."

"All the better for me." The prince sheathed his sword. "Now the next thing you have to be is *panku.*"

"I thought that meant 'family' in Angiran." Sulu carefully restored his sword to its sheath.

The prince had turned sideways, spreading his legs and squatting slightly. His head and back were so straight, you might have used them as a ruler. "It's a word with many meanings, but it originally was used for the stump of an old tree from which new shoots grow. So the roots reach back to the past, but the thing itself is fresh and new."

"All right," Sulu said, and copied the prince.

The prince let his hands hang loosely by his sides. "Now we draw. Like gunfighters back in the American

West. And it's quite acceptable for the slower person to move back and draw his or her sword."

But Sulu remained where he was. "I'm ready whenever you are."

The prince, watching Sulu intently, drawled exaggeratedly, "So make a move, Sulu."

"After you, Your Highness." Sulu mischievously twitched his fingers.

"I do believe you're up to something," the prince murmured. He started to move his right hand toward the sword hilt.

It was the moment that Sulu had been waiting for. Grabbing the sheath in his left hand, he tilted it up at a sharp angle so that, when his right hand clasped the hilt, he was pulling his sword downward out of its sheath rather than upward. At the same time, he bent his left leg and lunged forward. As the sword cleared the sheath, his left hand let go of the sheath and he clapped it against the dull back of the blade, adding even more force as he swung the sword up and in.

There wasn't any time for the prince to say anything as his body automatically stepped forward. But instead of delivering a downward slash, he found himself literally throwing his chest and stomach against Sulu's blade. It slapped against the padding of his jacket.

They stood like that, frozen in a kind of tableau, and for a moment Sulu wondered if he'd gone too far. Perhaps Sulu should have let the prince win as he'd expected to. Would the prince now explode into an imperial temper tantrum?

Suddenly Bibil gave a laugh. "Well done, Sulu." He began to applaud in the Angiran fashion with his palms held horizontally.

For his part, the prince simply looked in amazement at the blade that still rested against his torso. "I thought Lord Bhima had taught me every trick in the book."

That was high praise, since Lord Bhima had been the prince's fencing instructor back on Angira, and, according to the prince, was the best swordsman on all of Angira.

Sulu slowly straightened up. "You tipped me off when you said the draw was like a samurai's."

The prince took a step backward. "So you've killed me. But how?"

His right hand still holding onto the hilt, his left hand held the blade. He could feel the slight tingle from the magnetic field that protected his palm. "There may not have been anyone to teach me Japanese swordfighting when I was a kid, but some of the worlds had large libraries of old films. That's from a classic by Kurosawa called *Sanjuro*."

"I wish I had seen it as a boy." The prince raised his sword in a lazy circle and guided it expertly into the sheath. "It would have saved me many a drubbing from Lord Bhima."

Sulu started to take the sheath out of the belt. "I doubt if he'd approve of that little trick. It's hardly tournament form."

"Perhaps not, but he would be intrigued by trying to come up with a counter to it." The prince went into *panku*. "And it may be just the thing I need to deflate his ego a bit. You must show me how to do that."

"How about having some lunch instead. I can always show you tomorrow." Sliding the sheath over the sword, Sulu tried to hand it back to Bibil.

"No, please, Sulu." The prince stepped forward to

place his gloved hand on Sulu's wrist. "Show me how to do it so I can practice on my own then."

The prince had such a breezy manner that it was a shock to realize he could take anything so seriously—in fact, almost desperately. "It's just a little trick. Why is it so important to you?"

"It shouldn't be, but it is." Embarrassed, the prince let go of Sulu's wrist and his voice tried to resume its normal, languid tone, but there was still an anxious edge to it now. "Do you know what my family nickname is?"

"Your Highness." Bibil glared his disapproval.

"Sulu and I are both loners in search of something. He'll understand." The prince tried to draw his sword out in slow motion and bring his left palm behind the sword blade. But his arms wound up as a tangle in front of his face. "At home, I'm called the Shadow Lord, because I was of such an insubstantial character, as they say. And on our world that would be more of an insult than on yours."

Sulu looked down at his own shadow, remembering the lighting in the prince's own room. In the faint light favored by the Angirans, a shadow was neither as dark nor as sharp as it would be under normal Terran conditions. "I would think that the less you have of a thing, the more you would value it."

"To a mystic, yes; to a politician, no." Refusing to be discouraged, the prince sheathed his sword again.

Since the prince seemed determined to practice all day until he got the knack of the trick draw, Sulu decided that his stomach could wait. Walking over, he grabbed the prince's left hand and guided it to the sheath. "But your stock will have to go up. After all, you're coming back with all this knowledge to help modernize your world."

The prince watched as Sulu forced the mouth of the sheath to tilt downward. "All my learning will count less than a good, quick draw."

That earlier, boyish self responded to that idea as it had earlier to the challenge with the *sena*. "Then I'd love to visit your world," Sulu said wistfully.

The prince gave a little bitter chuckle. "And I wish I were free to stay on Earth another twelve years so I could take more courses and gather degrees like a bouquet of flowers." He drew his sword out again slowly, bringing his left palm up behind the blade. "It's a shame we can't trade places."

By a great effort of will, Sulu forced himself to be more pragmatic—for the prince's sake as well as for his own. "Well, at least I can teach you that little trick." Sulu squatted down to help adjust the Prince's legs. "Try bending your legs more when you take that step forward. The idea is to come in low beneath your opponent's sword."

It was a thoughtful Kirk who stepped into his quarters to meet with McCoy and Mr. Spock. After a good deal of reading about Angira and spending time with the prince, he was still no closer to a decision about the mission to Angira. "Sorry I'm late, gentlemen, but I let the prince talk me into a little fencing match."

McCoy stared at Kirk's fencing outfit. "What were you doing? Wearing him out for Sulu? Isn't there enough mayhem in the universe without trying to turn one another into swiss cheese?"

Kirk took off his fencing jacket. It had bound Kirk about the shoulders so that he pumped his arms now in slow circles, enjoying the luxury of being able to move freely once again. "It's the best way I can think of to get to know Prince Vikram in such a short time. He's a bundle of contradictions. He's got a real competitive edge when it comes to fencing; but beyond that . . ." Kirk simply shook his head.

McCoy crossed his legs. "I know. He's charming enough, but I don't see how anyone could expect him to pull Angira single-handedly into modern times. I just wish some of those bureaucrats would realize that they're dealing with people, not abstract sociological principles."

Kirk eased himself onto his bed. The prince had put him through a short but thorough workout. "I just wish they'd quit treating the *Enterprise* like a toy train that they can shuttle around at their convenience. First of all, we're supposed to drop the prince off on Angira and leave a small group behind to modify the astronomical charts."

McCoy laced his fingers together over his knees. "Well, at least it's a step in the right direction for Angira."

"But we're also supposed to take medical supplies to Beta Carinae." Kirk lay down, leaving only his feet dangling over the edge. "That means that the party we leave behind will be on their own."

McCoy kicked his leg up and down. "Take some free medical advice, Jim: Don't worry so much or you'll get an ulcer. You've seen the reports on Angira. The imperial government is as stable and progressive as they come."

Kirk frowned. "I'd still better send the most capable people.

"And for that reason I think I should be sent to

25

Angira." Spock turned the list of volunteers toward the captain as if he could read it at that distance. "And yet my name has already been crossed off the list."

Kirk rested his forearm over his eyes. "I need you, Spock. What if something happens on board the ship during the run to Beta Carinae?"

"You will deal with it as efficiently as you and the crew always do," Mr. Spock said smoothly. "The mission to Beta Carinae, while urgent, is not particularly hazardous. You can certainly spare me long enough for a short stay on Angira."

Kirk should have known better than to argue with Mr. Spock. He lowered his arm so he could look at his science officer. "Just why did you volunteer in the first place?"

Mr. Spock angled his head downward. His fingers smoothed the sheet of paper that contained the list of volunteers. "I confess to a certain professional curiosity."

Kirk found himself balancing on a fine edge. Even if Mr. Spock would never have admitted to such a Vulcan sin, he had a strong sense of pride. "That isn't a sufficient reason to let you leave the ship."

Mr. Spock took a deep breath and then let it out slowly. "I have already pointed out the lack of logic to such an assumption. May I ask the captain if there are any other reasons for refusing my request?"

McCoy shook his head in disbelief. "You really can't see it, can you?"

Mr. Spock blinked his eyes in annoyance as if McCoy had just tried to shine a bright light on him. "Perhaps you can instruct me, Doctor."

"I'd be happy to." McCoy let his foot drop to the

floor with a thud. "Spock, just how long can you hold your breath anyway?"

Spock frowned. "I fail to see what that has to do with my ability to revise the Angiran star maps."

"It's got plenty to do with it." McCoy leaned an elbow on the conference table and rested his cheek on his hand. "You're the last person that Jim should send to Angira with the prince."

Mr. Spock slipped into a more formal, rhetorical fashion—as if he knew just how much more it annoyed the doctor when he spoke that way. "The Angirans have asked the Federation to help them adjust their astronomical charts, which have become hopelessly complex. For one thing, their astronomers have created an elaborate system of epicycles to account for the movements of the planets. As a result of that and other erroneous theories, their astronomical maps are more exercises in geometry now rather than in astronomy. I should think they would be pleased that I can redo their charts more efficiently than any scientific team from the *Enterprise*. Besides, the fewer visitors, the less likelihood of violating some part of their elaborate etiquette."

McCoy tapped his fingers against his cheek. "It's not the quantity of visitors that counts. It's the quality. If revising the charts was the only problem, we could feed the data into the ship's computers and have the information for them in no time. But the revisions also have to be explained to the Angirans."

Mr. Spock drew his eyebrows together as if puzzled. "If I was sent to Angira, I would perform *all* my duties correctly."

McCoy sat back. "I wish you'd get it through your

thick Vulcan skull that correctness isn't the only virtue in the universe. There's also such a thing as tact."

Mr. Spock arched an eyebrow. "Perhaps if I saw you display it more often, I might understand it better."

McCoy closed his eyes. "Spock, I'm just trying to save you from yourself." His eyelids blinked up suddenly. "The Angirans invited us to revamp the charts because they have a passion for astrology, not for precision. They don't do anything—from the burial of the poorest peasant to the accession of an emperor—unless the stars are favorable. They wouldn't let Prince Vikram return until all the astrological signs were right."

"I'm already aware of that fact, Doctor."

McCoy leaned forward. "Well, I know you, Spock, and your obsession to tell the truth. You won't get through the first lecture without telling the Angirans just how stupid astrology is. And so they're going to be mad enough to stuff you into a cannon and shoot you back into space. And since the *Enterprise* won't be back from Beta Carinae for thirty days, Angiran time, you're going to have to wait quite a while for a rendezvous. So I repeat: How long can you hold your breath?"

Captain Kirk ran his fingers thoughtfully over his mouth and then lowered his hand. With the memory of that morning's fencing match in mind, Kirk said, "Whoever else we send, I think we ought to include Sulu."

Mr. Spock twisted his head slightly so that he could look at Kirk with his right eye—as if that movement could help him read the mind of his captain. "Mr. Sulu is junior to officers with more diplomatic training."

"But as chief helmsman, he has some knowledge of

astronomy." Kirk sat up, supporting himself on his hands. "And besides, he gets along with the prince, so he might be able to help the prince make the transition to living on Angira again. I want things to go without a hitch. Angira opened its door a little bit by sending the prince to the Federation for his education. Now it's opened its door a little wider by inviting us to help revise their astronomical charts. I want to make sure that the door keeps opening wider—maybe the acceptance of technical advisers or even an exchange of ambassadors."

"With all due respect to a fine officer like Mr. Sulu, I need no such help," Mr. Spock said firmly. "It would be a duplication of effort and a waste of a fellow officer's time."

The doctor was thoroughly enjoying himself. "Anyway, Spock, why would someone like you want to go down to Angira? You'll be surrounded by fops like Prince Vikram."

Except for the quickness with which he responded, it would have been difficult to tell what delight Mr. Spock took in correcting McCoy. "First of all, I am intrigued by any culture in the process of reforming itself; but I am especially interested in the way an individual like the prince can effect those changes."

"Come on now," McCoy sniffed. "I admit that Prince Vikram is an amusing fellow over cocktails, but a world shaker?"

Mr. Spock pressed his hands against the table. "'Fops' do not survive the jump from one era to another as the prince did when he left Angira for Earth. He has an unfortunate propensity to chatter and play the clown at times, but from our conversations, I have ascertained that he has also learned a good deal.

And that calls for a flexibility of mind and a firmness of purpose."

"Oh, yes?" McCoy smirked. "I gather from his own remarks that his family sent him off because he was the most expendable. His brothers and stepbrothers were needed to help his father control Angira. Now how can you expect anyone to listen to him?"

"That is precisely what I wish to see." Mr. Spock looked directly at the captain, as if the words were meant more for him than for the doctor. "Here is a person who now literally lives on the edge between two cultures, neither belonging wholeheartedly to Angira nor the Federation."

McCoy tipped his head back and looked down his nose at Mr. Spock. "A marginal man, Mr. Spock."

Mr. Spock's reply was calm and considered. "In effect, yes."

McCoy straightened up again. "Like yourself, in a way?"

Mr. Spock pressed his lips together in a thin frown. "The prince and I are hardly the same."

"For which the prince ought to thank his god or gods heartily," McCoy declared. He looked at Spock appraisingly. "I wonder how you'd handle a situation like the prince's. You'd need more than logic and reason."

"I think you underestimate both the prince and myself," Mr. Spock said quietly.

Kirk balanced the political objectives of the mission against the interests of his own science officer. Perhaps the doctor was closer to the truth than Spock was willing to admit. At any rate, it must be important to Spock, or he would never have insisted so strongly on going. As he stared at his first officer's carefully controlled face, Kirk wished he also had the ability to touch minds so he could understand what this mission really meant to Mr. Spock.

Was it worth risking both their careers? Spock seemed to think so; and so, despite his own misgivings, Kirk felt he owed it to Spock to send him on the mission. Perhaps he would regret it later. "Well"—he exhaled slowly—"a smart peddler puts at least one foot in the doorway. We'll shove in two: Mr. Spock and Mr. Sulu." He grinned at his science officer. "You can do the revisions while Sulu explains them to the Angirans."

"But just what are you peddling, Jim?" McCoy nodded his head toward Mr. Spock. "The Vulcan School of Charm over here or"—McCoy raised a fist and pretended to wave a sword—"Sulu's vegetable slicers?"

"Neither." Kirk smiled. "We are selling a certain kind of perspective. A-n-nd"—he drew out the word—"I would hope the grace to go with it."

Captain's log, Stardate 1831.5:

I have decided to detach our chief helmsman, Lt. Sulu, for duty on Angira with Mr. Spock. Their principal assignment will be to revise that world's inefficient astronomical charts; but their secondary task will be to cement ties of friendship further between Angira and the Federation. In the meantime, the *Enterprise* will continue on to Beta Carinae to deliver much-needed medical supplies.

Chapter One

Sulu had seen the palace many times in the prince's tri-d's; but he had not expected to see it in person. And the small tri-d's had not prepared him for its massive scale. Beginning with a citadel dominating the fertile plains below, the palace had grown until it seemed to have swallowed up an entire ridge of hills. Walls, pillars and even the delicate towers and spires had been hewn from stone the same blood red color as the hills, so that the palace of Angira seemed to sweep across the green plain in either direction without apparent end under the dwarf sun. He felt a sense of elation at having managed to come this far—almost as if he owned the view himself.

And when Sulu turned back to the prince's suite of rooms, the sense of power and wealth was almost overwhelming. The ceiling was of silver embossed with hunting scenes so cunningly done that the animals seemed ready to leap down from the ceiling. And the marble walls and pillars were intricately carved to resemble trees and shrubs. "It's almost like a forest that's had a magical spell cast on it."

The prince was dressing before a full-length mirror in an ornate, gold frame. "Next to politics, my people's greatest passion is interior decorating. We are fortunate they had only marble and silver rather than plastic."

"The collar, Mr. Sulu." Mr. Spock, as impeccable as ever, nodded toward Sulu's dress tunic.

Red-faced, Sulu looked down from the ceiling. Aware that Mr. Spock's eyes were calmly inspecting him for other flaws, Sulu felt like the rawest academy plebe again. As a result, his fingers seemed twice as large and clumsy as they did up the collar which had somehow come undone.

It was like the gracious Prince Vikram to forget himself and his own worries in order to put a friend at ease. "You see, Hikaru. You should wear the *soropa*. There are no buttons, seals or zippers to fight—only the pull of gravity." He held up his arms as his servant helped him wind the meter-wide, four-meters-long band of precious flame silk about his waist and loins. The tail end would be wrapped around his waist like a sash.

Sulu tried to smile encouragingly. "I should have learned how to dress myself by now." When Mr. Spock raised his eyebrows to remind Sulu of their conversation before they had beamed down, Sulu quickly added, "Your Highness."

Prince Vikram clicked his tongue in disappointment. "Must you begin the titles so soon?"

Bibil wound the silk cloth once around his master's

shoulder. "But you *are* the ninth in line to the throne," he said in a mild reproof. Though he fussed with the prince in his gruff way, he really seemed to care about him.

Annoyed, the prince shoved Bibil's hands away. "Which means I am never to have responsibilities, only to be carted out for state banquets like a floral display."

Mr. Spock's head turned ever so slightly—according to some precise table of courteous movements known only to himself. "But Your Highness does have responsibilities," Mr. Spock reminded him calmly. "The entire purpose of your studies within the Federation has been to help you modernize your world."

The prince draped the end of the cloth over his shoulder and eyed the effect in the mirror. "Yes, and I will certainly advise my people. And they will just as certainly ignore me. This is a world where the majority of people still believe that our world is at the center of the universe and all our stars and planets revolve around it. And even the bureaucracy regards paper clips and carbon paper as newfangled notions. How can I be expected to change all that?" The prince's face, reflected in the mirror, was furrowed in fear and worry.

In the short silence that followed, Sulu hunted desperately for something to say that might ease the prince's mind; but there was no denying it was an immense burden to bear and it was easy to see how such a lighthearted spirit as the prince's might be crushed underneath it.

To Sulu's surprise, though, it was Mr. Spock who was the first to try to comfort the prince. "It is never easy to be placed upon the border between two cultures, belonging neither to one nor the other." Mr. Spock spoke slowly and with great care as if he had already given the matter a great deal of thought. "Sometimes it seems as if one has been asked to balance upon the edge of a knife blade. No matter how one stands, no matter how one turns—the person will always be cut."

Prince Vikram studied Spock's reflection in the mirror. "Yes, just so. But then you live on this border yourself, don't you, Mr. Spock?"

Mr. Spock clasped his hands behind his back. "It is not unknown to me." If he even noticed Sulu's reflection thoughtfully studying his, Mr. Spock did his best to ignore it.

The prince fussed with the edge of his *soropa*. "And yet you persist?"

Mr. Spock stared at the back of the prince's head as if he wished he could impress his words directly upon the prince's brain. "As painful as life on the border may be, it is the place where change first begins for a culture; and something new and better can be created."

Bibil opened a jar and proffered it to the prince with a bow of his head. "As your father said when he sent you on your journey, we must find a way to combine the technology of the Federation with our own higher spiritual values."

The prince wriggled his index finger inside the jar and then raised a fingertip covered with gold paste. "I'd like to ask Great-Uncle Baruda what he thought of 'our own higher spiritual values.' The family locked him away in a tower for twenty years and then everyone forgot about him except for a few old servants who brought him enough food for himself and the *rastas*—they're rather like your mice—that he'd made into pets. Then the family rediscovered him quite by accident

35

during a palace revolt when everyone was looking for places to hide. He wouldn't let anyone in; and later when the revolt was crushed, he wouldn't come out." The prince stared at the precious paste as if it were mud. "Great-Uncle Baruda had come to like his pets better than humans. He said they were more dependable."

"I would say 'predictable' rather than 'dependable.'" Mr. Spock corrected him politely.

With a sigh, the prince touched his finger to his forehead and then dropped it, leaving behind the caste mark of the royal family of Angira. "Well, I can 'predict' what the *sinha* warriors will do when they see you, Mr. Spock." It was difficult to keep the prince's buoyant spirits down for long. "They will try to out-frown you. Shall I set up a contest between you and them? The victor could choose the destiny of this world: you, the Federation and modernization; they, a closed world and the status quo." He held out his hand and the ever-watchful Bibil wiped it with a towel. "You could win easily, I think."

It was the prince's way to tease everyone, but he hadn't reckoned with Mr. Spock's dignity. The science officer dropped his hands to his sides as he drew himself up straight. "Indeed? Since I have not studied Angiran physiology, I could not say."

Voices suddenly began to drone from beneath the window, the tinkling of dozens of little bells mingling with the sound. It seemed to Sulu like a hive of giant bees holding a funeral. When Sulu looked quizzically at the prince, he motioned Sulu to follow him to the window. "Those would be priests."

There, in a courtyard some twenty meters beneath

the window, several brown-robed Angirans were turning. Their voices rose in a steady drone as they pivoted endlessly, their hands hidden in long sleeves that fluttered like slim wings, and their heads covered by round straw hats a meter wide. The ringing came from small bells attached by long black ribbons to the guards of the swords that they whirled in the air.

"They belong to a mendicant order which stresses that individuality is merely an illusion, so they wear those big hats to obscure their faces." The prince shook his head. "They used to frighten me when I was small. They sound so sad when they pray and even sadder when they mourn."

Sulu leaned against the sill. "But why are they turning?"

The prince returned to his mirror. "They pray by chasing their shadows. In the old days, we used to believe that a person's shadow was the same as the soul. They'll whirl about for hours in ecstatic circles."

"And the swords?" Sulu wondered.

"They're not real swords. They don't have an edge. We call them shadow-catchers because the priests snare the shadow-souls of any dead who might want to work any mischief—especially before an important occasion."

At that moment, someone knocked at the door. "And now *my* inspection is to begin," the prince whispered to Sulu. And then, with one last quick check in the mirror, he turned toward the door. "You may enter."

Prince Vikram gave a start when he saw the tall, young Angiran in the doorway a pace in front of a horde of servants. A white, pantherlike head covered his skull, and the glossy hide hung down his back to be coiled around his waist over the light blue silks of a noble.

Sulu had read of the saber-toothed *sinha* of Angira; but this was the skin of one. At one time, it had been necessary for a noble to slay one of the deadly creatures to prove himself worthy of the warrior society which controlled the Angiran army and navy. But the creatures had become so rare in the last few centuries that other tests had been substituted and a lined cap of white silk, cut in the shape of a *sinha* skin, had replaced the pelt itself. That the young noble had found a *sinha* of such giant size said a good deal about his courage, persistence—and perhaps ruthlessness.

"You don't know how long I've waited for this day, Your Highness. As Master of Protocol, I wanted to be the first to welcome back my former playmate." The Angiran gave a slight bow of his head—so slight that Sulu suspected it was almost insulting in a court so bound with ritual that it even had a short ceremony for sneezing.

For his part, the prince did not even move his head when he spoke. "Rahu," he said with a delicate irony, "I can't tell you what a pleasure this is."

"Of that, I am sure," Rahu said. Then, with a careful twist of his head, Rahu scrutinized Mr. Spock and Sulu. "I have also been instructed to express our gratitude to you for escorting our prince during his long journey."

Before Mr. Spock could reply, the prince chided Rahu in the tone one would use for a child. "They are neither women nor servants. Do not use the low tongue with them." On Angira, as Sulu had read, there were two separate languages among the noble caste—one used by males and one by women and servants. But their universal translator had worked too efficiently for Spock and Sulu to have known the difference.

Rahu stalked into the room with all the wariness of a cat into a roomful of dogs. "They are not of the blood."

The prince stiffened ever so slightly, but he kept the same pleasant tone and smile. "Nonetheless, you will apologize. They are of a warrior caste as noble as your own. And"—he paused to emphasize his next words—"they are my friends."

"Can such a thing be?" Rahu mocked him with his eyes.

"Do you call me a liar?" The prince pressed his lips together into a thin, bloodless smile. "I warn you, Rahu. The next time we cross swords, I'll have your head, not just the tip of your finger."

"Now, now, I thought you two would have outgrown such talk," growled an Angiran in a deep voice. For a moment, it was impossible to see him among the servants in the corridor, but they scurried to either side quickly to reveal a middle-aged noble. Though shorter and broader than Rahu or Vikram, the Angiran seemed as solid and unshakable as an old oak tree with its roots sunk deep into the ground. "You must forgive me, Lord Rahu, but I couldn't resist hurrying here when I heard you were going to welcome the prince yourself."

It was difficult to say whether Rahu or Vikram was more surprised to see him. But it was the prince who managed to recover first. "Lord Bhima, you could always keep the peace between two foolish cubs."

"I only needed to remind you of your duties to one another." Then, with the effect of a great oak suddenly bending, he bowed his head deeply to the prince and then to Sulu and Spock. "And in this case, an insult to your escort reflects upon all of us." He glanced sternly from the corners of his eyes toward Rahu.

Rahu held his head up as if his neck and back had changed to stone. "I think you overstep yourself now, swordmaster. We are no longer children under your care. I will not bow my head to creatures who are attempting to take over our world."

Lord Bhima gave a deep grunt. "They represent His Highness's hosts and no matter what we think of their ways, we owe them some respect."

"And will they respect Angira and its ways?" Rahu asked sharply. "We've already seen the chaos that the emperor has created with his own madness. Now we're to have this pair whisper even greater insanities into his ear and bring him new, powerful weapons."

"That may be." Lord Bhima's voice was even and controlled. "But we mustn't forget our duties. How can we criticize the emperor for abandoning the old ways if we do so ourselves?"

"Do not lecture me," Lord Rahu snapped.

Lord Bhima planted his fists on his hips. "But you know how it is with teachers when they get old. They still treat everyone like children. I might even forget myself and take a reed to your backside, as big as you are now."

Though Rahu, as a *sinha* warrior, had a dagger stuck through the waist of his *soropa,* Lord Bhima gave every appearance of being able to beat him. The two stared at one another for a moment, but it was Rahu who finally dropped his eyes. Reluctantly, Rahu managed a slight bow to Spock and Sulu. "You have my apologies."

Once Rahu had done his piece, Lord Bhima swung around to study them himself. "So this is the miraculous pair who are going to change heaven itself."

"We are simply going to help your astronomers revise their charts," Mr. Spock corrected him. "Their system of epicycles—"

Lord Bhima chopped his hand at the air with gruff good humor. "Isn't it enough that you're going to put all us sword instructors out of work with all your modern weapons? We can always find jobs as butchers and poulterers. But what do you expect all those little nearsighted astronomers to do?"

Mr. Spock regarded the swordmaster with slight annoyance—rather as if he were being barked at by someone's pet mastiff. "There is a Prime Directive to prevent the introduction of our weapons. As for your astronomers, they will go on as before—but more accurately."

"Even if there weren't the directive, these gentlemen wouldn't do away with swordmasters," the prince assured his old instructor. "In fact, this one fences in a Terran style." He hooked a hand behind Sulu's arm and pulled him forward. "I think you'll find it interesting." He might have expanded more, much to Sulu's embarrassment, but Rahu spoke up suddenly.

"Perhaps we'll have time for such curiosities later, Your Highness," he said. "Since the official reception is to take place shortly, I thought you might like to get ready. I've brought along some help for you." He motioned with his right hand to the crowd of servants waiting in the corridor behind him. The gesture allowed Sulu to see that he was, indeed, missing the first joint to his index finger. "You have been away for a long time and may have forgotten much."

"I have not been away so long that I have forgotten who are my enemies and who are my friends. Faithful Bibil has been more than capable." The prince waved his hand for the other servants to leave, but they refused to leave until Rahu himself nodded lazily to them.

Without waiting for his own dismissal, Rahu turned. "I'll have a tray of food sent to you." And he crossed the room, passing by Lord Bhima in the doorway, to step out into the corridor.

Prince Vikram stared after him. "Rahu thinks it should be himself and not my father who sits upon the throne—just because my great-grandfather had the discourtesy to bludgeon his before the latter could stab him." He pursed his lips. "It's rather interesting that my father should appoint him of all people as Master of Protocol."

Lord Bhima shut the door. "He had no choice, Your Highness. There are many on this world who resent the changes your father has been making." He gave a disgusted snort. "Back in your home province, he's even raised an army of peasants and armed them with toys."

The prince glanced at Bibil. "The Hounds did well enough in my grandfather's time and they were all peasants."

"But they were led by officers chosen from the nobility," Lord Bhima said. "Your father's put peasants in charge and now they're strutting about as proud as lords. They think they're our equals."

"I see. On Angira, only nobles may order a slaughter," Mr. Spock observed with delicate irony.

"There's a way to do things." Lord Bhima looked at the science officer with thinly disguised contempt.

Before the two could start to argue, the prince spoke quickly. "And what other concessions has my father had to make?"

Lord Bhima swung back to the prince. "Your father's only averted a civil war by appointing members of the opposition to certain official posts. But there's talk that you've returned with the plans for all sorts of new weapons to tip things in his favor again."

The prince seemed genuinely pained. "When I went offworld, I gave my oath not to study any military technology."

Lord Bhima seemed so relieved that his normal reserve broke. "I told the others not to judge you by your light manner. I believed that you of all people would keep your word." He gripped the prince's arm in sudden elation. "I taught you the Code of the Warrior. When your father sent you away, I knew you couldn't be fooled. We may yet bring some order to this chaos your father has caused."

The prince stared at Lord Bhima's eager, hopeful face. He looked as if he would have liked to please his former master if he could, but it was impossible. Sadly, hesitantly, he shook his head. "It only seems like chaos, Lord Bhima. I've studied enough worlds to know that it is a terrible, anxious thing when the old order passes away. Take Terra, for instance. When China and Japan—"

Lord Bhima suddenly let go of the prince's arm as if he had just discovered it was leprous. "They are simply names on faraway worlds. I only know that we were far happier when this world was closed to all offworld traffic."

"One cannot have growth without some pain," the prince said as gently as he could, "but grow we must. If I have learned one thing in my studies of other worlds, it is that the alternative to growth is stagnation and even death."

"I fear death less than I fear the changes your father is making." Lord Bhima frowned harshly. "Offworld ways are not our own."

The prince studied his instructor as if he were just noticing the many silvery hairs and lines wrinkling the swordmaster's face. Perhaps for the first time in his life, the prince seemed to realize that his former teacher might not be the same energetic, wise master he thought Lord Bhima to be.

The prince squared his shoulders as if he were performing a task for which he had no taste. "With all due respect, Lord Bhima, the old ways are not better."

Lord Bhima sucked in his breath hard as if he had just taken a blow to his stomach. "What did they do to you out there in the stars? Did they take away your heart?"

"I had my eyes opened." The prince slowly raised one hand and held it out imploringly to the swordmaster. "Surely we can work together for the good of our people."

Lord Bhima stood very still and Sulu could only think of a lone oak tree he had seen once on a hill before a thunderstorm. There had been a tingling sensation in the air and it had almost felt as if the tree were bracing itself for the lightning to come. "I could never cooperate in the destruction of our world."

The prince stared down at his empty palm for a moment and then folded it across his stomach. "I'm sorry that we cannot be on the same side, Lord Bhima."

"And so am I, Your Highness." With a stiff little bow, he stalked out of the room.

"Poor Lord Bhima. It's a terrible thing to be a hero

when all the myths are dying." He clapped his hands together suddenly. "But you must return to your ship at once. I fear my father may have glossed over his troubles to save face with your Federation."

Mr. Spock took out his communicator but failed to raise his ship. "The *Enterprise* seems to have left as scheduled." He began to study the doors and windows with an eye for defense. "But I fail to understand why your father failed to notify you of such troubles."

"Face is everything with my people. They will not necessarily lie to you, but they will not rush to tell you the truth either." The prince bit his lip unhappily. "And you do not have your phasers." Only *sinha* warriors were allowed to carry weapons within the palace.

Mr. Spock slipped his communicator back onto his belt. "Hands and feet were used as weapons long before anything else. Both Mr. Sulu and I are acquainted with unarmed combat."

"Let us hope you will not have to prove it," the prince sighed.

The prince turned away from the door. "Well, Sulu, how does it feel to fall out of your twenty-third century into the seventeenth? You're now surrounded by palace intrigues and conniving villains."

Sulu hoisted himself onto a chair near the mirror. The chair was designed for longer Angiran legs, and Sulu's legs dangled in the air. "The stage seems set, but I wish someone would give me a script."

"Nonsense, you don't need a script. Simply let paranoia be your guide." The prince gave a light kick to a footrest so that it slid across the floor toward Sulu.

"Besides," Mr. Spock pointed out, "nothing has

happened yet." But Sulu couldn't help noticing that Mr. Spock placed a chair so he could face the door. His toes barely touched the floor.

The prince applauded softly. "Bravo, Mr. Spock. You learn quickly."

Sulu propped his feet on the footrest and settled back in his chair. "From what you've told me of the palace intrigues, slow students don't live very long."

As Bibil obligingly brought a footrest over for Mr. Spock, the prince lay down on a low, broad couch. "Yes, the penalty for failure is rather heavy." He placed his hands over his stomach. "I had no idea paranoia could whet one's appetite so much. I'd welcome even Rahu's tray."

Bibil scowled. "Why simplify Rahu's task?"

"After all these years of dreaming about an Angiran meal, it is sheer torture not to be able to eat anything," the prince complained. "Surely one bite couldn't hurt."

"Do you realize how much poison could be contained in just one bite? You're not to eat a thing." And Bibil extended his jaw stubbornly as if he were not going to take any contradictions from the prince.

There came a pounding at the door, and a woman announced, "A tray for the prince."

The prince glumly motioned Bibil. "Send the tray away."

"We don't dare insult Rahu yet. Not till we see how the land lies." Bibil went to the door and opened it. A woman stood there. On her head was a huge tray filled with steaming plates and bowls, along with a gold pitcher and cups.

The prince covered up his eyes. "Give me strength."

"Then this is just what you need, Your Highness,"

the woman grunted as she shuffled into the room. Her low cheekbones and small mouth made her eyes seem even larger and livelier, and she moved with an easy, well-muscled grace.

"Here, let me help you, little one." Bibil grabbed hold of the rim of the tray.

"No, no, I can do it," she insisted and, stepping up to a table, carefully lowered the tray.

The prince widened his fingers so he could peer through the cracks. "Oh, look at this." He reached over to pick up a diamond-shaped shell so thin it was transparent except for the faint rainbow tinge on the surface. "Rahu remembered all my favorites."

"Your Highness." Bibil fixed him with a stern look.

With a reluctant sigh, the prince set the shell back on the plate. "This is agony."

"Oh, don't be such a baby, Your Highness," the woman said.

The prince sat up to stare at her. "There's only one person on all of Angira who dared to talk to me like that. Urmi?"

The woman smiled and nodded her head as if pleased. "Yes, I've taken a post in the kitchen." She added with a nod to Bibil, "It helps being the niece of a famous old warrior."

The prince looked at Sulu. "When we used to visit Bibil's old village, this terrible creature made my stay simply miserable with her pranks." He lolled his head back on the lounge. "If you'd only known that you weren't plaguing a little serving boy from the palace, but an imperial prince."

Urmi smiled mischievously. "Oh, I knew, Your Highness. We all did."

The prince sat up. "But I was in disguise."

"You *thought* you were in disguise," she corrected him.

The prince collapsed back on the lounge. "Ah, you puncture one of my most cherished memories. All these years, I thought I put on such a marvelous performance."

"I wasn't going to let a terror like you walk around unsuspected." Bibil slapped the prince's shoulder as he went to Urmi. "And how is the family?" Bibil threw his arms around her and gave her a hug.

"We'll talk of it later," she said quietly.

"No, please, I think of your village as almost my own," the prince said. "I have so many affectionate memories of it when Bibil would take me there for the harvest festivals."

The woman seemed glad of an excuse to change the subject. "Even though I beat you at all the games?"

"She cheated," the prince insisted as Sulu and Bibil started to laugh.

"Only because you changed the rules to suit yourself," Urmi said snippily. "Did you try to do that with the offworlders too?"

The prince pretended to glare at her. "I was only a humble prince among the many royalty offworld."

"Ah." Urmi folded her arms. "And what did Your Highness do when he met an imperial prince from another world? Who went through the doorway first?"

The prince balanced the heel of his right foot on the toes of his left. "It depended on whether he was the eighth or ninth in line to the throne."

"I hear," Urmi suggested with a slight smile, "that there are worlds where even women rule."

"Yes, quite a few," the prince agreed cheerfully.

"But I still asked them what place they had in the line of succession."

"And if they were ninth like you?"

The prince pretended to flip a coin into the air. "We tossed for it, of course."

Urmi shook her head in mock sympathy. "How terrible to have the imperial dignity depend on random chance. No wonder you came home. Your pride must be badly bruised."

"I was looking forward to at least one day of being pampered." The prince lolled his head back upon the couch. "But not at the hands of Rahu."

She lifted up a plate. "Then feel free to indulge. I connived for this duty and switched plates just to make sure they were safe."

It was Bibil, however, who picked up the first shell. "Your Highness." And he popped it into his mouth, shell and all.

Urmi pivoted as if offended. "Uncle, how could you think I'd try to poison His Highness?"

He patted her on the shoulder while he waited for something dire to happen to him. "You are my favorite niece—"

"It's not much of a compliment, considering that I happen to be your brother's only surviving child."

"Let me finish." He left his hand on her shoulder, close to her throat. "But I would not trust my own dear, departed mother."

"Shame on you," she pretended to scold him. "Everyone loved grandmother."

"That's because she was always the first one to sample the plate." Bibil nodded smugly to the prince. "I think it's safe, Your Highness."

"At last." The prince looked apologetically at the

49

two Federation officers. "You must forgive my manners, gentlemen. But I have dreamed of this moment for years." And, saying that, he swept up a handful of the shells and began to pop them quickly into his mouth. "Oh, they're heavenly. Do try some." Mr. Spock refused, but Sulu could not resist and found that the shell crunched easily between his teeth, like wafer-thin candy, and the meat inside was like shrimp but with a nutty, sweet flavor.

"It's delicious." Sulu smiled to the prince.

"Yes, quite." The prince pointed to a dish of stuffed orange mushrooms. "Try that one next, will you, Bibil?"

Mr. Spock gave the prince a perplexed look. "You seem so very cheerful about a situation which borders on anarchy."

"Angira is one world only in the loosest sense. The average person here really identifies with his own clan first and Angira second." The prince watched Bibil intently. "Like Rahu, they count themselves as Angirans only when faced with offworlders."

"But that still doesn't explain your cheerfulness."

"There are only two possible reactions, Mr. Spock." The prince hardly waited for Bibil to finish swallowing before he picked up several mushrooms. "One either learns to accept the excitement of Angiran politics with a certain good-humored fatalism, or one becomes a hermit in the badlands and lives off roots and cacti." He lay down on a low, broad couch. "And," he added, "there is always the chance that we may all wake up some day and end this nightmare. Perhaps I'll have some small part to play in that process."

Mr. Spock nodded his head ever so slightly as if he approved of the prince's own choice. The prince seemed to have gone up in his estimation. "Indeed? And how long has this nightmare gone on?"

The prince swallowed quickly and reached for more. "For several thousand Earth years. We Angirans are a persistent lot."

The others had been paying attention to the prince during this exchange, but Sulu had been curious about the mushrooms themselves and had been examining one on the tray. When he looked up to ask Urmi about their natural habitat, he paused. For a moment, when she thought no one else was looking, another Urmi stood in her place.

Her mouth was still in the same cheerful smile, but her eyes were now focused on the prince as if he were a book whose pages she had to memorize quickly. And the reading wasn't very pleasant either. However, when the prince started to turn toward the tray again, her eyes took on the same cheerful look as before.

The prince gestured to Urmi. "But don't stand on ceremony, Urmi. You never did before."

"We were children then," Urmi reminded him politely.

"Then indulge a childish whim." The prince raised a plate and held it before her.

"Thank you, Your Highness." She helped herself to one of the shells.

When someone tapped at the door, Bibil called out, "Who is it?"

The voice came muffled through the door. "A priest come to purify the prince." And there was a faint jingling sound of a shadow-chasing sword.

"I don't think you'll have much luck, but you're welcome to try anyway." The prince motioned Bibil to open the door.

A priest stood there, his head hidden within a large, basket-shaped hat. His right hand, covered by a long, fluttering sleeve, held a shadow-catcher.

"So"—the prince wiped his hands hastily on a napkin—"where would you like me to stand?"

As the priest stepped into the room, Sulu craned his neck to get a better look at a shadow-catcher. Puzzled, he frowned at the prince. "I thought you said that shadow-catchers didn't have an edge."

Whipping the shadow-catcher over his head, the false priest shouted, "Die, traitor," and started for the prince.

Chapter Two

Without even hesitating, Bibil picked up the pitcher from the tray and threw it with deadly accuracy so that it caught the false priest squarely on the side of the head. The pitcher gave off a merry bong as it showered wine over both the false priest and the room.

But almost at the same moment, three *sinha* warriors came screaming into the room before the first assassin could even fall to the floor.

However, Mr. Spock had gotten to his feet and grabbed the back of his chair. Lifting its legs from the floor, he swung it in a low arc like a shot-putter to send it crashing into the second assassin.

The prince threw himself onto the floor and rolled toward the false priest's sword. In the meantime, Sulu had snatched up the footrest and, holding it by the legs, brought it down with a thud on the second assassin's head.

"Sulu!" Mr. Spock shouted.

Sulu turned just in time to catch a downward stroke

from the sword of a third assassin. It tore the silken covering of the footrest's cushion so that a fine, fluffy down flew into the air. The third assassin brought his sword around for a back-handed slash. But the prince had grabbed the sword by that time. It made an ominous jingling sound as he rose to his knees and lunged. The sword point slid easily into the back of Sulu's opponent.

He screamed, dropping his sword as he reached his hands behind him. Sulu brought up the footrest just in time to stop the fourth assassin from lunging at the prince's heart.

A vase in his hand, Mr. Spock came leaping over the prince's couch. He swung the vase at the fourth assassin, but the assassin managed to bring his sword up so that the vase broke on the blade.

He smiled in triumph as he readied himself for a backswing that would take off Mr. Spock's head. Suddenly he gave a grunt and a surprised look appeared on his face. The sword clattered from his hand and he turned slightly to reveal the slender dagger that had sprouted suddenly from his back.

"Urmi, you know commoners aren't allowed to bring daggers into the palace." Bibil seemed more shocked by his niece's impropriety than by the *sinha*'s assault.

"Be glad I did." She was drawing a second knife from the sash-end of her *soropa* as two more assassins charged into the room from the hallway outside. Side-stepping, she tripped the first one neatly and stabbed him as he fell.

In the meantime, the prince had freed his blade from his victim's back and turned to engage the last assassin. Urmi scrambled to shut the door and lock it while Sulu,

Mr. Spock and Bibil dragged a heavy dressing table across it.

"Who sent you?" the prince demanded. The grim-faced assassin tried a thrust at the prince's heart, but the prince deflected his blade easily, sliding his own along the assassin's blade like a guide so that the point rested against the middle of the assassin's chest where, presumably, an Angiran heart would be. "Who sent you?"

But the assassin did not look afraid, only angry and frustrated that he had failed in his mission. "Traitor," he spat, and slashed at the prince one last time. Vikram thrust his sword home almost as a reflex action and the assassin's sword dropped from his hand. "Tr—" he tried to say again as he slumped to the floor. The prince held his sword rigid so that the body slid off the blade.

Mr. Spock looked distastefully at the sword he had picked up. "I assume they haven't heard of conversation?"

"Angirans are impatient. They prefer a quicker, sharper wit—so to speak." He started for the door. "Even so, my father must be warned about the vermin running around in the corridors. The palace needs fumigating, I'm afraid."

The screams began to float through the great stone hallways—distant and thin so that they were almost ghostly. Bibil turned to the prince. "I'm afraid that your family and friends may be learning about it now."

"Not even Rahu would carry out a massacre on this scale." The prince stared at the wall as if he were trying to see through it to the other rooms.

"Why not?" Urmi retrieved her first dagger and tucked it away. "He has all of your family and their

55

supporters here at one time. And you're all off your guard, getting ready for the welcoming ceremonies." She reached down and took a sword.

"Rahu always wished to make a name for himself," the prince sighed. "His deeds will certainly go down now in the songs of voice masters."

"You may very well be the heir to the throne," Mr. Spock reminded the prince.

"Your Highness," a voice echoed down the hallway. "Your Highness." The sound of many feet reverberated down the great stone passageway.

"It sounds like more visitors." The old soldier stepped directly into the doorway and spread his legs.

The prince looked at Urmi. "Drop those weapons and you can probably claim to be some innocent servant."

"Thank you"—she joined her uncle—"but I'd rather stay with my present company."

"Please yourself then. I can see you will." The prince bowed his head to Spock and Sulu. "I should have warned you that people on Angira seldom die of boredom."

"We are far from dead," Mr. Spock reminded the prince.

"I thought you would be the last person to be an optimist, Mr. Spock." The prince faced the door with a sad, knowing laugh.

"I am simply observing the facts." Mr. Spock hid his annoyance by testing the balance of his sword.

"Your Highness." The voice grew louder and clearer so that they could tell it was an older man's voice and the footsteps were made by only one pair of feet. They had only been hearing echoes before. "It's Diwan."

"That's my father's servant," the prince explained to Mr. Spock and Sulu. He motioned for them to open the door.

The old man pounded on the door until they had pulled the dressing table away and shot the bolt back. When Urmi finally jerked the door open, an elderly man with the brown paste mark of a servant stumbled into the room, his *soropa* spattered with blood. When he saw Prince Vikram in the doorway, Diwan fell to his knees. Though both his hands covered his chest, they could still see the edges of a great gash there. "Thank the Many that you're still alive."

Bibil immediately knelt to support the old servant. "My father?" Prince Vikram demanded.

Diwan's knees sagged and he would have collapsed again if Bibil had not been holding him up. "Dead—as are all your brothers. Now they are massacring your father's supporters." He flopped a hand at his legs and they could see that his calves were coated in blood. "They were gathering for the assembly to greet you when Rahu's men attacked. The assembly floor is covered with blood now. It's terrible, terrible. You must escape, Your Highness. You are all that is left of the imperial line."

Bibil touched head and heart as if in prayer. "As bad as that?"

Diwan nodded feebly. "You must help the prince get away."

"How?" The prince pointed his sword. "We're five levels from the nearest gate and the corridors will be full of Rahu's men now."

Diwan clutched at Bibil's shoulder. "But you only need to go two levels down to the Old Chapel. You'll find a secret passageway that leads down to a hidden gate."

"But how could we reach the Old Chapel?" The prince gave a frustrated look toward the corridor. "We'll still need more warriors to fight our way through Rahu's men."

Urmi was standing in the doorway looking out into the hallway. "I know where you can find your own guard, Your Highness."

Both the prince and Bibil gave her puzzled looks. "What do you mean, girl?" Bibil asked his niece. "Who can we count on?"

"They once made the entire world tremble," she boasted. "The Hounds."

Bibil frowned. "I thought they would all have drunk themselves to death by now."

"Well, it wasn't for want of trying." Urmi laughed confidently. "But there are still some of them who have survived. And there's still a bite left in those old dogs yet."

The prince considered the possibilities. "It may be a fool's errand; but have I ever been anything else in my life?"

Diwan's voice, though thin, took on a new urgency. "In the chapel, there is a statue of the goddess of mercy. Touch her foot and the door will open."

"Yes." The prince nodded. "That would appeal to my ancestors' sense of humor."

Diwan stared at the prince desperately. "You must get to Kotah." Kotah was the name of the province which the prince's clan controlled, but, as Sulu recalled him mentioning, he had rarely gone there. Diwan stiffened for a moment as if he were trying to fight off the pain. "Kotah. Safe . . ." His voice suddenly faded away and his head rolled to the side.

Bibil closed the old man's eyes and lowered him to the floor. "He was a tough one in his own way."

"Well," the prince promised solemnly, "I'll see that it's put on his tomb—assuming we survive."

With Urmi leading the way, they trotted down the corridor. The cries seemed to grow louder and shriller. "The massacre seems to be spreading from the assembly room," the prince said grimly.

"Let's hope we can keep ahead of it." Sulu glanced behind them.

It was a quarter of a kilometer to the kitchens; and though they saw none of Rahu's men, they found the corpses of elegantly dressed Angirans—evidence that Rahu's men were nearby.

The palace kitchen was a cavernous place some hundred meters on each side. Dishes for the feast, waiting to be cooked, cluttered row after row of tables. But there was neither a cook nor a cook's helper in sight—as if they had scurried off to hide during the massacre.

The Hounds were heard before they were seen; their voices, used to cutting through the noise of countless taverns and battlefields, boomed merrily through the huge kitchen. Bibil grimaced as if embarrassed. "Old habits certainly die hard."

"Having a good time?" the prince asked curiously.

"Looting," Bibil explained.

When they entered the kitchen, they could see a half dozen small figures at the opposite end by the huge fireplaces. Fires were burning in over a dozen of them while whole sides of meat turned on spits, sending juices crackling and spattering into the flames beneath. The Hounds were sitting or, in some cases, lying before one with dozens of golden pitchers around them. One man turned a spit in between large swigs from the pitcher in his hand. Age had changed the fur of the half dozen Hounds from gold to a silver white.

"They're drunk already," Mr. Spock said to Bibil.

"An old Hound drunk is worth two *sinha* sober," Urmi said to him, and then, setting her hands around her mouth like a megaphone, she shouted, "We need your help." However, the men at the fireplace were too busy laughing and joking among themselves to hear her so she took a deep breath for an even louder shout. But Bibil put his hand on her shoulder.

"You have to know how to talk to old sword bait like these. 'Pretty please' just doesn't work." And he took a step out, spread his legs and took a deep breath, swelling out that huge chest of his. "At-TEN-SHUN."

Five of the men sprang instinctively to their feet. Only the man at the spit remained sitting, but he turned his head toward Bibil.

"Is it the Boy Wonder?" the man called.

"The same," Bibil announced in his loud parade-ground voice. He marched toward them in even, rhythmic strides. "And stand to attention when I order you to, Chit."

Urmi waited until there were some twenty paces between her and her uncle and then followed him, motioning the others to come after her.

"We're not in the service anymore," Chit said sullenly. "And you're not the youngest sergeant-major in the Hounds. The Hounds don't even exist. We were disbanded, remember? So don't try to give us orders."

And the other former Hounds glanced at one another sheepishly and then sat back down, one by one.

"You're still in the service of the emperor." Bibil stopped about ten meters away from them. As Sulu neared them, he could see that the fur of each man was silver with age and their gray *soropas* and aprons were spattered with grease and soot—as if they performed the most menial and dirtiest of kitchen chores.

Chit picked up some kind of roasted game bird from the floor and took a huge bite with studied casualness. "A proper emperor would know how to treat his old soldiers."

Bibil planted a fist on either hip. "You once were soldiers. Now you're nothing but thieving old scum."

Chit took another huge bite from the breast of the bird. "I'm surprised they ever let you back on this world. I thought they were going to keep you in exile." He rested a foot on top of a footstool and shoved it toward Bibil. "Still, you always could smell out a party." He pitched the bird to Bibil. "Help yourself." And he broke into such a broad welcoming smile that Sulu realized he had only been pretending to be sullen before.

Bibil caught the bird neatly in one hand and took a bite since it seemed to be expected. "Chit, I thought you were going to retire to your farm." He looked toward a man with one eye. "And I thought you were going to run a tavern, Bacha?"

Bacha slapped his leg in embarrassment. "Oh, well, you know how things are."

Chit prodded Bacha with his toes. "He drank up all his own stock."

Bacha twisted around and gave a tired, bitter smile.

"Well, at least I got to enjoy it and that's more than you can say." He turned back to Bibil. "He gambled his farm away."

"It was the inflation, I tell you," Chit insisted indignantly. "Ever since this emperor started modernizing things, he's been printing money on paper." He turned and spat into the fire. "It isn't even worth using in the shithouse."

A third man with a scar across half his face took a drink sourly from the pitcher. "Gold coins are scarcer than kind hearts now. And the paper money's worthless and so are pensions."

Chit jabbed a finger at Bibil. "But that crazy man on the throne wants his taxes to be paid in hard currency, so you wind up having to sell double the crops just to get enough coins." He gave the spit a quick, savage turn so that the juices went flying into the flames with a loud crackling sound. "Now what's a person to do?"

"I would have been better off dying in battle." Bacha shook his head. "I'd rather be part of a funeral monument than be a live old relic."

And, looking at them by the fire, Sulu couldn't help feeling a kind of sadness—as if they were whales left stranded on a beach by a sea that had vanished all too quickly.

Bibil contemptuously threw the bird onto the lap of Chit. "When Urmi told me there were some of the old Hounds still alive in the palace, I thought my problems were solved. But what do I find? Six drunken old wrecks feeling sorry for themselves." He started to pivot. "Come, Your Highness."

"His Highness?" The scarred man squinted his eyes as if he had trouble seeing beyond Bibil. "Is that the young prince you've been nursemaiding?"

"Who else? And with Lord Rahu hot after his blood."

Chit dumped the bird on the floor and hastily wiped his hands on his apron. "Tell the lad to come forward."

"Go on," murmured Bibil.

They walked toward the fireplace while the small group of men set down their wine bottles and meals. Chit squinted at the prince. "Well, he's got the look of his grandfather."

"Who doesn't?" snickered the scarred man. "The old he-goat—"

Bibil cut him short. "Jata, we don't have the time to reminisce now. We have to escape."

Chit pointed at Sulu and Mr. Spock. "And what are those?"

"Offworlders," Bibil said. "They came to help us."

"More like make this world into a worse mess," grumbled Jata. "This is the first time in ages that we've had enough to eat and drink. Why should we leave?"

"Not since Agra"—Bibil nodded toward Jata's scar —"where you picked up that little decoration."

"That was something then." Jata shook his head at the prince. "Now your grandfather knew how to treat his troops right."

Bibil concentrated on Jata. "He gave you a medallion himself, didn't he?"

"For being the first man on the wall." Jata took on a distant look as if he were remembering better, more glorious times.

"And now," Bibil said quietly, "his grandson's come to you."

Jata suddenly seemed to remember where he was. "A lot of good his children and his children's children have done us."

"And what happened to that medallion?" Bibil demanded sternly. "Did you put it over the hearth so your children and grandchildren could see it? Or did you pawn it?"

Jata wiped at his nose uncomfortably. "Times were hard."

"You mean you needed a drink," Bibil snorted. "Even if the old emperor had been alive today, you'd still be where you are." He sighed. "And here I've been telling His Highness how you chased every army you ever faced off the battlefield, and now look at you. Nothing but a bunch of dirty old thieves who couldn't chase away a pack of children."

"Here now." Chit raised a warning finger. "Watch that kind of talk."

"The old emperor provided for you." Bibil's voice took on a frustrated edge. "It's not his fault you squandered it all like so many bandits."

The prince touched Bibil's arm. "Come along, Bibil. I think we're going to have to look for help elsewhere."

"Now hold on," Chit said. "We didn't say we wouldn't help. We just wanted to think about it."

"We have very little time," the prince observed to them, "and it is not in me to beg."

Bacha rose from the bench and pointed at the prince. "Now *that* is spoken just like his grandfather. He's one of the bloodline all right."

Chit ripped off a drumstick from the bird and waved it at Vikram. "So you're the one they call the Shadow Lord?"

Jata nudged Chit. "Look at that sword of his. Can't you see he's armed for the part?"

Chit irritably rubbed the spot that Jata had just hit. "What part?"

"Why, the Lord of the Underworld where all the shadows of the dead go." Jata looked at the prince as if he expected him to laugh. "Now how's that for a play on your name?"

The prince, however, could only manage a feeble smile. "I've never been important enough for anyone to bother with a joke like that."

Impulsively, Chit tore off his apron. "But you are now. I don't know about you, lads, but I'm sick of the sight of dishwater and garbage." He wiped his hand across one of the blackened stones above the cooking fire. "We'll be shadow hounds for a shadow lord."

Laughing, Bacha became caught up in the same fancy. "If we had any sense, we would have gone underground long ago."

"Let's get ready," Jata called to the others. They threw down whatever they had in their hands and reached for the blackened stones.

His face clumsily blackened, Chit rose with sooty palms and started for the prince. "You'll want to be prepared too, Lord."

But the prince stepped back. "It isn't time for me to go into mourning yet."

"Humor them," Bibil whispered.

Chit held out his black palms. "So what will it be, Lord?"

The prince leaned forward. "This should give the Many quite a start when They see me."

"And if They don't treat you right, we'll kick Them off Their thrones and put you in Their place." He wiped the soot carefully over the prince's face.

Then, their faces blackened like masks, the Hounds snatched up kitchen knives and full jars of wine. "Fall in now," Chit ordered the others. With all the excitement and eagerness of small boys, they formed into a single column and marched smartly toward the door.

Sulu, Urmi and Mr. Spock had been gathering food into sacks and putting water into bags made from the bladders of some large animals.

As they followed the Hounds, Sulu murmured to Mr. Spock, "They must have fought their last battle twenty years ago."

The science officer arched an eyebrow. "More like thirty, I should think."

"What can those old fossils do against Rahu's men?" Sulu wondered.

"Probably very little," Mr. Spock sniffed. "I suspect it will come down to our own skill with these outmoded weapons. Are you ready?"

Sulu adjusted his sweaty palm's grip on his sword hilt. "Not really. But I don't think I have much choice in the matter."

They had gone only some fifty meters from the kitchen before a half-dozen of Rahu's men found them. They were not *sinha* but seemed to be from Rahu's own household since they wore metal cuirasses engraved with the rayed sun that was the emblem of Rahu's clan. They were armed with sharp-edged halberds.

Sulu tensed and raised his sword in both hands so that it was parallel to his torso. Though Sulu had had plenty of practice and theory with a sword, he had never actually used it against an opponent who wanted to kill him.

But before Sulu could even engage, wine jars flew at Rahu's men. Most of them shattered against the floor, but a few found their mark. And then the Hounds rushed past him. "Angira, Angira."

Chit ran straight toward the points of the spears and

the halberd blades, but just before Rahu's soldiers could lunge, he dropped to the floor, sliding in under the shafts and slipping his blade up under the armor of the first man.

With a shout, he tumbled backward off of Chit's knife and Chit was slashing at the legs of a soldier to his right. The other Hounds were almost as wild and reckless. What the Hounds lacked in youth and energy, they made up for in cunning. In a matter of minutes, four of the halberdiers were down, and the other two were running off.

Sulu lowered his sword to stare as the Hounds began to loot the corpses. "They're crazy."

"Suicidal is a better word," Mr. Spock corrected him.

"Well, they don't quite recite a rhymed couplet with every thrust and parry"—the prince leaned against the wall—"but they do get things done. Do you suppose d'Artagnan was more like this than the dandy in Dumas?"

"Well, I don't know how many copies he would have sold with this version." Sulu watched as Chit leapt to his feet. Then, throwing back his head, Chit let out a howl that echoed down the hallways.

"The world hasn't heard that cry in a long time." Bibil massaged the fingers of his right hand as if his arthritis were bothering him slightly. "They're the likeliest sweepings for the prison, and yet give them a proper cause and they'll rise above themselves every time." Bibil paused proudly and nodded to the prince. "And the cause is you, lad."

The prince held up his sword wearily as if this were an old argument between them. "Oh, no, you don't. All my life, I've tried to put as much distance between myself and the throne. If I had been born the son of a farmer, you would never have kept after me the way you did. I can't help who my parents were. The throne is a burden that I do not want."

"Neither beasts of burden nor princes have any say in what weights they carry." Bibil fixed him with a stern eye. "Whether you like it or not, this is the brighter side of your heritage and more valuable than gold or palaces."

"That is simply an irrational illusion that should have nothing to do with me." The prince looked to Mr. Spock for support.

Mr. Spock had been watching the Hounds strip the armor and weapons from the dead. He faced the prince now. "That isn't strictly true, Your Highness. Certain illusions have been necessary in the growth of a group identity. 'One king, one nation' has proved a useful phrase in forging many little feudal states into a nation with one identity. The same has been true of certain worlds."

The prince frowned. "But what is logical about that?"

Mr. Spock slid his sword back into his belt. "Societies do not always develop along logical lines."

Bibil used the back of his hand to slap the prince's arm. "There, you see. You can't avoid the throne now."

"But I can certainly give it a good try," the prince snapped.

Armed with halberds and swords now, the Hounds fought several more skirmishes with Rahu's household troops; and though the elderly veterans had less and less energy with each fight, they still managed to send

Rahu's men running. By that time they had traveled two levels down.

Bibil gave a disbelieving laugh. "We've made it. I can see the chapel." He pointed his sword at an ornate door of patinaed bronze.

Suddenly a woman screamed; and though it was difficult to tell distances in the winding corridors, she seemed to be nearby. The prince halted abruptly. With a pained, anxious expression on his face, he listened to the woman. "We just can't run off and leave that poor woman to Rahu's men."

Bibil's nostrils widened as he inhaled. "I don't like it any better than you do, but we have to think with our heads, not our hearts. We can't save everyone in the palace."

"Agreed," Mr. Spock said. "Our primary objective is to get you to safety."

The prince twisted sideways as if the screams were a magnet drawing him toward it. "That's easy for you to say, gentlemen, but I couldn't live with myself if I turned my back on that."

"You may not live at all if you don't come with us right now." Bibil looked the prince up and down critically. "Don't let all our little victories go to your head. So far we've only met and scattered sword bait. *Sinha* are made of sterner stuff."

But the prince's confidence was unshakable. "You go on ahead and locate the secret passage. I'll join you when I can."

Urmi cocked her head to the side as if pleasantly surprised. "So you're not nearly as selfish as you pretend to be."

The prince raised and lowered his shoulders. "Every

69

now and then I get an attack of high ideals—usually at an inconvenient time."

She gave him a grudging smile as if he had just gone up in her esteem. "No, beneath all that foolishness, there really is something there." She suddenly placed a hand beneath her throat and gave a mock cough. "And I think it must be catching. I'll go with you."

The prince saluted Sulu with his sword. "Coming, d'Artagnan?"

Sulu's instinctive reaction was to say yes; but, much to the prince's disappointment, Sulu was disciplined enough to glance at Mr. Spock. And the Vulcan was frowning in disapproval. "Your Highness, our small group can do little to stop the slaughter in the palace. We can do far more when you are safe in Kotah."

The prince lowered his sword self-righteously. "But I might be able to save a few people. And what value can you place on a life?" He started down the corridor. "Shall we proceed, Urmi?"

Jata let out a whoop. "Now there's a real emperor." He fell in behind Urmi and beckoned to the rest of the Hounds to join him.

"Children think they're invulnerable," Bibil sighed to Sulu and Mr. Spock. "So I guess older, wiser heads ought to go along to pick up the pieces."

They ran for several hundred meters down dusty, dimly lit corridors until they turned into a long hallway with false pillars set into the walls. Between the pillars were niches with dust-covered busts that frowned at the group racing by now.

Urmi, who was in the lead by then, slipped as she reached the end of the hallway. At first Sulu thought that she had simply lost her footing on the slick marble floor. But she rose from her hands and knees, wriggling the fingers of her free hand uncomfortably and looking about for something on which to wipe them. Impulsively she went over to the left half of a set of drapes that covered the exit and wiped her hand across the blue material, leaving behind dark, red stains.

She was using one of the drapes to wipe off her knees as they crowded toward the entrance to a large, domed room some fifty meters in diameter. Only a few of the fat yellow candles had been lit in the chandelier and the few pieces of furniture in there were covered by old cloths as if the room were rarely used. But some twenty-odd corpses lay scattered across the floor so that the white marble tiles were now covered with large red pools.

Right at their feet lay a man with his eyes opened in terror, his mouth contorted for an angry shout that would never be sounded now. Urmi took a ragged breath and nodded to the corpse. "He was one of the men from the kitchen."

Chit carefully stepped into the room and paused beside the body of a young woman. "And this was one of the nursemaids. What harm could she do to anyone?"

"Let's ask her killers, shall we?" Despite the uncertain footing, the prince hurried across the room toward another hallway from which the screaming sounded.

When they rounded the corner into a wide corridor, they found a dozen *sinha* using a bench as an improvised battering ram as they tried to break down a wooden door. Behind the door, they could hear people begging the warriors to go away. But that only made the *sinha* swing the bench even harder against the door.

Bibil tried to yank the prince back behind the corner. "Get back, you young fool, before they see you."

Chapter Three

The Hounds ranged themselves on either side of the prince and Bibil, leaving only a few meters on the right. "Come along," Urmi said to Sulu and Mr. Spock. "It looks like we're to have the flank of honor."

Sulu stepped up between Urmi and Mr. Spock and swung his sword up. In his nervousness, he glanced at Mr. Spock, who was waiting as calmly for the charge as he would have for a meal. Sulu looked back at the *sinha*. "It's strange," he said out of the side of his mouth to Mr. Spock. "I've never actually seen an opponent in the flesh before."

Mr. Spock turned sideways and swung his blade up. "And if you wish to glimpse another opponent, I suggest you concentrate, Mr. Sulu."

Sulu watched the *sinha* run toward them. The eyes of one *sinha* seemed to lock on him and Sulu watched as the angry, scowling face grew closer and closer. He had fought and killed before, but that had been done at astronomical distances with the *Enterprise*'s weaponry, not at arm's length.

Sulu had thought, perhaps, that at some magical moment—perhaps by the grace of some fencers' angel —he might receive all the buoyant confidence of a d'Artagnan or a Cyrano. At the very least, he thought he would feel the competitive excitement and determination he felt during a tournament. But he felt neither —only a tightening of his stomach as if someone were drawing his bowels into a knot. He could feel the sweat on his palms loosening his grip slightly and he had to remind himself to breathe.

"Rahu! Rahu!" The *sinha* swung his blade in a waist-high arc and Sulu swung his blade down in a parry. It was a shock when the blades met. It seemed as if Sulu could feel not only the strength of the other man's wrist but his determination—even his eagerness to kill Sulu. The *sinha* almost immediately disengaged and stepped back, eyes appraising Sulu for some weakness or flaw.

Sulu should have been doing the same, but instead he could not help glancing at Mr. Spock, who was fencing capably if not brilliantly. But then, Sulu realized, Mr. Spock was probably treating this as some new problem of mind-and-body relationship. He was simply letting his body move through the motions it had been taught.

The hiss of a blade slicing through the air brought Sulu back to reality. He saw the glint of something silver coming down at his head from his left side. He parried the blow, knocking the *sinha*'s blade further to the left, away from the *sinha*'s side.

What happened next was more instinct than plan. While the *sinha* was recovering for another blow, Sulu

74

dropped his left shoulder low and whipped his sword down and around almost in a full circle so fast that his wrists began to ache with the strain. And then the sword seemed to be rising of its own will as if it were drawing Sulu's arms up with it.

And for a fraction of a second, the *sinha* did not seem to know what to do against a blade that was coming at him so close to his body from beneath. The angle was too awkward to knock Sulu's blade to the outside away from his body. The *sinha* tried to bring his own blade down, but it meant raising his own sword at an absurd angle so that his parry lacked real strength. When their blades met, Sulu did not feel the stiff resistance of before and he let his blade slide off the *sinha*'s sword and into the *sinha*'s body.

Sulu's blade caught the rim of the *sinha*'s cuirass and it served as a guide as Sulu swept it across. The sword paused for a moment as it sank into the *sinha*'s flesh, but then its sharp edge sliced easily across the belly as if it were slicing silk.

With a scream, the *sinha* toppled backward. And Sulu was standing there with his blade hovering in the air. He stared at the blood on the sword, realizing that he had really killed a man. He felt more shame than elation.

And then Sulu's own awareness began to expand outward again so that he began to hear the clashing of weapons around him. He looked to his right. Mr. Spock was still fencing with the other *sinha*, who was content to wait till his superior reach gave him an opening. Mr. Sulu brought his blade up over his shoulder, timing his blow for when the *sinha* was exposed and then he struck. Blood covered the *sinha*'s shoulder and he stepped back.

"It's not tournament rules," Sulu said to Mr. Spock, "but I guess that doesn't matter."

"Survival is what counts," Mr. Spock said with a slight smile.

And then Sulu turned to see what had been happening around him. Urmi had killed her own opponent, and two more *sinha* were dead. But three Hounds had also died and Chit was down with a slash across his leg. In the meantime, the prince was being pressed back by two *sinha*.

One of them squinted at the prince and then gave a sudden, exulting shout. "It's Prince Vikram. Hey, we've got the prince."

Urmi's slash caught the shouting *sinha* in the throat. But too late, excited shouts answered from a nearby corridor. Bibil lunged past the prince and the *sinha* barely escaped being skewered. He parried Bibil's thrust, but left himself open to the prince's sword. And the prince didn't hesitate to lay his chest open.

Bibil yanked at the prince's arm. "Come on."

"But the people—" The prince pointed his bloody sword at the room.

"Can't you get it through your thick skull?" Bibil snapped. "We'll be lucky if we get out alive ourselves now."

A dozen more *sinha* had appeared at the opposite end of the corridor. And there were more shouts in the distance. Chit had torn off part of his ragged *soropa* and bound it around his leg as a tourniquet. "Go on, Your Highness. We'll hold them off."

"I can't leave you like this." The prince shook his head. "I'm the one who led you here."

"We didn't have to follow." Having found some last new source of energy, Chit slowly shoved himself

76

upright with the help of his halberd. "Your Highness, we're as likely a crew for the executioner's sword, but we do know how to die gloriously." And though he was too proud to beg out loud, his eyes pleaded silently for the prince to understand.

"I won't forget you." The prince raised his sword in a mock salute.

"Why? We're just some old fools who outlived their usefulness." And Chit turned to meet the new group of *sinha*.

"Come on, lad." Bibil pulled at the prince's sleeve. The prince turned, stumbling into his servant. Tears had half blinded him. Sulu hooked his right arm through the prince's left arm. "I'll lead you."

Halfway back to the chapel, the prince shook off Bibil's hand. "I can see now." He drew a long, shaky breath. "But I'm not sure I want to. How could I have led those men to such senseless deaths?"

"Well," Bibil sighed, "keep that in mind next time you want to play at being a hero. People can die for your mistakes."

Sulu hadn't expected the Hounds to hold the *sinha* for more than a few seconds, but they seemed to be giving a good account of themselves, if the clashing of steel behind them meant anything.

"There wasn't any reason to die for me. I'm just a creature like any of them." The prince rubbed his forehead as if both puzzled and pained.

"That you are," Bibil said, "but sometimes a person represents an ideal."

"But it's foolish." The prince glanced behind them as if he could see through the stone to where the Hounds were making their last stand.

"Then we should all be such fools," Bibil panted.

"Do you think they're dying just so you can become a . . . a professional student?"

Mr. Spock paused in front of Bibil and the prince. "Your Highness, you cannot help what sentiments other people might project onto you."

Bibil jerked his head at Mr. Spock. "What do you know about it?"

"I speak from experience," Mr. Spock said coldly. "People are continually asking me to play roles in petty emotional melodramas in which I have asked neither to be cast nor directed."

Urmi came up to Mr. Spock. "What kind of offworld double-talk is this? Just a while ago, you said some illusions were necessary."

Mr. Spock's nostrils widened slightly in annoyance at having his own quotes thrown back at him. "Whether the prince wishes to participate in the illusion is quite another thing. I was merely providing him with enough information so he could make his own decision."

Bibil took the prince's arm and tried to guide him around Mr. Spock; but the prince refused to budge. "Well, the prince also has responsibilities."

"Which have to be determined by reason and logic," Spock stated firmly. "Not by one's emotions. It is morally repugnant when you try to bully someone, using guilt as a club."

The prince perked up. "Well, if it's been done to you, you certainly don't seem any worse for wear. But tell me the secret, Mr. Spock."

Mr. Spock hesitated—as if he felt he had already inadvertently confessed too much. "One uses logic and reason to make objective choices."

"Don't use objectivity as an excuse for selfishness," Bibil insisted stubbornly.

Mr. Spock, however, could be just as stubborn in his own way. "The same might be said of responsibility—or rather what people try to claim your responsibilities are."

Bibil leaned his weight on his left leg and cocked his head to the side. "Are we discussing the prince's predicament, or your own?"

Mr. Spock lowered his hand. "The terms of the argument may change, but not the argument itself." Mr. Spock leaned his head forward as if to emphasize his point. "Emotions can be worse tyrants than any emperor and they provide the excuse for the most terrible abuses. I am merely asking you to respect the prince's decision."

Bibil squinted an eye first at Mr. Spock and then at the prince. "I don't know which is worse: the fool who knows his duty and refuses to accept it or the fool who won't even admit it." He jabbed a finger at the prince. "No matter what you claim, I know your heart's Angiran."

"But my legs are most definitely not"—the prince began to run as if he wished to escape from all of them—"and they will be carrying the rest of me far away from Angira."

They raced down the corridors as quickly as they could, arriving at the chapel out of breath. Bibil threw himself at the door and shoved it open, waving them through the doorway hurriedly. Then he shut the door.

The chapel was a small room with a low ceiling, about forty meters square. The walls had been left rough and unfinished, though they seemed filled with a bewildering array of statues jammed together on various altars. The statues were in many styles of carvings from different ages of art, as if assembled through countless generations. A solitary candle hanging from the ceiling cast a dim light over the room.

The prince pointed toward a statue whose *soropa* had been wrapped about its head so that its face was hidden in shadow. "That's supposed to be the Lord of the Shadows, the Judge of the Underworld." In the statue's hand was a shadow-catcher like the prince's.

Sulu gave a shiver. "But I don't think he can tell a joke quite as well as you do."

"Oh, I think he has quite a sense of humor. Think about the people he chooses to take underground and the ones he chooses to spare."

Mr. Spock stared about the chapel. "Yes, but which one is the goddess of mercy?"

The prince scratched his forehead. "I don't know. We'll have to look. But perhaps there's something to be said for monotheism."

"Mr. Sulu and I can try to barricade the door while you search." Mr. Spock motioned Sulu over to a nearby bench.

Bibil strode forward to the main altar and peered intently at one statue. "By the Many, I never expected to see this."

"Did you find the goddess of mercy?" The prince swung around excitedly.

"No, your grandfather." He pointed toward a stern-faced statue holding one hand up with fingers delicately curled around an orb with an eye. "I'd never thought he'd end up keeping company as holy."

"I rather suspect it was my grandmother's idea." The prince began to inspect another side altar.

But the Angirans still had not found the statue by the time Mr. Spock and Sulu had dragged a heavy wooden bench over toward the door. Mr. Spock picked up one of the sacks of food and motioned for Sulu to do the same. "We'll be needing candles in the passageways. Extinguish the candles on the right side, Mr. Sulu. I'll take the ones on the left."

Sulu had managed to fill his sack full of candles when Urmi gave a shout. "I found her."

She was standing by one of the side altars, her hand hidden in a regular forest of statues. "But it's very small."

"Yes, well, mercy has little to do with Angira," the prince said as he strode over to Urmi.

Her hand pressed and pulled at one foot. "No, it's not that one." She began to push and jerk at the other one.

There was a click and Urmi stepped back from the altar as chains began to clink and old stones began to groan against one another. Faintly, through the heavy door, Sulu could hear excited shouts from the *sinha*.

"I think they've heard the entrance opening," he said.

"Then we'd better hurry." Bibil picked up a heavy gold candleholder and waved Sulu and Spock toward the altar.

The marble block that had formed the front facing for the altar was sliding down now, revealing steps leading downward. The heavy bronze door rattled in the doorframe as the *sinha* tried to get in. First the prince and then Urmi stepped through.

"We'll have to jam the mechanism if we can," Mr. Spock said as he crouched down and stepped onto the stairway. The bronze door had begun to ring with a deep, bell-like sound as the *sinha* tried to batter it down.

Bibil almost shoved Sulu through the opening and

followed him onto the steps. Mr. Spock had already found the mechanism that closed the block. He yanked at the chain as soon as Sulu and Bibil were on the steps beside him and then disabled the pulleys.

There was the sound of water dripping in the distance. Bibil held a candle above his head so that they could see the passageway overhead. Small little bumps covered the ceiling and they could see drops of moisture at the very tip of some. The texture gave the red-colored stone the appearance of flesh, and Bibil gave a grunt. "This passageway must have been built back in the first days of the original citadel."

The footing was rougher here than in the chapel. Water had created small nodules underfoot, and grooves, so that the going was more uncertain and it was hard to shake off the illusion that they were traveling down a damp, fleshy throat.

Bibil had led the way downward for some hundred steps before he turned around, motioning the prince past him. When Urmi would have gone by, he thrust the candle at Urmi so that she stepped backward into Sulu's arms, almost knocking the two of them down. "Hold her," Bibil growled. And the startled Sulu obeyed.

Handing the candle to the prince, Bibil relieved her of her sword and then gave her a quick yet thorough search. But there were only the two daggers in her sash.

His nostrils widened as he drew in a long, slow breath. "Now suppose you tell us what you were doing in the palace?"

"Trying to survive." She squirmed to break free from Sulu's grasp, but he held on.

Bibil slipped her sword through his sash and then held the daggers out on his palm. "With this arsenal?"

She grew still. "One . . . one needs protection."

"Daggers are like emperors. One is fine, but having two of them at the same time leads only to trouble." He closed his hands around the hilts of the daggers. "Whom did you mean to kill?"

"No one," Urmi insisted.

"I don't think—" the prince began, but Bibil merely sliced at the air for silence.

"There are some children who are born to be servants and others who are not," he explained, never taking his eyes off Urmi. "And if ever there was a more difficult, headstrong, rebellious child, it was Urmi. She would never take orders from anyone—no matter how often she was switched."

Urmi lifted her head defiantly. "You've been off gallivanting among all those elegant worlds. You don't know how bad things have gotten here."

"What do you mean?" the prince demanded. "Before I left, my father showed me all his plans for modernization. He was going to create all sorts of new factory complexes."

She twisted her head around to stare contemptuously at the prince. "And did he tell you what the lives of the factory workers were going to be like? You work from sunrise to sunset and then creep back to a little wooden box surrounded by families in other little boxes. And whether you're inside the factories or out, you have to breathe the fumes. And the water's so polluted now that the few surviving fish don't swim; they crawl."

The prince stiffened indignantly. "Then why don't you people leave?"

"How?" Urmi's voice broke with anger. "They owe money to the companies for rent, for food, for clothing —for everything. They've just exchanged one form of slavery for another. Only instead of being owned by the landlord, they're owned by the company. The ones who can afford it send their children back to the villages like mine did. But most of them need the money, so their children work right beside them—and die. The factories just chew up people and spit out coffins."

"What about your parents?" Bibil asked sharply.

"I only know what I was told when their funeral urns were brought back to our village. Father was killed in a factory accident; mother died spitting out blood." She jerked her head resentfully at the prince. "The people say now that it's better to sit in your grave and wait to die than to go into one of those cities."

Bibil tucked the daggers away in the sash end of his *soropa.* "Your parents deserved better deaths than that." His voice ached with grief.

The prince looked at them both in genuine distress. "You must believe me when I tell you that such conditions were not my father's intentions for the workers. Someone must have been lying to him about their standard of living."

Urmi's forehead wrinkled skeptically. "I'd like to believe you."

Bibil squared his shoulders as a new thought occurred to him. "At the moment, you have to explain your actions, not the late emperor's. Were you thinking of taking your revenge, child?"

With a sudden elbow to Sulu's stomach, Urmi twisted free of his grasp. "The daggers were only for self-defense."

Bibil raised his sword. "Give me a proper answer, girl."

The prince placed his hand on Bibil's wrist and forced him to lower the weapon. "Never mind, Bibil."

"But—" Bibil began to protest.

"We'll sort things out later—if we ever get out of here." He handed the candle to Bibil. "If Urmi had wanted to kill me, she had plenty of opportunities back in the corridors."

"I'm just trying to protect you," Bibil grumbled.

"Yes, and I'm grateful." The prince signed for Bibil to go on. "But let's not get carried away. I won't have you killing your own kin just on a hunch."

Urmi eyed him like a sharp trader inspecting a gem for flaws. "When you visited our village, I remember thinking how eager you were to be liked—just like a young puppy. I felt sorry for you then. Uncle Bibil used to tell us how vicious the court was so I didn't see how someone as soft as you was ever going to survive."

"I often wondered that myself." The prince gave her a grudging smile.

"There's more to you than you think, lad." The wick flame flickered as Bibil motioned them on with the candle. "You just have to believe in yourself."

The passageways led downward for several hours, twisting sometimes to the left, sometimes to the right. The moisture seemed to increase, giving the stones a bloodlike color. And every now and then they would pause, studying the passageways. At one of the forks, Bibil shrugged apologetically. "I've never been down here, Your Highness."

"It's all right, Bibil. I'd rather starve to death here than be left to Rahu's tender mercies." The prince chuckled sourly. "With a little luck, he may have a stroke out of sheer frustration at losing me."

After about an hour of wandering, Bibil shook his head. "This can't be the way. We should have been going up by now. We'll have to retrace our steps."

With no choice, the party headed back the way they had come until they were once again at a fork in the tunnels. "Here, let's try the right one."

But after thirty meters, the passageway began to lead downward again. "Maybe it was some other fork in the tunnels," Bibil said doubtfully.

"I'm beginning to think my ancestors are descended from moles." The prince touched the walls. "I had no idea the tunnels were this extensive."

"I'm beginning to wish they hadn't been quite so industrious." Sulu tried to laugh.

Bibil suddenly gave a satisfied grunt. "Good, it's starting to go up again."

They went through more than half the candles before the ceiling suddenly lifted overhead. They found themselves at the entrance to a large room. There was an iron gate barring their way, but it swung open at a push of Bibil's hand. It creaked on rusty hinges and stopped about a meter away from the stone wall. The ceiling itself disappeared into the darkness above them, leaving only mysterious, rusty chains dangling down.

Sulu craned his neck back so that he could just make out a pulley. "What's this room, Your Highness?"

The prince shook his head. "I have no idea. Do you, Bibil?"

"Only rumors, Your Highness." Bibil stepped out into the room and something crunched under his foot. He took a step backward so that they could see it was the bones of a hand, and the hand was joined to a skeletal arm.

Mr. Spock squatted down. "Fascinating. This arm has been hacked off."

Bibil swung the candle toward the left. Running

along the room were small alcoves, about a meter in height. Heavy iron bars stood in front of the alcoves. "What are those for?"

"Prisoners," Bibil said distantly.

"Some of them are still occupied." Sulu pointed toward one alcove where a skull lay amid a heap of bones.

"Bibil, I think it's time you told us about those rumors." The prince gripped an overhead chain.

Bibil stepped over the arm and walked forward several paces. He paused beside a table. The wood was obviously very old and there were dark, ominous stains on its surface. Chains led from rings on the floor, ending in manacles. And, in a neat array on a smaller table, lay a series of knives, lancets and needles. A small furnace with large pipes led somewhere up into the ceiling. "Vischa the Mad was said to have built a torture chamber."

"He lived over a thousand years ago. And this equipment doesn't look this old." The prince angrily let the chain swing back and forth.

Bibil gave an embarrassed little cough. "It's been used occasionally since then."

The prince suddenly shoved the table over in sheer disgust. Knives and other metal objects clashed on the ground. "How recently?"

"Your grandfather's time, I would say. But no one's been sent here since then," Bibil was quick to add.

"But it could be utilized again." The prince frowned in distaste.

"By Rahu," Bibil insisted stubbornly.

"Or myself—if I had the throne." The prince wiped his hands on the front of his *soropa* as if they suddenly felt unclean from touching the table. "This is something the history books don't mention about my grandfather."

"It was perfectly acceptable by the standards of that time," Bibil argued.

"And who determines what's acceptable? Whoever's in power?" The prince waved a hand over their heads. "Did those poor, brave fools know they were dying for . . . for this?" He flung his hand out toward the cells.

"There is a darker side to ruling," Bibil said. "And sometimes some of this is necessary."

"Not with me, it isn't."

"All right, then, change it," Bibil said angrily, "but don't just sit back and whine. It's all very easy to criticize. It's harder to do something about it. Don't use this as an excuse to run offworld the first chance you get."

There was a sharp clicking sound, and Bibil immediately swung around, holding the candle over his head. But there was only a pile of bones in one of the alcoves.

"What was that?" the prince asked.

"I don't know." Bibil turned slowly. They could see more tables and torture devices looming like so many misshapen monsters. And then, faintly in the distance, they could make out a green gleam—as if made by two slitted eyes.

"Curious." Mr. Spock was still examining the amputated arm. He held up the ulna. "I was wondering what this was doing out here when everything else seems to be in neat order. But I believe now that this was dragged away from some other area." He turned it over in his hands. "And it looks as if it's been nibbled—and by something large. But the markings puzzle me a bit. They don't look as if they're made by the teeth of a large rat or rodent."

Bibil and the prince glanced at one another. "That's because we don't have rats on Angira," the prince said. "We have *kik-kiks*."

"What's that?" Sulu stood beside Spock, examining the arm curiously.

"It's a kind of beetle with large mandibles. It's almost as common as the cockroaches are on Earth. But ours are larger and they fill the same ecological niche that a rat would occupy on Earth."

Bibil swung around. The pair of eyes had been joined by a second. "The beetle has the luminescent markings on its back so that they look like eyes."

"Rather like those," the prince finished for Bibil. "But usually they're only found singly or in pairs."

"There's another rumor, Your Highness," Bibil said.

"I don't think I want to hear it, Bibil."

"I think you should, Your Highness. It's said that they travel in hordes down in the dungeons. That's one of the reasons why people stopped using this place."

Mr. Spock rose. "Legend or not, I suggest we find the exit."

"I don't think any of us would disagree." The prince pointed. "Isn't that a doorway over there?"

Bibil started forward, the others bunching in close behind the light. Sulu couldn't help noticing that the two creatures kept pace with them cautiously. But the large black opening only proved to open on a room full of old wooden frames.

"They look like beds," Sulu said.

"They were—at one time. Probably for the guards

and the jailers. But something's gnawed away the bedding and the leather thongs that would support the mattress."

"Maybe they were stripped." Sulu suggested.

"Those markings on the wood are similar to the markings on the bone I examined." Mr. Spock pointed to the small triangular holes marring the wood.

"I rather dislike the habit that rumor has of becoming fact down here." The prince shooed them out of the room. "Shall we find that exit, people?"

They circled round the room, finding another chamber of cells—these with even lower ceilings so that the prisoners could only have squatted, bent over. And they were forced to pass by larger, more hellish machines constructed with, as Mr. Spock observed, an almost scientific fervor for protracted torture.

The prince glanced, rather embarrassed, at a large cage inset with needles placed at strategic points so that a prisoner would have to stand rigid or be stabbed. And yet the needles were short so that the prisoner could not throw himself or herself on a point and end it all. "I rather wish my ancestors had used half their imagination on astronomy. Or even gambling."

Eventually they found another metal gate, but unlike the other, this one was locked. Bibil pulled at it. "It's no use. It's locked."

"Perhaps the keys are around." The prince turned.

"I don't know if we have the time to search." Sulu pointed. There were now nearly two dozen green "eyes" surrounding them. And more arriving with every second.

Chapter Four

The prince shook the gate in exasperation and then, after a pause, rattled it again. A pebble fell to the ground. "Something's giving."

"It's the hinges." Mr. Spock went up to the massive hinges. They seemed half-dissolved in rust already. "I believe the stone has become damp around the hinges so that it's starting to crumble." Slipping his sword from his belt, Mr. Spock began to use the point to pry at the stone; it gave, falling in bits and pieces.

But the beetles were gathering behind them. There seemed to be nearly a hundred pairs of eyes in the room and more were scurrying into the room every moment. Sulu and the prince began attacking the other two hinges.

Urmi caught at Bibil's arm. "Uncle, let me have my daggers back. I'll go crazy if I just stand here doing nothing."

Bibil shook his head slowly. "We needed a fighter up above or I would have taken your weapons away then. I don't want to take the risk now," he explained in a soft, patient voice. "Try to understand, Urmi. The lad's always deserved better than he's gotten. Now that he has a chance, I intend to see him sitting upon the throne."

Urmi cocked her head to one side as she studied her uncle. "You really mean that, don't you?"

"I'm not just being ambitious for him. I know the prince better than anyone else. He'll make a far better emperor than any of his brothers and stepbrothers"— Bibil paused and then raised his voice so that the prince could hear him over the clinking of steel on old, crumbling stone—"whenever he finally faces what he is." But though the prince stiffened, he pretended to ignore his servant.

"If you don't give me my weapons back, he may never get that opportunity," she tried to reason.

"You always were able to wheedle things out of me." Bibil adjusted his grip on the melting candle. "Well, you can have your weapons—but on one condition."

"What's that?" Urmi asked cautiously.

Bibil fixed her with a hard, demanding stare. "You have to promise to help me put the prince on the throne."

Urmi reared her head back. "He's a tool of these offworlders."

"I thought you were involved in some kind of mischief," Bibil grunted triumphantly. He placed a hand on his niece's shoulder and spoke in a low, urgent voice. "Now listen to me, child. I've raised that boy. I've coddled him. I've even cuffed him when I had to. He's been like my own son. I don't intend to see him come to any harm."

"And I don't intend to let our world come to any

harm either," Urmi warned him. "Oh, your prince is likable enough, but I've listened to him talk. He's a puppet for these offworlders. They'll use him to exploit our poor world."

The prince wiped at the mixture of sweat and dust that now caked his face. "Urmi, at this point, I would be happy if we survive. I don't care about the throne."

"If you survive, you will *be* the emperor," Bibil promised, and pointed the candle at his niece. "But I'll compromise with your conscience, girl. Give me your oath that you'll help the prince reach Kotah."

Urmi frowned. "He's too tainted by offworld ways. His clan will never accept him."

Bibil smiled grimly. "Then you don't have anything to worry about if you help him reach Kotah."

She gave an exasperated sigh. "All right. I give my word to you that I'll help him." She held out her hand, wriggling her fingers at him. "So give me my weapons."

"Remember your promise now. As a little girl, you were guilty of many things, but never of lying." Bibil pulled the daggers and sword from his sash-end and handed them to her.

As soon as she had the daggers stowed away in her own sash-end, she joined Sulu, jabbing her sword point behind the middle hinge.

Bibil hung his candle closer to them so they could see better. "I suppose the beetles have been eating one another up till now."

"When we provided a four-course banquet," the prince grunted. "How thoughtful of us."

Mr. Spock began to use his sword as a kind of crowbar. The rusty hinge began to inch away from the wall with a massive groan. Parts of its surface fell away in flakes of rust.

"This time, we'll try it in unison." The prince stood with his sword braced by the middle hinge while Sulu squatted down by the bottom hinge.

When Mr. Spock had slipped his blade further behind the top hinge, he nodded to the others. "On the count of three." He braced one hand behind the sword blade to give it better support. "One . . . two . . . three."

They pried at the hinges, grimacing. The crumbling stone fell in a small shower of particles and pebbles now. "For the love of heaven, hurry," Bibil urged them.

The floor behind them was fairly seething with eyes now and, on the very edge of the circle of light cast by the candle, Sulu could see a large six-legged beetle. It was a third of a meter long with legs that were double-jointed. Its body was housed in a thick black carapace topped by two large oval spots glowing on the back—it was the spots which gave the illusion of eyes. Its mandibles swung out in an arc as wide as Sulu's hand like a big, ugly pair of pincers. The head seemed to be mostly muscle that was designed to close those mandibles and hold on. Its heavy wingcase suddenly flipped up and then snapped back against its carapace with a loud click. It was a loud, ominous sound—like the revolution of a cylinder in an old nineteenth-century six-shooter.

Sulu gave a shudder. "Once one of those babies bites into you, it doesn't look like it's easy to get them to let you go."

"One has to hack off the head and then pry the mandibles apart," Bibil advised.

Sulu, the prince and Urmi began yanking at the hinges almost frantically, and though Mr. Spock was more controlled, he could be seen to be pulling even harder than before.

The light suddenly flickered and dipped as Bibil swung the candle in a wide arc. "Hah. Get away," he shouted.

Sulu glanced over his shoulder to see that the beetles danced backward, snapping their mandibles with ugly little clicks. Mr. Spock's blade snapped suddenly and he fell backward.

"Here." Bibil pulled out his own sword and tossed it to Mr. Spock. Flinging down the useless hilt of his old sword, Mr. Spock caught the hilt of Bibil's.

Hurriedly setting his new blade behind the hinge, Mr. Spock began tugging again.

"I think it's giving," Sulu grimaced.

"Then pull," Urmi's voice said almost shrilly. While she was quite capable of facing any regular foe, she clearly did not relish facing a horde of beetles.

Sulu tugged until he thought his own sword blade would break. A shower of grit and small lumps of sandstone fell on their feet. The hinge gave grudgingly, resentfully, groaning all the while as it came away from the wall—leaving a spot wide enough for a person to slip through sideways.

"Forgive the lack of etiquette, Your Highness." Saying that, Mr. Spock grabbed the prince by his shoulder and unceremoniously shoved him through the gap. He beckoned Sulu and Urmi to follow after the prince.

More beetles were trying to dart forward. "You next, offworlder." Bibil backed up by the gate, swinging his candle. The beetles scuttled off again. Spock slipped through the gate. The bars were too widely spaced to stop the beetles, but at least their group was through now. Bibil followed a moment later and thrust the candle into Sulu's hands. Taking another candle from one of the sacks, he lit it from the first. "Keep going," he said. They were in a small alcove from which three corridors led.

"Which way?" Sulu asked.

"Your guess is as good as mine now. But any way that leads upward would probably suit us." He held out his hand to Urmi. "I'm afraid an old warrior feels naked without a sword."

"I gave you my word, didn't I?" Urmi said resentfully.

"And you can keep your daggers. I just want the sword," Bibil insisted. And reluctantly his niece handed the weapon to him.

"Bibil." The prince seemed genuinely alarmed. "I don't want any more foolish heroics for my sake."

"Let an old man with tired legs form the rear guard, Your Highness." He motioned them to go on.

"But—" The prince started to protest.

"I'm only willing to put up with so much nonsense from you." He gave the prince a shove down the tunnel that almost sent him sprawling on his hands and knees.

"Go on, Mr. Sulu," Mr. Spock said quietly.

Sulu set forward at a trot, passing by the prince. But the prince, scrambling to his feet, kept pace at Mr. Sulu's heels. Urmi and Mr. Spock came along after them with Bibil following, twisting sideways every now and then to glance behind them.

They could hear the click of beetles' mandibles and there was a clacking sound whenever one beetle raised and lowered its wingcase in a threatening display. Occasionally there would be a swirl of glowing spots as one beetle attacked another and more joined in to attack both combatants. But such fights were only a slight eddy in the steady flow of beetles that followed them.

When they reached the next fork, Mr. Sulu paused. "They both look like they lead down."

"Let's try the one on the right," the prince urged.

And they plunged into it. To Sulu's relief, the floor swung upward after only ten paces. "Faster," Bibil urged from behind them, "the beetles are gaining."

The thought of those ugly mandibles immediately made Sulu pick up the pace. He only slowed when he came to the next fork. "The right one again," the prince suggested.

And they swung into it, but this one dipped after only twenty paces and began to slant downward. "Should we try to go back to the other one?" Sulu called.

"We can't," Bibil said. "And for heaven's sake, hurry. They're gaining on this downslope."

The clacking seemed to grow louder as if the beetles were bumping into one another in their hurry to catch them. But the tunnel swung upward almost as abruptly as it had gone downward and they began running even faster, trying to put more distance between themselves and the beetles.

They passed through two more forks, each time taking the right. Ahead of them lay another fork. "The right one again?" Sulu panted. By now they were all gasping for breath.

"Wait," Mr. Spock said. "I feel something from the left one."

Sulu paused and felt something brush his cheek faintly—like a ghostly bit of velvet. They had been running through the tunnels for what seemed like such a long time that at first it seemed hard to believe that there was any other existence against the damp, stagnant air.

And then, as if from some half-forgotten page of a history text, Sulu remembered what it was. "It's a breeze." He plunged eagerly up the left tunnel. This one slanted upward sharply and it took its toll on their already tired legs. But they scrambled upward, hands pawing for some grip, heedless of how many times they might slip and bruise themselves on the stones.

"Wait," Urmi said in alarm. "Bibil's falling behind."

"No, no, go on without me," he called.

Sulu paused long enough to look below. Bibil's legs were already cut as if the beetles had slashed him.

"Go on, Mr. Sulu," Mr. Spock said. "I will assist him. Getting the prince to safety is our first priority."

But after Sulu had climbed another ten meters, he found himself staring at a wall of rocks. He looked hurriedly for some side passage but the way was blocked by a pile of stones—except for a small crack through which a faint breeze was blowing.

The prince squeezed up next to him in the narrow passageway. "There must have been a landslide." He began pulling at the stones. Rocks began to clatter down below.

Urmi, unable to join them because of the narrow space, paused. "Pass the candle to me, Sulu."

Sulu handed the candle behind him and started to help the prince. "Look out below."

"I'd rather have a few bruises," Urmi said grimly, "than a set of mandibles sunk into my leg." She picked up a stone in her free hand.

"Get back there." There was an ugly clattering,

followed by noisy crackings and squishings. Bibil was using a rock to smash the beetles.

Mr. Spock gave a grunt and Urmi cried out. And Sulu jerked up sharply at the pain in his shoulders. The beetles were skittering over the ceiling in an ugly luminescent flood that neither Bibil, Urmi nor Mr. Spock could stem. It seemed that for every beetle they crushed, a dozen more took its place.

"There's a space," the prince gasped.

It was a narrow hole, but they went on tugging at the rocks, though their fingers had already been scraped raw and bleeding. The space gradually began to widen, large enough for one person to crawl through. They almost didn't need the candle because of the soft, eerie light from the beetles' wingcases.

"How is it coming?" Bibil asked from below.

"It's going to take a while," Sulu shouted down to him.

He paused to look behind. The beetles were now crawling up over one another's backs, surging upward toward them, and Bibil's legs were now almost hidden by beetles. Bibil hefted the stone in his hand. "You'll need time," he said.

"Bibil, don't do anything foolish."

"I'm through taking orders, Your Highness." Bibil raised his sword in one last salute. "Just remember. Go to Kotah. You'll make a far better emperor than even you suspect." And suddenly he charged back down the corridor, sword slashing and stone swinging. The flow of beetles paused, and then swarmed backward toward him. Bibil kept on grimly fighting and crushing, but the beetles covered him up to his chest now.

"Bibil," the prince called.

Mr. Spock went on smashing at the beetles that

scurried back along the ceiling. "Your Highness, we must not waste the time that Bibil is buying for us."

There were still several dozen beetles that tried to attack them, but they worked to enlarge the hole until it was big enough for one person to crawl through. The prince looked behind them. "Bibil, it's done."

But there was no answer from the figure covered in a living cloak of beetles. And even as they watched, it toppled over into a horde of *kik-kiks.*

"Bibil, you old fool," the prince murmured.

"Your Highness, go through the hole," Mr. Spock said quietly.

"But—"

"You would be the most likely to know where to find the door and how to work it," Sulu urged.

And the prince, three beetles clinging to his back and legs, squirmed through the opening.

"Go on, Mr. Sulu." Mr. Spock thrust the candle into his hands. "His Highness will need light."

Taking the candle back from Urmi, Sulu crawled through the hole, trying to ignore the fiery pain in his chest as a beetle sank its mandibles into him. Nearly a dozen beetles had crawled through the opening, but Sulu ignored them as he stumbled on. Urmi kept right at their heels as they found the prince by the doorway.

"The device that would open the door is usually to the left, but of course there are always exceptions." The prince was feeling all the stones around that side. Sulu and Urmi began to feel to the right with their free hands. Beetles darted up the walls, trying to seize their wrists.

There was a large crashing of stones and rubble and at the very edge of the light from the candle, Sulu could see that Mr. Spock had reclosed the hole. He made his way slowly up to them, bleeding from nearly a dozen cuts, his fingers closing around the neck of a beetle clinging to his leg.

Suddenly, Sulu's fingers brushed a small knob, cleverly plastered and painted to look like stone. "I think I've found something." He pushed and prodded at it. "But what do I do?"

Urmi smashed a beetle that tried to snap at Sulu's hand.

The prince stepped up behind Sulu. "Try pushing it to the right." He shoved the knob in that direction, and hidden pulleys and gears began to turn and move. And then stopped abruptly.

The prince jabbed at the knob several more times. "Come on. Come on. Work for us."

And gradually, groaning all the while as if the machinery were breaking down, the pulleys and gears began to move and the door slowly began to swing in. Throwing down her rock, Urmi impatiently grabbed hold of the door's edge and tried to pull it open faster. The prince added his strength to hers and, after setting down his candle, Sulu joined them.

Sulu could feel almost a physical hunger to see the light again and breathe the fresh air—though the air that was coming to them reeked faintly of smoke. But they kept on tugging.

And suddenly they were stumbling outside. The prince was searching by the side, and as Mr. Spock limped through the opening, the prince pushed some other projection. This time the door swung shut more quickly.

They were standing in a gulch through which a

narrow, muddy stream ran. A huge column of black smoke rose from the old citadel, hovering like a giant moth spreading its wings. The prince, however, stared at the door that had closed. "Bibil, if you weren't dead, I'd have you hung for what you just did." He wiped clumsily at the tears in his eyes. "Of all the people who have died today, I will feel your loss the most."

Sulu set the edge of his sword against the neck of the beetle hanging to his chest and took an immense satisfaction in severing its head. "You were close to Bibil, weren't you?" he asked sympathetically.

The prince bent over patiently while Mr. Spock and Urmi removed the beetles there. "He fussed and scolded a bit more than I liked, but he was my only true friend in the palace. Even the ninth heir has some uses within the palace"—the prince managed a weak smile —"if he can be controlled. But I could always count on Bibil to act for my interests and not for his. You wouldn't think that such a tough, practical man could have a soft spot for the runt of the litter."

Urmi used the tip of her sword to pry apart the mandibles of the last *kik-kik* clinging to the prince. "Why do you always run yourself down?"

The prince straightened, examining his clothes, which, like Sulu's and Spock's dress uniforms, were now in tatters. "Because I noticed at an early age that earnest young princes do not reach their majority."

Urmi knelt to bathe her own cuts in the stream. "Is that why you joke all the time?" She looked at him with new interest.

The prince flopped down beside her and began to wash the soot from his face. "Perhaps your uncle was a poorer judge of character than he thought."

A change in the breeze sent a thick cloud of smoke rolling down into the gulch. "In any event, we must get Your Highness away from here," Mr. Spock said. He surveyed the gulch. "How far away is your clan's province?"

"To the west is the great plain we saw from my window." He pointed in the opposite direction toward the hilly country. "It's fifty kilometers through the badlands. My family usually takes a more leisurely trip along the river to a mountain pass but that doubles the distance. And the river and the pass will be the first things Rahu will seek to control."

Mr. Spock dabbed some water on a jagged slash on his leg. "The safest thing to do would be to hike a short distance into the badlands and find a place to hide until the *Enterprise* returns." He straightened up. "In view of the circumstances, I am sure the Federation would grant you political asylum."

When Sulu had finally pried the dead beetle's head from his chest, he came over to the stream. "Then you can do like you said you wanted to do and take courses for the rest of your life."

"Amazing." The prince lifted his arm from the water, letting the drops patter down from the matted fur of his arm. "A few hours ago, I would have killed to achieve just such a dream. And now you gentlemen are presenting it to me on a silk cushion."

Urmi shook her head as if she could not quite believe her ears. "They'll keep you there until the next time they want to take over Angira."

The prince clicked his tongue in exasperation. "They're not out to exploit either me or Angira."

Urmi held up an apologetic hand toward Mr. Spock.

"Don't misunderstand me. You offworlders have fought well; but it was in your own self-interest to get away from the palace."

"What do they have to do to convince you that they're sincere?" the prince asked in exasperation.

Urmi extended her jaw stubbornly—much like her uncle—as if it were a family mannerism. "They could promise to leave as soon as they could and never to come back."

"You mustn't take such a narrow view, Urmi," the prince chided gently. "Whether Angirans like it or not, they are a part of a galactic community now."

"You might as well know it now," she warned Sulu and Mr. Spock. "Angirans will never accept you as their own."

With an almost insolent casualness, the prince dangled his feet into the stream. "After what's just happened, I think Mr. Spock and Sulu are inclined to take that as a compliment rather than an insult."

Before Urmi could make any kind of reply, the screams began again. Orienting himself by the sun, Sulu judged that the sound was coming from a different part of the palace from where the slaughter had first begun.

"It would be just like that fool Rahu to burn what he didn't want." The prince looked up at the palace walls. There came a scream and he stiffened. "Or to kill." The prince's chin dropped to his chest while Urmi's words sank in. Finally he raised his head and, with a sigh, the prince turned to Mr. Spock. "Your suggestion is as sensible as usual. And yet I must respect Bibil's last wish and at least return to my home province."

"To claim your throne?" Urmi asked. She looked as if she didn't enjoy the idea at all.

The prince held up a hand. "Let me finish, Urmi. Once I'm there, I can perhaps determine if one of my brothers or stepbrothers has survived. If not, I will find someone to take my place as the claimant to the throne. My house has plenty of collateral lines, thanks to a great-grandfather who was ever at the whim of his glands. In either event, I will see to it that I am free to leave by the time the *Enterprise* returns." He clapped his hands together. "And since I shall use the route through the badlands, I can leave you gentlemen safe and settled whatever might happen to me. We'll be passing by Bibil's old village, so I can see that you're well supplied."

Mr. Spock did not look up as he finished cleaning the last of his cuts. "I confess to a certain scientific interest in how you and Kotah will react to one another."

The prince seemed surprised. "But it's more logical to leave me. Why risk your lives on my account?"

"Why not?" Sulu shrugged.

"Spoken like a true cavalier." The prince clapped his palms lightly together in the Angiran fashion.

Mr. Spock frowned as if he disliked being associated with Sulu's romantic streak. "Our orders were to escort you safely home. Since the palace now belongs to another tenant, we must then see you to your clan's province."

"Mr. Spock, I think you're capable of rationalizing anything." The prince wagged a finger at him.

Urmi pointed a warning finger at him. "If you think you can work some sort of mischief here, you're wrong. I won't let you put your puppet on the throne."

Mr. Spock clasped his hands behind his back. "Whether the prince leaves or stays, he will make that decision on his own."

The prince lowered his head. "But just who am I then?"

"That is something only you can discover," Mr. Spock said quietly.

The prince gave a soft laugh. "It's the old eternal question, isn't it? Though I am neither melancholy nor Danish." Sulu thought he was simply staring at the ground, so he was surprised to see that the prince seemed to be studying his own faint shadow. Suddenly he raised his fingers above his head so that the silhouette of a crown appeared there. "The Shadow Lord has become the Shadow Emperor."

Lord Bhima woke upon his bed. He tried to rise, but his hands and feet were bound, and then he remembered Rahu. The young lord had been carrying on a casual conversation, it seemed, with several others about a hundred meters from the prince's room. He had walked up to Rahu, a line of poetry running through his head. It had been composed by a young courtier some five hundred years ago, who had been forced to commit suicide for some minor breach of etiquette. "Beware the hidden edge to a smile," he had written.

Lord Bhima had approached the group warily, as he would a nest of flame vipers. "Lord Rahu." He'd nodded his head slightly. "If I might speak with you."

"Yes, of course." Rahu had inclined his head slightly to the others. "If you'll forgive me, gentlemen," he said. But in actual fact, it had been he who was dismissing the others.

Lord Bhima had waited until the others were some ten meters away. In the intricate forms of politeness within the Angiran court, it was assumed they would pretend they had not heard—even if they had. "You are not to behave again in such a discourteous way to our guests."

"You puzzle me, Lord Bhima." Lord Rahu had folded his arms across his chest. "I have often heard you complain about the contamination from offworld."

"That has to do with ideas, not with people," Lord Bhima had corrected him.

"That is your mind speaking, not your heart." Lord Rahu had studied him. "I know you—perhaps better than you do yourself. Your sense of duty prevents you from doing what you really want: to restore this world back to the old ways."

Lord Bhima had hooked a thumb through his sash-end. "I speak of virtues, you speak of privileges. In either case, we both must serve the throne."

Rahu's nostrils had widened slightly. "And if one were to choose between this world and the throne?"

"Events must not be allowed to come to that," Lord Bhima had warned him.

"And should we simply roll over on our backs while a treacherous emperor lets these offworlders take over our world?" Rahu had drawn himself up. "I had expected more of you, swordmaster."

Rahu had touched upon Lord Bhima's own secret fears. Nonetheless, Lord Bhima had reminded himself of the Warrior's Code, by which he had tried to live all these years. "I will fight any attempted takeover by them, but," he had added, "in the proper way."

"You are too much the gentleman." Rahu had frowned. "Critical times call for critical measures."

"If it cannot be done properly," Lord Bhima had said, "then it should not be done at all. Now if you'll excuse me, Lord Rahu, I must prepare for the welcoming ceremony."

He should have taken several steps away from Rahu so that he was out of arm's reach before he turned his back on the ambitious lord. But he'd been preoccupied by the enigma of the prince and his visitors. He'd realized his mistake when he heard Rahu draw the dagger. He had tried to turn, but he was already preparing himself for the stab of the blade. So he had been rather surprised when it was a heavy pommel instead that smashed down against the base of his head.

He pulled and tugged at his bindings now, but the leather thongs cut into his wrists and ankles. So then he tried to wriggle his arms and legs slowly to get some slack. In the distance, he could hear screams and shouts. At first, he told himself that the commotion was probably nothing—only some of the sillier of the servants who panicked at the slightest excuse. But as he listened more closely to the shouts, he could detect the note of fear in them, and the outrage. And he knew with a terrible certainty that something worse was going on.

He managed to sit up. Yes, he was in his room, surrounded by all his familiar things, and so it seemed impossible for the terror to be happening outside. He glanced around the room for something with an edge, but all his weapons were locked away in the fencing hall. For once, he regretted being so dutiful. He glanced at the polished bronze surface of a mirror. His tastes were inclined to simpler lines rather than the intricate gold frame, but it had been a gift from the emperor after Prince Vikram had beaten Rahu so decisively in that match long ago.

Lord Bhima struggled to his knees. Part of the frame had a slight edge to it. Perhaps he could make use of that to free himself. It took him a long time to make it over to the mirror, even longer to knock the mirror down by lying on his back and using his feet to kick it from the wall. And then it took a while to grasp the mirror in his hands so he could begin to saw the thongs against the edge.

There was not nearly so much noise as before, but just when he thought things were settling down, he would hear a solitary scream. What madness had Rahu created?

He couldn't know that until he was outside the room, and he couldn't do that until he was free. He almost had the bonds cut when he heard the footsteps. Hastily he crawled back toward the foot of his bed. There was no time to hide the mirror.

The door was flung open and a young *sinha* officer stepped into the room. Lord Bhima could have wept to see the blood staining the officer's cape and forearm. Worse, his sandaled legs seemed to be covered in red up to his knees, as if he had waded through blood. In his hand was a sword—though that was forbidden even to a *sinha* warrior.

Rahu followed a second later. His pelt and limbs were also bloodied and there was an odd, sad air to him. "I am sorry you were inconvenienced, Lord Bhima."

Lord Bhima tested the thongs. It felt as if they would break now with one quick tug—if necessary. "You look like a butcher," he said accusingly to Rahu.

"Yes, one might call me that." Rahu sheathed his own sword. "But I did it for the sake of Angira."

Lord Bhima scowled. "The foulest deeds often carry the fairest reasons."

"So be it." Rahu stared down at his bloody hands as if they belonged to someone else. As a child, he had always been so fastidious about keeping clean. He looked suddenly at Lord Bhima. "I have been willing to risk everything today—including my reputation."

"What did you do?" Lord Bhima demanded sternly —as if Rahu were once again one of his pupils.

And like a small boy, Rahu lowered his head slightly. "We attacked the emperor and his family while they were still taking their places in the assembly room."

Lord Bhima sucked in his breath. "You slaughtered them."

"It was a battle," Rahu said sharply. The distinction seemed to be important to him. "They fought well even though they were bare-handed. But," he added almost apologetically, "I suspect our losses would have been heavier if you had been there."

"Why spare me, though?" Lord Bhima shook his head, trying to clear the tears away from his eyes. "Did you come to gloat?"

Rahu came forward impulsively. "I cannot ask you to condone what I've just done, because I know you wouldn't. But I would ask that you be pragmatic. Our goals are the same as yours, after all. We seek to preserve our world's honor and heritage."

"What honor is left now?" Lord Bhima demanded.

"Our heritage then—and our identity as Angirans," Rahu argued. "Or would you have the best of our youth travel offworld and become aliens to us? And would you allow our world to slide into anarchy? You know the reports as well as I do. The peasants are ready to revolt. This world needs a strong hand to guide it back to sanity."

"My oath is to the emperor," Lord Bhima insisted stubbornly.

Lord Rahu swallowed anxiously. "And there is none now. The line is extinguished."

Lord Bhima's eyes widened in disbelief. "You were that thorough?"

"You trained me to finish a task once it was begun." Biting his lip, Rahu stood over Lord Bhima. "So be our conscience now, Lord Bhima. You can guide and temper the Restoration."

And Lord Bhima's own doubts and uncertainties with the dead emperor now filled his mind. He had been forced to stand by and watch in anguish as the emperor had slowly and methodically ruined their world. In his madness to modernize Angira, the emperor had ruined many noble families and alienated the peasants. Worse, he had poisoned their world with all of his modern factories and mines.

He had hoped that Prince Vikram might be able to heal their world's wounds, and so he had been disappointed when Prince Vikram had sided with the offworlders. He seemed likely only to increase the destruction of their world. And so, though he despised Rahu for what the ambitious young noble had done, he decided that Rahu was right in this much: Modernization could not be allowed to continue. So their goals were similar.

And suddenly Lord Bhima found himself toying with the idea that he might be able to stop some of Rahu's zealous excesses. Perhaps he might even heal some of their poor world's wounds. And wasn't one man's honor less important than the salvation of their world? The Warrior's Code had always emphasized that the interests of society came before those of an individual.

"And if I refuse to join you?" Lord Bhima asked cautiously.

Rahu licked his lips nervously like someone about to take a last, desperate throw of the dice. "I will set you free in a place of your own choosing and you will then be able to travel where you like for an entire day before my *sinha* begin to hunt you."

Lord Bhima realized he was flirting with his own death. "And if I choose Kotah?"

Rahu drew closer in his eagerness to convert Lord Bhima. "You would be taken to the border." He nodded his head slightly. "You see, I understand the way your mind works, swordmaster. You must be given a real choice, or you will never choose to help me."

Lord Bhima considered the matter. His own death would not bring back the emperor. Nor did he care to defend a cause which only brought harm to their world. Besides, going to Kotah would only prolong the slaughter. In fact, Rahu, left unchecked, might plunge this entire world into a blood bath. He knew his former pupil well enough. But where did honor truly lie in this affair? All his life, he had drawn strength and guidance from the Warrior's Code; but either alternative seemed equally dishonorable. And suddenly he felt weak and lost like an abandoned child.

"Considering what has just happened, I would need more than your oath if I were to join you," Lord Bhima said bitterly.

"And what if I placed the imperial seal and all of the imperial symbols in your hands? I could do nothing without your approval." Rahu could not help smiling slyly. He had known his quarry and what bait would attract him.

Lord Bhima studied him. "And why should you care what I think, Rahu?"

"Because I value your opinion"—Rahu shrugged— "and because I am not a fool. Your presence would enhance any regime."

"I rather think both our reputations will be dragged down." With a sudden sideways pull of his arms, Bhima broke the thongs that bound them. At the same time, he swept his legs outward, catching Rahu from behind so that Rahu tumbled into his lap.

With his left hand, Bhima caught Rahu's wrist so that the sword point was held away. But Bhima's right hand closed around Rahu's throat. The *sinha* lieutenant raced from his position by the door with his sword raised over his head.

"Don't," Bhima growled. His hands tightened around Rahu's neck. "I can crush his throat easily."

Rahu made strangling noises and waved the tip of his sword at the lieutenant, as if to warn him to stay away. When the young officer had stepped back, Bhima looked down at Rahu.

"I've done this to show you that I do, indeed, have a choice in the matter. And I will always have one. I won't allow myself to be used by you and then be discarded like so much old rubbish. Do you understand me?" He could feel Rahu struggling to nod his head despite the hand constricting his throat. "I will help you, Rahu, because I would end the suffering in our world." He released Rahu and the young lord rolled away, lying on his hands and knees, coughing and gasping.

With one hand around his neck, Rahu lifted his

sword. Lord Bhima calmly swung his legs around, holding his ankles apart as best he could and then waited for a sword stroke. One way or another, he would have Rahu's answer. He was almost disappointed that Rahu did not deliver a death blow but, instead, brought the point down with precision so that it cut through the thongs. He had always dismissed such displays of swordsmanship at tournaments as so much showmanship, but he had to admit that it sometimes had its uses.

"Then it's a bargain," Lord Rahu rasped.

"Lord, Lord," a *sinha* burst wildly into the room at that moment. "Prince Vikram barricaded himself within the Old Chapel, and when we finally broke in, he was gone. There must be some hidden passageway out of there."

Rahu tried to say something, but could not for a moment. He had to cough several times before he could find his voice once again. "Well, find the entrance."

The messenger spread his arms. "Lord, we've searched all over for it, but we haven't discovered it yet."

"If he's gone into the lower levels, he may not live for very long." Lord Bhima threw the severed ropes away.

"I, for one, refuse to trust to ghost stories to do my work for me." Rahu rounded on his heel apprehensively. "Lord Bhima, will you keep your bargain with me? Or will you maintain a hollow loyalty to that other family? I will abide by the terms of my original offer and give you free passage."

Lord Bhima began to rub the circulation back into

his numb ankles. If it had been any other son of the emperor but Vikram, he might have reconsidered things. But as it was, he had little heart to defend some idiot who was half an offworlder already. "No." He sighed, feeling suddenly very old and tired. "I'll help you, Rahu."

Lord Rahu seemed pleasantly surprised by his answer. "Lord Bhima, I will head to the river with my army. We will probably catch the prince there. But I want you to locate the secret passageway in the Old Chapel." He nodded to the lieutenant. "Round up a dozen men and assist Lord Bhima."

Lord Bhima was looking down at his own *soropa*. The blood from Rahu had already stained his own clothes. It was, he thought to himself, one of the hazards of dealing with a murderer. And though he told himself that he had made the right decision, he could not shake off a strange sense of doom. "And what will you do with him?"

"I will do whatever is necessary to save this world," Lord Rahu said quietly.

"No." Lord Bhima shook his head firmly. "That poor fool can't harm you. Lock him away in the palace someplace, but don't add his death to your crimes."

"Pity has little place in the Restoration," Rahu warned.

"I will salvage this one small bit of honor," Lord Bhima insisted.

Rahu mulled that over and then he raised his shoulders and let them drop. "I had been looking forward to the news of his death. But I'm willing to forgo that pleasure if I can gain your support. If you can capture him alive, then do so."

Lord Bhima nodded his head to Rahu. He owed him that much now. "Thank you, Lord." He should have felt lighter of heart after having struck that bargain for the prince; and yet he felt only more uneasy—like some simpleton in a tale who's only fooled himself when he thinks he's gotten the better of a deal with a demon.

Chapter Five

It was hot within the gulch as they walked along with weapons in hand. And the smoke rolled down from the palace walls, hanging in the gulch so that they coughed as they hiked along the rocky floor. About a half kilometer on, they halted abruptly. Eight bodies lay smashed on the floor of the gulch and one lay half within the stream, its blood rising in plumes that flowed downstream, turning the water red.

Urmi craned her neck back to look at the high palace walls hanging on the very lip of the gulch. "They must have thrown them from the top of the battlements. Or maybe they just decided to jump."

The prince gave a shudder. "Their features are too crushed to be recognizable, but from their expensive *soropas*, I'd say they were nobles."

Urmi stared at the corpses. "Well, at least their deaths were quick enough."

Skirting around the bodies, they made their way for

another kilometer along the gulch until it finally widened into a rocky valley about a kilometer wide. And the prince followed the stream until he could point to the southern end of the valley. "The same emperor who built the chapel also founded a monastery. In ancient days it was filled with saints. But like many other virtues nowadays, holiness seems to be in short supply."

"How do you know?" Urmi demanded. "You've been gone for ten years."

"I doubt if Angira could have changed that much," the prince said dryly.

Ahead of them, on the right bank of the stream, was a large handcart with wheels of wooden planks hammered and then trimmed into two large circles. "Whom does this belong to?" Sulu asked.

The prince paused to pick up what looked like a large bowl of straw a meter wide at its mouth and nearly a third of a meter deep. "The monks. See. Here's one of their hats." He indicated the straps on the rim. "You saw some of the order this morning."

Curious, Mr. Spock peered over one side of the handcart. "It would appear that someone was doing the laundry." He touched a shallow basket filled with soap.

Sulu picked up another of the half dozen straw hats that littered the ground. By now the blood in the stream had been diluted to pink, but it was still noticeable. "They must've been frightened by the sound of fighting and run away. Or maybe they even saw the blood." He tried one hat over his head and could barely see through the interstices of the tightly woven straw. "I guess they left these behind so they could see where they were running."

Sticking her dagger through the sash-end of her *soropa*, Urmi began to go through the robes. "It might be wise to wear these during our trip."

The prince lowered the hat. "I suppose we ought to disguise ourselves from pursuers."

"Rahu's men won't be the only threats we might meet." Urmi's voice sounded strained as she leaned her stomach against the side of the handcart. "Times have changed. And we have changed with them."

Sulu placed his sword's edge on the side of the handcart where Urmi made a point of ignoring it. "Before we let you lead us anywhere, I think you'd better tell us a little more about yourself, Urmi. How close was your uncle to the truth? Are you a spy?"

She paused, her hands tightening like claws around the robes.

"Are you?" the prince demanded.

She closed her eyes as if she had been pushed once too often. "Yes." She started to shove robes around again at a furious rate; but she didn't select any. "But not the kind you think. We don't want to overthrow anyone. We just want to protect ourselves. We have that right."

The prince frowned as she dragged a robe out and measured it against him. "Do not address me in the nobles' tongue."

"No, this hem is much too short." She put the robe back into the cart insolently. Apparently, she had used the nobles' tongue again because the prince went on frowning. "What're you going to do if your face freezes like that? They'll wind up using you at some temple to scare off demons." It was almost as if she were trying to take out her frustrations on the prince.

119

The prince's lips wriggled themselves into a smile. "Well, you did fight by my side, so I suppose that does make you my equal in a way."

Urmi seemed surprised at that admission—as if she had been expecting almost any other reaction but that. "Well, at least there's one thing to be said about your stay among the offworlders. You really aren't like the other nobles."

"That's about the kindest thing anyone's said to me today." He leaned against the cart. "But what did you mean about 'protecting your rights'?"

Urmi held up another robe. "We had to band ourselves together against the bandits and the taxmen. Your father started to farm out taxes to collectors who bid for the right. And they don't care how they collect their money, so they use bullies and thugs. Sometimes they even take more than they should. And if you complain to the officials—"

"The petitioner loses his or her head." The prince took the robe from her. "Yes, I know my father's attitude toward criticism."

"And then there are a lot more bandits nowadays." She turned back to the cart and selected a robe for Sulu. "We had to form a militia for self-defense even if it was illegal."

Sulu held it up against himself with one hand. "That still doesn't explain what you were doing in the palace."

With a disapproving frown, she took it from him and gave him another to try. "Once the militia was formed, we began to contact other villages and the workers in the cities. Your father had the right idea about improving Angira, but was going about it in the wrong way."

"I'm sure my father would have been delighted by your help," the prince said dryly. He began to wind the ribbons of his sword around the blade near the hilt so that the bells would not ring as much.

"And if the emperor didn't go along with it?" Sulu asked.

"That remained to be seen," was Urmi's honest reply.

"Do we have any reason to trust you now?" Mr. Spock asked.

She glared at him. "I gave my word to my uncle." She looked back at the prince. "You're not the only one who will keep faith with him. I'll help you reach Kotah. After that, my obligation is ended."

"So I can feel safe enough to turn my back on you until then?" the prince asked wryly.

"If I have to kill you, it will be face-to-face," Urmi promised solemnly.

"You were impudent, disrespectful, but, as your uncle said, you were not a liar. I believe you, Urmi." With forced cheer, he scrutinized Mr. Spock. "Do you know, Mr. Spock, I detect a religious aura about you."

Mr. Spock picked through the robes. "I am more interested in what people do *not* detect."

"Yes, those dagger-shaped ears." The prince presented the hat to Mr. Spock with an elaborate flourish. "This should do nicely."

The robes hid everything, with a hem that trailed along the ground. For easier walking, they slung the hats on their backs by means of the straps, while the robes were bunched up around their waists. When the robes were allowed to hang down, they would hide their weapons; and the long, flowing sleeves would hide the offworlders' naked hands. For her part, Urmi had used strips torn from a robe to fashion wrist bands for her daggers.

When they were ready, she led them to the northern end of the valley where a narrow track zigzagged up the steep slope. Because their large hats and robes forced them to take short steps, the trip seemed to take forever.

Halfway up the trail, the prince stopped. "This is no good, Urmi. I don't see any spies about, so I suggest we put our hats back and tuck up our robes."

Urmi let her hat hang by its straps behind her back. "I guess it's safe enough for a while."

They found the going was easier when they had taken off their hats and rolled their robes up around their waists.

At the top of the path, they paused, as much to catch their breath as to take in the view. Filling the plain below them were the red tops of tall mesas. Squat, blocklike shapes—some as high as fifteen stories—thrust up from the orange soil. Bands of yellow and orange and pink decorated the sides, but red seemed to predominate, streaking everything. And the mesas seemed to stretch on to the horizon.

"The view is as enchanting as ever," the prince murmured.

Sulu shaded his eyes and stared at the flat-sided mesas that rose from the plain like high-rises, and the broad spaces between them like avenues. "It looks like an abandoned city."

The prince pointed to the tops, which seemed to end in crenellations or even conical spires. "But at least this is a city where everyone lived in a castle."

"An abandoned fairy tale then." Sulu grinned back.

The prince gave a sad, knowing little laugh as he gazed at the crumbling tower shining in the sun. "As the poet says, 'All grandeur decays and all magic passes away.'" He paused and then added, "And so have all the kings and queens who lived here." He could not resist turning to Urmi. "Is there a lesson here for me?"

"Of a sort." Urmi raised her left leg to scratch it. "But it's more likely the story of some fool of an emperor who had such grandiose schemes that his own people turned against him."

The prince kicked a pebble over the edge. They heard it clack as it fell. "Then the moral is to leave this world to you and Rahu so you can work out your own destinies."

Mr. Spock stepped brusquely to the edge of the path. "And how far do we travel?" He was careful to accent the last word as if they had all forgotten.

There was silence for a moment, as if the others still wanted to enjoy the scenery. But when Mr. Spock turned around expectantly, Urmi sighed. "It's fifty kilometers. Then the path climbs up another ridge."

"Then may I suggest we move as far as we can while there is still daylight?" Mr. Spock said. "Since Angira has no moon, Mr. Sulu and I will have trouble walking just by starlight."

"Do you always have to be so pragmatic, Mr. Spock?" the prince asked. "I fear the charms of landscapes and moons are wasted on you."

"I won't squander precious time sentimentalizing physical phenomena, if that's what you mean." Mr. Spock started down the path at a brisk pace.

The path wound through slender pillars of sandstone

that stood like trees from which the branches as well as the leaves had been blasted. Bars of light alternated with bars of shadow so that it seemed sometimes as if they were walking along a meandering series of piano keys.

On the floor of the plain, the path widened into a broad, rocky avenue between two huge mesas. As they entered the first canyon, Urmi looked at them defensively. "Would you mind telling an ignorant peasant why you might want to take over my world?"

"I hate to tell you this, Urmi," the prince said pleasantly—as if he really didn't mind at all, "but there are far nicer worlds for them to conquer than Angira."

"Then why don't the offworlders just leave us alone?" Urmi asked as she skipped over a rock.

Mr. Spock looked at her as calmly as if they were merely strolling through a park after dinner instead of escaping from Rahu. "In the long run, it is far better to add new and healthy partners. That is one of the chief principles upon which the Federation is based."

"Tell me another story." Urmi arched a skeptical eyebrow.

Mr. Spock spent the better part of an hour trying to explain the Federation to Urmi. Suspicious and stubborn, Urmi tried her best to establish that its principles were simply propaganda. And her sharp questions had backed Mr. Spock through space and time until he was now trying to explain the *Meditations of Surak* and the *Works of Mencius*.

The prince and Sulu, on the other hand, walked on ahead, watching the alterations that the late afternoon sun created in the canyons. The shadows seemed to rise up the sides and the colors at the very top seemed to change. The reds seemed to deepen to almost a vermillion while the lighter hues seemed to fuse into a somber orange. And the topmost peaks and spires seemed to glow like frozen tongues of flame.

As twilight filled the canyons, it seemed to Sulu as if the maze of canyons would stretch on forever; and the mesas themselves took on a timeless quality, as if they had been created in this eroded state and would always stay this way. If Sulu took a breath here, he could hold it forever until he himself turned into stone.

"Well," the prince sighed, "at least some of the magic still lingers in the fairy tale." He halted and looked behind him.

"And so," Mr. Spock was saying in his earnest way, "the alternative to growth is stagnation and decay. And it is equally true of a collection of worlds or just one."

The prince beckoned to the two stragglers. "You might as well take a rest, Urmi. Your ears will wear out long before Mr. Spock's tongue. Why don't you enjoy the view instead?"

"I suppose so." She scratched her forehead self-consciously. "But I still find it hard to believe that they can help themselves by helping us."

The prince shrugged. "Even if Angirans have not learned to conquer their selfishness, other people have."

"Then I must be too stupid to understand." Urmi laughed a little too loudly. "But I can see how you could've fooled someone as gullible as the prince."

Her tone was joking, but Sulu guessed that she was still smarting from her debate with the prince and Mr. Spock. At an early age, Sulu had learned to recognize the resentment and even the hostility that lay underneath such a tone. He had met with it in a variety of forms from colonists during his family's travels. His father had told him the hostility had come from the colonists' own insecurities rather than anything Sulu had done. And long ago, Sulu had learned to counter it with a determined, even aggressive cheerfulness.

"What do we have to do to convince you that we don't want your world?" Sulu tried to laugh.

She made a soft hissing noise as if in mock exasperation. "You could go home and never come back."

The prince turned around and backed along the stony ground so he could face Urmi while he spoke. "People like Sulu and Mr. Spock don't have one measly little planet that they call home. They have the whole galaxy."

"Everybody has a home." Urmi flapped an exasperated hand at the sky.

"Not space travelers. We have points of origin rather than homes." Sulu stopped the prince before he fell into a water-worn ditch.

"You were born on a spaceship?" Urmi asked with sudden interest.

It was an easy thing for the prince, with his long legs, to simply step over the ditch, but Sulu had to jump. "No," he said from the other side, "but I might just as well have been. My mother was a scientist who studied crop production so we were always moving from one world to another."

"Where were you born then?" Urmi sounded more curious than anything else now.

"Earth," Sulu said, "but I didn't really know about it except through books—and my imagination." Sulu chuckled at the memory. "When I was a kid, I built it up as really something. Instead of wilderness and struggling farms, there would be green hills and mansions and castles. And instead of dirt farmers, there would be gentlemen and ladies and everything would be perfect. So I kept after my parents until they decided to take me back to the ancestral homelands. That was a mistake." Sulu paused as he remembered that trip.

"What happened?" Urmi asked as she easily strode over the ditch.

Sulu waited until Mr. Spock had joined him on the other side of the ditch before he went on. "You have to understand how idealistic my dad could be sometimes. He insisted I do without a universal translator. He said the only real way to think in Japanese was to speak it. So I tried to get by on my English and bad Japanese."

"But you told me you were named after a character in a classical Japanese novel." The prince straddled a flat rock.

"That doesn't mean I read it in Japanese." Sulu climbed up beside him. "We used it a little bit at home for ordinary, everyday things and I thought it was enough." Sulu added, "But sometimes it wasn't. Taxi drivers would take me out of my way to pad the fare. Clerks would wait on everyone else before they'd wait on me. And I can't tell you how many times the old people would scold me like I was dirt beneath their feet."

"I don't understand that, though." The prince leapt from the rock. "When I was there, I never had any trouble. In fact, they made me feel very welcome."

"There's a double standard—at least in Asia." Sulu picked his way, using smaller stones as steps. "A stranger doesn't have any face to begin with—so it doesn't matter. Mistreating you would have been just as bad as mistreating some idiot child. But I and my family were supposed to fit in and speak the language like 'real people.'"

"Instead of grunting like an animal?" the prince suggested. "At least that's what Bibil called it. He was always after me to hold our conversations in Angiran so our tongues wouldn't get rusty."

"So you have no . . . roots?" Urmi sounded stunned. The pause before the last word had not been hers but the universal translator's. She had probably used the term *panku,* with all of its meanings, and the translator had to take a fraction of a second to find a word suitable for the context.

But Sulu had remembered the almost mystical connotations the prince had described—a stump that bears new shoots, a source and so on. "No," Sulu said quietly, "I have no *panku.*"

"But that's like . . ."—this time Urmi struggled for words sufficient to express her horror—"like a world without a sky."

"So 'home' is as much a foreign concept to me as a 'moon' would be to you," he explained good-naturedly.

"'Moon?'" Urmi looked to the prince for interpretation.

The prince held a fist up in the air and moved it in a slow circle. "It's a smaller version of a planet that reflects the light of the sun even at night."

Urmi wrinkled her forehead as if she suspected it was another offworlders' hoax. "That sounds impossible."

"Not at all." And Mr. Spock looked quite prepared to provide an explanation, but Urmi waved her hand hastily at Mr. Spock.

"Never mind. A moon isn't as hard to understand as the situation you're describing." She stared at them quizzically. "It sounds terrible to be an outsider like that."

"I'm afraid it's the price one must pay to learn about things such as moons and planetary rings." The prince's sandals slapped against the hot, gritty rocks.

"The cost is still a relatively small one," Mr. Spock said to Urmi as he followed her down the rocks.

The prince cocked his head to the side curiously. "Perhaps I lack your philosophical detachment about such isolation, Mr. Spock. I find it rather like being in a glass cage: You can see and hear everything—but never touch or be touched."

Urmi's voice was softer. "You mean here, on Angira?"

"Or in the Federation." Straightening his head, the prince resumed walking.

Urmi gave a shiver. "I'd rather live in the dungeons with the *kik-kiks* than live in an exile like that."

The prince fussed with the robe that lay wadded up around his waist like an inner tube. "I want some semblance of a normal, carefree life. I want to live on a safe, sane world where everyone isn't bent on trying to stab everyone else in the back."

As if she were determined to defend the honor of her world, Urmi caught up with him in three quick strides. "You make Angira sound like a pit of flame vipers. But we fight for what we believe is right."

The prince cleared his throat. "In the Federation, it is possible to fight with something more than swords. There are laws and courts."

"We're not a bunch of big-lunged orators," Urmi

declared proudly. "We're willing to die for a just cause."

"And so are they, but they do not whip out a sword the moment they suspect they are losing the debate." The prince pretended to slash at the air for a moment before he lowered his hand.

Her puzzled eyes searched his face. "Do you hate it here so much that you'd prefer a life in the glass cage?" When the prince didn't answer her, she rounded on Sulu. "If you're one of the homeless, how do you deal with it, Sulu?"

Sulu took his time while he considered several possible answers. His first inclination was to guard his own privacy, and yet he could sense Urmi's confusion and even hurt. After the escape from the palace, he felt he owed her more than a curt answer.

"You become a chameleon," he said finally.

Again, Urmi looked to the prince for help in understanding his friends. "A what?"

"It's a creature that can change color"—the prince paused and scratched his cheek—"like a *kita,* but it's a reptile."

Urmi swung her head back toward Sulu. "You learn to hide?"

Sulu brought the toes of his left foot up behind the heel of his right—walking slowly and with precision while he hunted for an answer. But it was difficult—perhaps because he was now moving through psychological territory he had rarely explored. "No, you learn to read people's moods and attitudes and to fit in."

"A toe licker?" Urmi asked scornfully.

"Not at all." Sulu lifted a hand up from his side and brought it down again. "You can be yourself. It's just that moods and attitudes of one world are different than those of another. They're like a language, in fact. And you learn how to express yourself in that language." He tried to shrug nonchalantly. "If you do it well, you get a reputation for being cheerful."

"Like Sulu here." The prince glanced at him shrewdly. "But in your own imagination you slip into fantasies of being a musketeer—and you claim that world as your own and you shape it as you see fit."

"Yes," Sulu said in surprise, "I suppose I did."

"It still doesn't sound right to me," Urmi frowned.

Sulu sighed. "As a kid, I guess I just got tired of always being different. I wanted to pass for one of the other colonists." He looked at Mr. Spock. "I guess I never had your strength of character."

"You never had my training," Mr. Spock suggested, much to Sulu's surprise. It was the kindest thing that he could ever recall Mr. Spock saying directly to him.

Urmi wrapped her arms around herself as if she had finally understood how truly alien they were, and it made her feel terribly cold. "You three are harder to understand than ten thousand moons."

"You flatter me, Urmi." The prince touched his fingertips to his chest. "I shed no light at night." As if eager to change the subject now, the prince took Mr. Spock's hand. "It's getting rather dark now, and since Angira lacks the civility of a moon to guide us, you will have to do with my hand, Mr. Spock. And perhaps Urmi will be so kind as to take Mr. Sulu's. I can attest to the fact that he washes his hands when he can."

Her cool, leathery palm closed around Sulu's hand. "How do you people manage to see through such tiny eyes?"

"Now, now," the prince pretended to scold her, "don't mock the handicapped. They can't help it if they were born with such beady little eyes."

"No, I guess not." Urmi gave Sulu's hand a guilty squeeze. "I shouldn't make fun of the handicapped *and* the homeless."

It had been a frustrating day for Lord Bhima. He had spent most of his time exploring the Old Chapel in a fruitless search for the secret passage. And in the end, he had given up and simply padlocked the chapel door so that no one else could go in or out. It had been nearly sunset when he had decided to inspect the land around the palace. But it had taken them most of the evening to reach the gulch.

And until just this moment, Rahu's band of young fanatics had been inclined to regard him as a madman. They seemed to resent having to follow him about when they could have been covering themselves in glory by marching with Rahu's army. But they were now coursing about like fine, purebred hunting dogs that had just caught the scent of their quarry.

When Lord Bhima joined the *sinha* lieutenant by the mouth of the gulch, he noticed how cautiously the lieutenant bowed his head to Lord Bhima. He still seemed to be unsure of a man who had not rallied to their cause until after the massacre had taken place.

Lord Bhima held his torch so that he could look at the tiny drops of dried blood on the ground. "So you found signs of someone's being wounded?"

"Yes, Lord. And they seem to lead that way." The lieutenant pointed toward the badlands.

"A wounded monk would head for the monastery,"

Lord Bhima mused. Suddenly he frowned at the young officer. "Why aren't you wearing your cape over your chest?" The other dozen *sinha* had clasped theirs in front of them, but the young officer had hung his bloody one around his waist by his sword and dagger.

"It just gets in the way," the lieutenant said. There was a slight curl to the corners of his mouth as if he felt superior to the cloaked Lord Bhima.

"The sun will be setting soon. It's clothing, not virtue, that keeps out the cold. Put it on," Lord Bhima ordered. He put all the authority he could into his voice.

The corners of the lieutenant's mouth pressed into a thin, contemptuous smile; and, for a moment, it looked as if he were even going to argue with Lord Bhima. "I'll be warming up soon enough when we begin our pursuit."

Lord Bhima saw that he had sunk even lower in the lieutenant's estimation. Well, he wanted obedience, not admiration. "This is a direct order, Lieutenant. I want you to wear your cape around your shoulders. I won't have you showing off just to impress your men."

"Yes, Lord." Reluctantly the young lieutenant undid the clasp so that he could lift his cape to his shoulders.

"And when you're finished, form up the men." Lord Bhima looked at the badlands. "And be sure to send a scout ahead of us."

"As you wish, Lord." The young officer turned to obey.

Lord Bhima watched the officer speculatively. The three regiments of *sinha* had once provided the noble cadets who officered the army. As such, they had been as much an elite social club as a training school. But

Chapter Six

Though they hardly paused for any sleep, it still took them a night and half the next day before they left the mesas behind, climbing up through a gap that snaked through the side of a new ridge of mountains. Its curving sides looked like clay molded by some giant child's hand and then left to dry.

It was several hours later that they stumbled on the remains of the massacre. Urmi, who was in the lead, casually took a large stride as if she were merely stepping over some large rock. Sulu, who was right behind her, looked down to see the skull lying on the rocky floor.

He stopped so abruptly that the prince almost ran into him. "What happened here?" he asked the prince.

The prince's eyes widened as he looked ahead of them. Bones lay scattered all along the sides of the gap and along its floor. They seemed to glow in the shadows like the letters of some strange, deadly alphabet. "I don't know."

"A battle or massacre." Mr. Spock picked up a skull. Some sharp instrument had split it almost in two. "Several years ago from the look of things." He pointed to sharp scratches on the skull. "These are made by some animal's teeth so I would surmise the bones have been scattered partly by scavengers." He looked up at the arroyo walls, studying the bands of color. "But from the markings on the walls, I would say this area was subject to flash floods and they would have dispersed things even more."

Urmi turned. "I should have warned you, but we've gotten used to the sight." She motioned to the bones. "It was a caravan coming to our valley; but the bandits got to them."

The prince walked forward slowly, as if trying to estimate the size of the caravan. "There are at least ten skulls here." He pointed to small whitish lumps that lay up ahead of them. "And it looks like even more up ahead. So it wasn't a small caravan."

"The bandit bands have gotten larger and bolder." Urmi waited impatiently. "They even raid the valley now."

The prince took the skull from Mr. Spock's hands. "But they were never that daring."

Urmi adjusted her grip on her food sack. Like all their sacks, it was much lighter now. "It's not just a few criminals or runaway farmers anymore. To start his land reforms, your father simply confiscated the lands from many of the lesser nobles and paid them only a fraction of what they were worth. And these nobles and their followers became bandits."

The prince set the skull back down. "I should have known. The blame always seems to come back to my father and his plans for modernization." He straightened up. "But these poor traders should have been buried, Urmi."

She looked about absently as if the bones no longer meant anything more to her than the rocks themselves. "Wake up, Your Highness. Those courtesies belong to an Angira that's vanished. We barely have time to take care of our own dead."

The prince turned to Sulu. "Now I know how one of those people feels in a Terran fairy tale when they come back after a night among the fairies and find twenty years have passed by in the real world." He looked back at Urmi, almost pleading now. "As bad and violent as things were, you make the past seem positively kind and benevolent now."

"I remember those times—they seem like a dream now. But that was many, many deaths ago." She stalked toward Mr. Spock almost tauntingly. "Do you still want Angira in the Federation?"

Mr. Spock brushed his hands on his robe. "I do not mean to sound callous to the suffering of your people, but the Federation has helped worlds that have been much worse than this. Mixing pride with despair may be the deadliest of sins. It is certainly the most misguided of philosophies."

Urmi halted almost wistfully. "I'd like to believe that there's hope."

Mr. Spock nodded at the sky. "I wish I could show you those worlds. I think that's the only way you'd trust me."

Urmi hesitated as if she were torn between her own convictions and the hopes that Mr. Spock held out to her.

"Why do you keep on fighting the truth?" the prince asked softly.

Urmi came out of her reverie, staring first at the prince and then at Mr. Spock. "No," Urmi said, "no. You won't have me fall under the same spell as the prince." And saying that, she spun around and started to walk along with quick, short strides through the bones—as if she were eager to get away not only from the scene of the massacre but from Mr. Spock as well.

Another ten kilometers found them climbing a pass. "We're only three kilometers from Urmi's valley now," the prince said.

Before the prince could say anything more, Urmi held up her hand suddenly. "I think you should put on your hats."

The prince set his hat over his head. "Why, what's wrong?"

"There's a song lizard who's usually singing its head off at this time of day but it's quiet."

"Could it be dead?" Sulu asked.

"None of the local people would kill it." She looked behind her but Mr. Spock and Sulu had already set their hats on their heads. The landscape was immediately screened by a dense weaving of straw. "There may be bandits about. If they are, they may still be too far away to get a good look at the offworlders. Let's hope for the best."

"But it's broad daylight," the prince protested. "Surely the bandits wouldn't dare come this close to the valley right now."

Urmi lowered her robes. "They would if they're Lord Tayu's men. He thinks he still owns the valley."

Sulu and Spock were quick to copy Urmi, but the prince stood there surprised. "Lord Tayu? But he comes of such a fine, old house."

"His family's bloodline wasn't any protection from confiscation."

The prince slowly lowered his own robe. "My father certainly has been busy making things miserable for everyone, hasn't he?"

"Some people have a knack for it," Urmi snapped. She looked at Sulu and Mr. Spock. "Now remember," she said quietly, "move slowly in the robes or you'll trip over the hems."

The prince added. "And keep your heads bowed slightly. We must seem like monks who beg for our daily meal now. So we must think humbly, or"—the prince could not help turning his head mischievously toward Mr. Spock—"in your case, priggishly, Mr. Spock."

They continued through the pass and down the other side of the ridge. Every now and then some pebbles cascaded down the sides—though whether a lizard did it or some larger creature, they could not tell. What made it even worse was the slow pace that the robes and hats forced them to adopt.

Urmi led them into an arroyo that wound its way down the next set of ridges. The stones seemed to gather heat so that the air rose in heat waves that made the outline of the few bushes and weeds waver. It was hot even when the arroyo's curving sides closed in, reducing the sky to a thin narrow strip above them.

Despite the shade, Sulu was sweating heavily in his robes. "They certainly do their share of penance," Sulu murmured to the prince. And as the walls of the arroyo seemed to close in, he couldn't shake the feeling that they were insects slowly crawling into some trap.

It was a relief, then, when the arroyo suddenly

widened. Its sides seemed to peel back in huge curving sheets like billowing curtains. When they rounded the bend, they found themselves on the eastern edge of a large, flat stone bay several square kilometers in area. Ahead of them was a shallow pond some fifteen meters across, fed by a sluggish stream that wriggled through another arroyo to the southwest.

Beginning on the western edge of the pond and spreading outward to fill the bay were thousands of stone markers, some as small as a meter and made of crudely piled rocks, while others soared up two meters high and were of elaborate stonework. There were so many that they looked like the bristles on a brush.

They crossed the rocky dirt to the bottom of the pond. Kneeling, they raised water in their cupped hands to splash it on their faces—though the need to keep on their hats made it awkward. Then, after they had taken a drink and refilled their water sacks, they rose.

"We only have to cross that ridgetop and we'll be in my valley," Urmi tried to encourage them.

"What is this area?" Sulu asked in a low voice so that they couldn't be overheard.

"It's our cemetery," came Urmi's hushed reply. "My people have been using it for nearly a hundred generations."

"And what are the jars?" Sulu pointed to the hundreds of jars that were scattered all about the cemetery. They were colored brown and were about a third of a meter high. Their tops were sealed with bright orange clay. "Are those offerings?"

"In a manner of speaking, yes," Urmi's voice was edged with irony. "They are infants brought here to die because their families are too poor to feed them." She

140

swung around to face them. "There are hardly any children under the age of five in the valley."

"If anything would convince me how miserable people are, this would. Children are—or rather were—precious to us." The prince seemed drawn to the edge of the cemetery.

"But isn't there something that can be done?" Sulu asked, horrified.

"Do you think we'd do this if we hadn't already tried everything?" Urmi's voice sounded strained—as if she were in pain. "The taxes and rents are already so high that we cannot feed any more new mouths."

Suddenly the prince bent and lifted up a small skull and a handful of pottery shards. "The scavengers have been breaking the jars and getting to the corpses. But the priests are supposed to protect them." He set the skull and shards back down.

"How can you expect the priests to do their duties when everyone else fails in theirs?" Urmi gripped a stone marker carved in the shape of a man's head. "There are jars like these in every shrine and temple. Only the potters seem to make money nowadays. And do you want to know what happens to the older children?"

The prince placed his hands over his ears. "No, I don't."

Urmi reached up under his hat and grabbed his hand to pull it away. "They're sold as slaves." Her voice broke on the last word.

Since it was useless to try to shut Urmi out, the prince dropped his other hand. "I'm . . . I'm sorry, Urmi. I apologize for what's been done to your people."

Before Urmi could say anything, a great shout rose

from the middle of the cemetery and a dozen ragged men popped up from behind the stone markers. Another dozen trotted out of the southwest arroyo to cut off their retreat.

"Bandits," Urmi hissed.

Some were in worn, cracked boots, while most of them wore sandals, but there were two who were even barefoot. And here and there among the dirty rags of their *soropas* and cloaks, Sulu thought he saw the glint of gold thread. Someone had made an attempt to sew large emblems on the fronts of their *soropas*, but the cloth had been so clumsily cut and sewn that it was difficult to tell what the emblems were supposed to represent—though they looked vaguely like some many-petaled flower.

A small Angiran padded forward. On his head was a long, floppy hat like a stocking cap. Sulu couldn't help noticing that his fur, like the fur of the other bandits, was darker than any of the Angirans in the palace, and it lacked a certain luster. Several even had bald spots as well as a rheumy red line outlining their eyes.

The little man paused two meters from the prince and puffed himself up with self-importance. "Kneel, you leeches, for Lord Tayu." Urmi had been right. Apparently the scout had not gotten a close enough look at them to tell that they weren't priests.

Urmi touched Sulu's arm and then nodded her hat toward Mr. Spock. The three of them knelt on the rocky dirt, careful to keep their boots covered by the robes. But the prince was a bit slower to obey and the man in the cap tripped the prince so that he fell on his back. "Leeches that are slow to kneel get shortened by a head." And he raised his sword over his head.

A monk's robes, Sulu realized, were not the best

clothing to wear for a quick defense. By the time they had pulled up the robes and gotten out their weapons, the prince would be dead.

But the prince himself flung up a hand. "Wait. What's happened to Lord Tayu's hospitality?"

"It's been a long time since anyone spoke of that." A ragged man came toward them. His fur was as dark and lusterless as the rest of his men's so that it seemed to blend into the leather vest he wore. The only bright bit of color was his short cloak of tattered if expensive silk, and some attempt had been made to keep himself cleaner than the others. "I had more monks visiting me in those days. They once praised my piety. Strange how the flattery ended at the same time as the donations."

"You are welcome to share what I have." The prince tried to sit up but the man in the cap jabbed his sword at him and the prince remained only halfway up.

"I had intended to anyway." With an almost lazy arrogance, Lord Tayu motioned for the man in the cap to raise his sword. "It's hard to collect what's due to me."

The prince sat all the way up. "Due to you?"

"My taxes, leech." Lord Tayu snatched up the nearest sack and began to rummage through it. "You don't think a piece of paper from the emperor can really take away lands that have been in my family for generations?" His hand reappeared, holding a small chunk of cheese. He bit into it hungrily, glancing away from the prince as if Lord Tayu were embarrassed.

The other bandits grabbed the other sacks, elbowing and jostling one another to get at what little food might be there. With angry shouts for the others to wait, the remaining bandits on the arroyo's walls began to climb down.

The prince gave a sad shake of his head. "I'm truly sorry for you, Lord Tayu."

Lord Tayu lowered the cheese as if he were finally aware of the spectacle he was making. His fingers wiped at his mouth in a clumsy attempt to groom himself. "Wait till we have a real emperor like Lord Rahu."

The prince's spine snapped straight as if he had just been stung. "You don't think you can rule over the valley again after what you've done to them?"

"They're rebels who refuse to pay their taxes." Lord Tayu handed the remainder of the cheese over to the man in a cap, who wolfed it down hungrily.

"And the caravan?" the prince said indignantly. "Were they rebels too? Or are you going to tell me that wasn't your handiwork?"

Lord Tayu whirled around as his men began fighting among themselves over the sacks. "Try to remember who you are," he shouted at them. He threw his own sack over to them and started a new, wild scramble. He looked back at the prince. "No, the caravan was my doing. They should have paid me what I asked. People had to be taught a lesson. I might not live on an estate anymore, but I am still the lord here."

"But to slaughter them?" the prince demanded. "You're no better than a mad animal now."

Lord Tayu's eyes narrowed dangerously. "Spare me the sermons, leech. My men can't survive on them." He leaned his head back as a new thought came to him. "But where are your begging bowls? They say a monk without his begging bowl is like a viper without its fangs."

"We were forced to leave our monastery hastily. There has been trouble at the palace."

Lord Tayu curled his fingers around the hilt of his sword. "Or you're scouts sent to trap us."

With a violent shove, the prince rolled into Lord Tayu, bowling him over so that he went head-first into the pond. Mr. Spock was the first to get to his feet, but it took time to raise his robes so he could pull out his sword.

And even as the prince was trying to scramble to his feet, the man in the cap was raising his sword for a deadly slash. "You must sample our new style of hospitality."

But then the little man gave a start as the dagger sank into his chest. Spinning around, he tumbled backward into the pond. Sulu had been so busy raising his own hem that he hadn't noticed Urmi take the daggers from her sleeves.

Lord Tayu rose, spluttering from the pond. "Kill them," he bellowed to his men.

Prince Vikram had his sword out by then. With a twirl of his wrist, he unfurled the ribbons from around the blade. The bells jingled as he met the first man, skillfully parrying the clumsy slash, and then let his blade slide down the other's to sink the point into the bandit's throat. The second bandit skidded to a desperate halt so he could take up a proper fighting stance; but he was so off balance that the prince easily countered the bandit's awkward parry and stabbed him as well.

The other bandits stopped and stared as their comrades fell to the ground. Urmi ran up beside him, a dagger in her right hand. "If we can hold them off long enough, our sentries will hear the noise and the militia will come."

"Let's hope their hearing is sharp enough." Sulu

stepped up beside the prince while Spock took his place on Urmi's left.

"And let's pray their feet are fast enough." The prince flung his hat from his head.

Lord Tayu stared from the pond. "I know you from somewhere."

Prince Vikram shifted his grip on his sword. "My father once said that the difference between a bandit and a lord was the title. I'm afraid that you've proven him correct, Lord Tayu."

"Prince Vikram?" Lord Tayu started to wade through the water.

"We both seem to have fallen on hard times, Lord Tayu." The prince smiled grimly. "Please meet my friends." They each took off their hats, letting them dangle down their backs by the cords.

"Quite a menagerie you've brought from offworld." Lord Tayu glanced down as the corpse of the little man in the cap bobbed against him. With a shove, he sent it drifting away. "But why the robes? You were never very pious before you left."

The bandits had begun to circle round them and the four travelers shifted back to back to meet an attack from all sides. "One sees an interesting side to people when one travels as a priest."

"That's true, but you were never the adventuresome sort." Lord Tayu rose from the pond, the water streaming down his clothes onto the stones. "I rather think you're running away." With a grin, he drew his sword. "So that means there's trouble at the palace and you're worth something to someone. Maybe even my lands."

"I rather think you'll have to take me first." The prince smiled.

Lord Tayu signed behind him and a bandit raised his spear. "Surrender," Lord Tayu said, "or your companions die." His face had already taken on a cheerful, absent look as if he were already on his estates once again.

Urmi threw her second dagger almost at the same time the spearman threw his weapon. It was Spock who knocked her down. The spear blade entered the flesh above his hip with a sickening, wet, smacking sound. They heard Urmi's dagger clatter on the rocks. For once, she had missed.

"Mr. Spock." Sulu caught him and lowered him to the ground.

Mr. Spock seemed surprised at how quickly his legs had collapsed from underneath him. He held out his sword to Urmi. "I think you'll be able to make better use of this than I will now."

Urmi sounded almost annoyed with Mr. Spock as she took it. "Why did he do that? I thought he didn't have any use for me."

The prince motioned for Sulu to rise. "Urmi," he said impatiently, "the offworlders can still be loyal to a comrade—even if they don't agree with her. And, after all, you saved Mr. Spock's life. He was only trying to return the favor."

Urmi stared down at Mr. Spock. "It's strange to think that someone born so far away would come here to save me." Shyly, hesitantly, almost as if she expected him to turn her fingertips to ice, she patted his shoulder. "Thank you."

"There were other reasons that brought me here, but"—he grimaced—"the effect was just the same."

"Go on. What are you waiting for?" Lord Tayu pointed his sword at them. "Capture the prince."

"Alive," the prince called playfully. "Don't forget to tell them to take us alive."

"Lord?" One of the bandits looked to Lord Tayu.

Lord Tayu nodded his head impatiently. "Yes, alive if you can." He added with a meaningful look at the prince, "But dead if you have to. I think even his head will be worth something."

"You always were the shortsighted one," the prince grunted.

The first attack was more of a test. The bandits closed, crossed blades and then retreated warily. They had all seen how easily the prince had disposed of two of their number.

"Do you think we have all day?" Drawing his own sword, Lord Tayu rushed at the prince. The prince parried the first cut and then brought his blade down as Lord Tayu tried a backhanded slash from below.

"Your wrists have gotten stronger since we fought last time," the prince grunted.

Lord Tayu stepped back. "We were boys in a tournament in those days. Swordplay was only a game then."

Four bandits charged in then and Sulu's own world instantly narrowed in focus as he turned to face two swordsmen. He was a little more confident this time, after having won the swordfight in the palace. He parried the first cut; but before he could even congratulate himself, he saw the sword darting in from his right. He deflected the second bandit's thrust and then had to meet the first bandit again.

It was a strange, brutal kind of intimacy that Sulu found himself sharing with the two bandits. He could see the spots and tears on their *soropas,* hear the stamping of their feet as they shifted and lunged, smell their sweaty fur. The first bandit had even less of a chin than most Angirans, so that his face had a mashed-in look. The second had a way of grimacing as he fought so that one side of his face twisted up, wrinkling the black skin around his nostrils. Sulu felt at that moment as if their images were fixed forever in his memory, so that he could have drawn every hair and every blemish. And he was sure they could have done the same with him. It was a far cry from reading the lights and meters of a control panel of the *Enterprise*.

There really wasn't time for the niceties, he decided. He parried the first bandit's slash close to Sulu's body so that the first bandit was now leaning forward. It was a simple thing then to trip the bandit and shove him into the second bandit so that the two went sprawling. Two quick slashes disabled them both.

Two more bandits tried to close in with him even as the first pair were crawling away. Sulu fought on the defensive while his left hand fumbled to lift his hat's cord over his head. Then he could grip the hat by its rim. The straw was too flimsy, of course, to be useful as a shield, but it did help mask his own blade.

He flapped his hat at one bandit so that the bottom edge raised and the bandit retreated cautiously. It gave Sulu just enough time to swing the hat around to deflect the sword blade of the other bandit and disable him with a slash across his sword arm. Then he brought his sword in front of him again as the first bandit tried to thrust at him. The blade ripped through the straw, sliding past his body by only a few centimeters. Sulu didn't hesitate, but thrust his own sword through the hat. The point tore through the straw and he felt his sword jar against something and then slide onward.

The bandit yelled in pain and Sulu slid his blade free. There was blood on the point and he lowered the hat in time to see the bandit stagger back, clutching at his stomach. From somewhere to his left, another bandit screamed—Urmi's work. The prince himself was still busy with Lord Tayu.

Panting for breath, Sulu turned back to the other bandits. But they weren't nearly as enthusiastic as they had been before. Finally, a large man with a huge cutlass started toward Sulu. And Sulu tensed. The man's cutlass was large enough to break Sulu's own blade if he wasn't careful. But on the other hand, it ought to be a clumsier weapon. It would be a test of Sulu's own quickness—and perhaps his luck.

Suddenly a smooth, round stone, about the size of Sulu's thumbnail, rattled on the ground between them. Two more stones rattled and one of the bandits cried out, raising a hand toward his bloody head.

"It's the villagers, Lord." The large man fell back toward the other bandits. "We have to get away."

Lord Tayu's face took on an angry, frightened look— almost as if he had lost his estates a second time. "I'm not finished yet."

"But Lord—" The large man broke off to curse as a rock hit his shoulder. A dozen more stones fell among the bandits and Sulu could see the slingers on top of the arroyo's walls.

Lord Tayu dismissed them with a wave of his left hand. "Go on. Run away if you want. That's all you're good for anyway."

"Hey," Urmi almost crowed in delight. "It's me, Urmi." She waved a dagger over her head.

Gaunt men and women, half-skeletons themselves, began to run through the cemetery toward them. Their fur was just as dark and dull as that of the bandits, but more of them had bald spots and the fiery, red-rimmed eyes. A few were armed with spears, but most held only rakes, shovels and knives—which they held in positions better suited for work than for fighting. Even so, they could kill the bandits by sheer weight of numbers.

Gathering up their wounded, the bandits were dashing down the same arroyo that the prince and his group had traveled. And the militia gave gleeful shouts as they streamed past the cheering Urmi.

"You've just condemned yourself to death," the prince said to Lord Tayu. "Because if I don't kill you, the peasants will."

"I intend to take you with me—one way or another." He swept his sword in one last, desperate slash designed to decapitate the prince.

But the prince simply squatted down, sliding his sword up across Lord Tayu's stomach. Lord Tayu lowered his left hand to his stomach, trying to hold in his entrails. His eyes glazed with pain and still he fought to speak. "I'll be waiting for you . . . by the gates to the underworld." He brought his right hand down in a clumsy cut that the prince easily parried. And then he fell forward over the prince.

Urmi and Sulu helped the prince slide out from underneath Lord Tayu. "It's nice to know that one has something to look forward to in the afterlife." When the prince rose, his robes were covered with Lord Tayu's blood.

An earnest young man came over to them. On his head was a battered wooden training helmet and in his hand was a sickle. "Keep your mouth shut," Urmi whispered fiercely to the prince. "Let me do all the talking."

"Urmi, what's the news?" the young man asked.

"I'll tell you back in the village, Schami. I want to tell the story just once instead of a dozen times."

Schami pointed toward Sulu and Mr. Spock. "And just what sort of companions did you pick up?"

"Offworlders," Urmi explained, and then paused before she added, "and my friends."

"It's a bad sort of joke, Urmi." Schami frowned.

"It's the truth," she insisted proudly.

Schami made the sign against evil. "They say people change when they leave the valley—and not in the right ways either." He nodded to the ragged prince. "And who's this? Their keeper?"

"A bodyguard," Urmi ad-libbed quickly. "And a fool who almost got us killed by leading us into a trap. You won't get any bonus from us."

"You're not my employer. They are." The prince jerked his head toward Sulu and Mr. Spock.

Urmi drew herself up in mock indignation. "And I'm the guide and they'll listen to me."

Schami laughed and clapped the prince on his shoulder. "You may be handy with a sword, but Urmi is handier with her tongue. A smart person gives up when he's outmatched." And he began to recall the rest of the militia.

Chapter Seven

They had been climbing steadily along the zigzag-ging track all that day so it was a surprise to Sulu when it suddenly sloped downward. "Steady," Urmi called to the others who were helping to carry Mr. Spock on a litter improvised out of cloaks and spears.

They made their way around the other side of the mesa and Sulu could see, in the fading daylight, a series of sandstone shelves held suspended like the waves of a sea by some powerful magic so that they did not crash down on the valley below. A hundred kilometers long but only some twenty kilometers wide, the valley had been formed by a river that snaked its way between the mountain ridges before it plunged into a steep gorge.

Along the river's banks, the fields showed as a smoky green. "After the badlands, I'd almost forgotten what the color green looked like," Sulu said to Urmi.

"There are eleven villages in the valley," Urmi explained. She pointed to a cluster of lights immediately below them about five kilometers from the northern end of the valley. "That's my village, where they raise the greenest crops and the brightest children."

"And the biggest liars," one of the militia women grunted. "My village has the best of everything."

That touched off a heated, if friendly, debate among the militia. "It's noisy," Urmi said to Sulu and the prince. "But it's home."

Sulu was a bit surprised by the lush valley below. From what Urmi had been describing, he had been expecting drought conditions. "It looks like you grow enough crops to feed yourselves."

"But we never get to keep much of what we grow," Urmi said pointedly. "Most of it goes to pay for our rent or all of the emperor's many taxes."

Sulu clicked his tongue sympathetically. "It must drive you crazy to be surrounded by all that food and not be able to eat it."

"That's criminal," the prince declared.

Urmi looked at Sulu but her words were meant for the prince. "Yes, I wanted you to see this for yourself. Now you know why we have to fight."

As the track wound its way down through the shelves, they began to pick out more details in the nearest village. Its small whitewashed houses looked like so many little boxes tumbled together. They seemed to have been built on the owners' whims so that there was no order to the streets, only twisting, winding lanes between the houses. Green and orange and purple fruits were drying on the flat thatched roofs.

Herds of *gaya*—long-haired, goatlike creatures, some three meters long—walked leisurely along the paths toward a nearby village, their heads nodding content- edly. The farmers, too, were finally leaving their fields, their hoes or rakes over their shoulders. Some of them were washing on the banks of the river, but others were trudging wearily into the village.

"What're these execution posts doing here?" The prince pointed to several posts dug into the slope. There were small nicks in the wood, as if from arrowheads, and there were dark, ominous stains on the poles and the ground.

Urmi refused to look at the posts. "The emperor declared that all the land not used for farming around a village was his."

"But that's ridiculous. You get your firewood from here and you catch small game." The prince looked shocked. "It's always belonged to everyone."

"Not anymore. Now we have to pay for licenses." Urmi smiled wryly. "Otherwise we are accused of being thieves. The first time the tax collector surprised us."

"So we keep a watch—as much for tax collectors as for bandits," Schami explained. "The emperor will have to pay for all of his big plans without that little extra bit of money from us."

In a more somber mood, the militia reached the floor of the valley where they divided into groups, each heading for its village. But Sulu and the others stayed with Schami.

Sulu knelt to examine the nearest field where broad, yellow-leafed plants were growing.

"What're these?" Sulu asked Urmi.

"That's *amma*—the green gold of Angira," Urmi declared proudly. "It's tough enough to grow most anywhere and doesn't need much sunlight. In fact, it grows so quick, the farmers like to tell a story about a man who used to harvest a crop in his closet."

"I suppose the broad leaves help it gather in the sunlight." Sulu shaded his eyes as he looked up at Angira's dwarf sun. As the prince had said, the world received less sunlight than Earth. "It might do well on other worlds with a short growing season."

Urmi pulled at her lower lip. "Yes, I suppose so. It would certainly be worth their while to try. You can get six cuttings from one plant. And then the fibers can be used for a whole lot of things. And at the very least, you can uproot the plants and eat the tuberlike roots."

"Really?" Sulu looked ready to step into the field to examine one of the plants. "I wish I'd had time to check it in the ship's library."

"You may have more than enough time to study it, offworlder," Schami said. "Your friend doesn't look like he's in a good way."

"I was hoping to get some volunteers to be bearers," Urmi said.

"Tired of our hospitality already?" Schami asked them.

"We have urgent business in Kotah," Sulu said quickly.

A rickety bridge of planks spanned the river and they marched across it to Urmi's home village. Because Schami had sent a runner on ahead, there was already a crowd of several hundred people waiting excitedly by the gates of Urmi's village. Sulu couldn't help noticing that the villagers all had the same half-starved look as the militia, and their fur seemed just as dull and dark. Some had huge naked patches of skin, while others had eyes centered within large bloodshot circles. At the very front of the crowd, standing very self-consciously, were a dozen men and women with orange bands tied around their arms.

156

"Who are they?" Sulu asked Urmi.

"Members of the Committee," she answered back. "They're drawn from all the villages of the valley."

A squat man suddenly strode forward. In his hand was a spear with a blade of an ornate design on top of a new shaft of pale wood. As they drew closer, Sulu could see the purple ribbon around the man's neck.

Urmi saw it at almost the same time and she turned sharply to Schami. "When did they make Mumtas the voice of the people?"

"About thirty days ago. He was doing all the talking anyway," Schami said. "Why, what's wrong?"

"Because he's an egotistical fool," Urmi snapped.

"You're welcome to try to impeach him." Schami shrugged. "But I warn you, he has a following through all the valley."

Mumtas raised the spear melodramatically into the air and then thrust it point first into the dirt. "You've carried out a dangerous and risky mission like the brave woman you are and done far better than anyone could have hoped. And so, in the name of the Committee, I say a hearty 'Well done, Urmi.'" And he raised his right palm parallel to the ground and brought his left one down lightly on top for quiet applause. The other villagers did the same.

Urmi held up her hands. "I'm not some dancing clown."

"But you have brought us hostages of immense value." Mumtas beamed at her, but now that they were closer, Sulu could see the cold, hard appraising eyes in Mumtas's face.

"You can't imprison them." Urmi said angrily. "I made a promise to my uncle."

"You don't have the authority to make promises like

that. Only the Committee does." Mumtas made a point of indicating the people behind him.

Urmi looked beyond him. "Listen to me. Even if I hadn't made that promise, we have to let them go. They have much to do in Kotah."

Mumtas rocked upward on the balls of his toes as if he were trying to give himself even more height. "And just what are their plans there?" He made a wringing motion with his hands. "Are they going to teach the nobles how to squeeze even more money out of us?"

The crowd stirred angrily. "No more of that," someone shouted.

Sulu eyed the nervous, excited crowd. "It won't take much to turn them into an ugly mob," he said to Urmi.

"Not if I can help it," she said to Sulu and then, spreading out her arms, she patted the air with her hands. "Wait. You haven't heard the news yet." When the crowd was silent again, she lowered her arms solemnly. "The emperor is dead and so are all of his court." Her further words were drowned out by the loud cheer that spread from the front of the crowd and rippled toward the back and sides. Some people tossed up their hats. Others squatted down and then leapt into the air as if they had been catapulted. Still others did an impromptu little hopping dance.

Urmi turned slowly, glancing embarrassedly at Sulu and the prince. The prince had done his best to make his face into a blank mask, but the muscles on his jaw worked as if he were clenching them. Urmi faced the crowd again. "Listen to me," she tried to shout. But they couldn't hear her in the midst of their celebration. She cupped her hands around her mouth like a megaphone. "Listen to me!"

The Committee members turned and made silencing motions with their hands. But even so, it took a good while for the happy people to quiet down.

Urmi looked around contemptuously. "You're a fine lot of fools to start a party before you hear all of the news. You've just climbed out of the mud wallow and jumped into the manure pit. Lord Rahu wants the throne now and if he has his way, he'll make things like they were a hundred years ago when you couldn't even leave the valley without your lord's permission. These offworlders can stop him."

Mumtas closed his hands around the shaft of his spear. "I say let the nobles kill off one another. The fewer the better." He looked over his shoulder toward the crowd and there were growls of approval.

Urmi glared at them. "But Rahu's a mad animal. He'll attack the workers and the farmers as well. You have to let these offworlders through so they can stop him."

"All the more reason to keep them as hostages." Mumtas yanked his spear from the dirt and brandished it triumphantly over his head. "It's not every day that two men fall from the sky into our valley." And the crowd began to cheer.

Urmi frantically motioned for silence again. When she had it, she looked at them disgustedly. "You people can't see beyond your own noses. We're not just one village or one clan or one valley anymore. We're part of Angira."

"Oh, yes," Mumtas sneered, "and the whole of Angira will march to help us when Rahu visits us." He waited for the jeers and laughter that he knew would come. "No, we can only count on our own kind and," he lowered his eyelids significantly at Urmi, "you can't always be sure even then." He jabbed his spear toward Sulu and Mr. Spock. "Disarm them."

Militia suddenly grabbed Sulu's and the prince's arms and took away their swords.

Urmi looked desperately toward the rest of the Committee. "You know I'm not some flutterbrain that gets scared easily. I risked my life when I went to the palace and for that you need a level head and caution. So you can believe me when I tell you that we have to let them go—as much for our own sake as for Angira's."

There were anxious conversations among the Committee members and the crowd itself. And for a moment, it seemed as if Urmi might have her way. But, like an actor sensitive to his audience's moods, Mumtas sensed the change in the crowd. He raised his hands above his heads. "A sharing session," he shouted suddenly. "I call for a sharing session."

"I've had a long, tiring journey," Urmi said. "I would like a short rest."

Mumtas swept an arm back and forth in front of them as a sign of negation. "This matter is too important to wait. How often do two treasures like these"—he nodded to Sulu and Mr. Spock—"fall ripe into our hands? Between Kotah and Rahu, we should do quite well."

Urmi let out her breath in an indignant gasp. "You can't be serious."

Mumtas was all smiles now. "The palace isn't the only place for intrigues."

"And I say I need time to catch my breath and collect my thoughts."

"Fine, let's have a sharing session to discuss that idea," the squat man said.

Urmi's lips tightened like someone who knew she had been boxed into a corner. "Very well then."

Mumtas turned triumphantly to the guards. "In the meantime, take our visitors into protective custody and put them in the stables."

"And have them witch the animals?" Schami pretended to object.

"You'll do no such thing to them." An older, more compact version of Bibil limped from the crowd. "When two creatures come from so far away to our village, you can't put them in a stable. They'll stay in my house."

Mumtas scowled at Puga. "You stay out of this, Puga."

"When the village's reputation is at stake, it's as much my business as it is yours." Puga spread his legs as if getting ready for a fight. "A big spear doesn't make a big warrior."

Mumtas stiffened as several people laughed in the crowd, but before he could say or do anything, Urmi jerked her head at him. "I'd advise you to fight one war at a time."

Mumtas forced his mouth into an artificial smile and pretended to give in with gruff good humor. "All right. At least until we decide what to do. And I'll post guards outside." He motioned the guards to follow Puga.

"Don't worry. That's my grandfather," Urmi said to Sulu. "You'll be safe enough with him while I knock some sense into the Committee."

"I hope so," Sulu said. "As nice as your village is, I'd like to see other parts of Angira."

The crowd parted hurriedly, forming a lane into the village itself. And, staring at the villagers' faces, Sulu realized they were more frightened than hostile. A number of them touched head and heart as if to ward off evil. But when Sulu tried to reassure them with a smile, a child began to wail as if Sulu were going to gobble the child down. "So much for public relations," Sulu said to the prince.

Outside Puga's house were a series of racks about a third of a meter apart from one another. On each of the racks lay the broad leaves of the *amma,* drying out. And over the doorway was a bunch of some kind of tiny yellow flowers for a bit of color. Reaching a hand up, Puga snapped off a handful of the brittle stalks. "There's nothing like some of my herbal tea to make you feel like a new person."

The house itself was little more than a box five meters on each side that had been built around an open, central hearth, though there was a hood to catch the smoke and a flue rising through the center of the roof.

When Mr. Spock was laid down on the dirt floor of Puga's house, Puga waved the flowers at the bearers. "Now shoo," he said. "You've had enough of their faces and I'm sure they've had enough of yours."

"But we're supposed to guard them," Schami said irritably.

"Well, you can do that from outside." And he chased the militia away as if they were only small children.

Then, after he had bolted the door shut and lowered the shutters, he shuffled over to where they were sitting beside the warmth of the hearth. Ducking his head under a lamp hanging from the central roof beam, Puga studied the prince by its dim light. "I thought I recognized that face," he whispered. "It's a little longer and a little leaner, but it still has some of that same impish look." He bowed his head. "Whatever I have is yours, but it's a poor enough welcome for you, Your Highness."

The old man tried to kneel but the prince stopped him. "Whatever troubles I've had, you've just made up for many of them."

"And my son, Bibil?" Puga asked in a trembling voice.

The prince looked away as if he had been dreading this moment. "He died helping us escape."

Puga's chin sank to his chest and his torso swayed as if someone had just added more weight to an already heavy load. "Well," he sighed, "my son lived thirty years longer than anyone expected. And when he told me he was going offworld"—the old man shook his head—"I thought for sure that was the end of him."

The prince swallowed. "It would have been very lonely out there without him."

Puga struggled to lift his head so he could stare at the prince. His eyes searched the prince's face for a long while before he finally gave a firm nod of his head. "Yes, I think he stamped you."

The prince dropped his head guiltily. "I wasn't able to bring his body out. I'm sorry."

Puga squared his shoulders. "It doesn't matter." Setting the dried flowers down on a short, wide stone beside the hearth, he shuffled across the room to an old chest and lifted the lid.

He took out a number of carefully wrapped objects and set them to the side as well until he lifted out a flat object. Two boards on small hinges covered the front like little doors. "I paid a traveling teacher to write this up for us when Bibil first enlisted." He added with shy pride, "But I put the hinges on myself." He opened the hinged doors so they could see Bibil's name in crude block letters. "We always expected to be burying this instead. They don't usually ship a soldier's body back home."

"No," the prince said huskily, "they don't."

Puga shut the doors again anxiously. "I've let it get dusty." He gave it a quick wipe before he put it back inside the chest.

The prince crossed the room. "If I reach Kotah, I swear that you won't have to worry about money."

"If you don't mind, lad, I would rather take care of it myself." The old man took out a sack that clinked.

"What's that?" the prince wondered.

"Bibil's medals from his campaigns. He told us to sell them for the metal, but I've always kept it to buy his coffin." He gave it a little jingle. "This should be enough for a headstone, don't you think?"

The prince shifted his feet uncomfortably as if he already suspected what the answer to his question would be. "Surely your neighbors wouldn't resent a burial?"

"Times are hard." Puga returned the sack to the chest along with the other things. "You've seen the people here. They don't get enough to eat, so their fur's darkened or even fallen out in patches."

"Then those are symptoms of malnutrition?" Sulu asked.

"Yes." The prince's fingertip traced the outline of an eye in the air. "As well as the redness around the eyes."

Puga shuffled over to a meter-high jar that sat beside the hearth. "I don't mean to speak ill of the dead, but

164

the emperor never seemed to have the slightest clue as to what was happening in the countryside."

The prince sighed. "He meant to help folk and yet he's hated so much."

"Well, lad"—Puga started to use a dipper to fill a kettle with water— "people suffered—whether it was his doing or not."

The prince got up quickly. "Here, let me help you like I used to."

Puga raised the dipper in protest. "But in those days you were simply the nephew of Bibil's 'friend.' Now, well." He raised one shoulder and began to pour water into the kettle again.

"Now I am far less than I once was." The prince took the kettle and dipper from the old man. "So let me help like I used to."

"As you wish." The old man surrendered the dipper with a smile. Turning slowly, he began to walk toward a shelf where a few cups and plates were stacked.

There was something likable about the open, generous old man, and Sulu rose. "Here, let me do that. Can I get the cups?"

"No, no." The old man patted the air with his hands. "You're one of my special guests. You shouldn't."

"But I insist," Sulu said.

The old man had a cheerful, wheezy laugh. "I've so much help today that I feel like a lord myself."

Sulu collected four cups from the shelf, under the old man's supervision. When they returned to the hearth, they found the prince had already hung the full kettle on a hook over the fire. "Set them here." The old man squatted and slapped his palm against the stone where the flowers already lay. When Sulu had done so, the old man nodded his thanks and then glanced at the prince. "Are you trying to reach Kotah?"

As if it were a familiar routine, the prince began to break off the tops of the flowers and crumble them into the cups. "Yes—before Rahu can catch us. Now there's a real horror of an emperor for you. He wants the days when a lord could flay a peasant for laughing too loud."

Puga gathered the dry flower stalks and threw them into the hearth fire where they flared instantly into flame. "But at least people know what deviltry to expect. They never knew what new madness your father would try."

The prince dusted off his hands. "The more I learn about modernizing Angira, the more impossible it seems."

Despite his pain, Mr. Spock struggled to speak—as if what he had to say was very urgent. "There are many worlds where change has been accomplished peacefully," he said in a weak voice. "Merkat is a thriving member of the Federation now and yet, not very long ago, it was at the same technological level as Angira."

The prince rested his elbows on his knees and slowly hid his face in his hands. "I would like to help my people, but they need an emperor as strong as my grandfather was—not a fool like me."

In the meantime, Puga had opened a pantry of wood so old, it almost shone like gold. Sulu couldn't help noticing how empty the shelves had been; and yet Puga had recklessly filled a bowl with fruit and little buns until the pantry itself was empty.

Puga brought the bowl over to them and placed it proudly in front of them. "Child, if I've learned one thing after all these years, it's that someone has to begin to do the right thing sometime."

The prince looked up. "Even if he's only a weak clown?"

With a rag wrapped around his hand, Puga lifted the kettle from its hook and poured the water into the cups with well-practiced flicks of his wrist. "You know my brother served as a Hound in your grandfather's time."

"Yes, so Bibil said."

Puga set the kettle to the side. "Well, before the battles, your grandfather would vomit with fright, but you'd never know it from the tales nowadays." He grasped the prince's arm. "This is the stuff of heroes right here." He let go of the prince and slapped his own arm. "And this is too. Heroes are simply ordinary people doing their duty."

"Well, I'll keep that in mind," the prince said awkwardly.

"Do more than that. Keep it in your heart," the old man urged. And then, picking up a cup of tea, he took one of the smallest buns from the bowl. Lifting the bun almost ceremoniously, he bit into it to show them it was safe. And then he took a sip of tea. "There, now please enjoy yourselves."

With the remaining water in the kettle, the old man cleansed Mr. Spock's wound and then applied a poultice before he bandaged it. It was only when he had finished tending to his guests that Puga spoke with the Prince about events within the valley and of what little the old man knew of the outside world. And though Mr. Spock and Sulu tried not to eat too much, the old man insisted that they have more—as if it were now a point of honor with him.

"No stranger ever left my house hungry," he insisted, and the prince nodded his head for them to take more.

After several hours, the prince was softly telling the old man about his travels with Bibil when they heard the knock on the door.

"It's me," Urmi said. "Open up."

"Coming," Puga shouted and tried to rise, but he sat back down. "Ah, these old bones just don't quite work the way they should."

"I'll do it." The prince rose quickly and went to the door, unbolting and opening it. Urmi had changed from her robes to a *soropa* of homespun cloth and a cloak of some wool-like material. "Is it time to go already?" he asked Urmi.

"Yes." Urmi was careful to keep her voice under control. "To the stables. Mumtas was more persuasive than I was."

"Urmi," Puga said angrily, "they're our guests."

"I tried." Urmi slapped her sides helplessly. "But you can't expect me to go against the Committee no matter how foolish I think they are."

The old man's nostrils widened and he glared at his granddaughter. "You ought to be ashamed of yourself," he said furiously.

"Orders are orders," Urmi tried to argue.

"Yes?" Puga suddenly thrust his hands up toward the prince. "Please help me up." When he was on his feet again, the old man limped toward the pallet in one corner. "I'll be with you in a moment."

Schami shoved past Urmi. "But you aren't a prisoner and you aren't in the militia, old man."

"Then I just joined one of them. Take your pick." Puga gathered up a blanket. "I intend to see that these offworlders are taken care of."

"Urmi?" Schami appealed to her for help.

She shrugged. "You ought to know my family by now. We each do what we think we have to."

Lord Bhima sat in the lee of a rock, contemplating the nude corpse of Lord Tayu. The peasants had simply left it exposed so that the carrion lizards had been savaging it. He would have liked to order the *sinha* to build cairns for Lord Tayu and his men, but Lord Bhima could not afford to tip his hand just yet.

It was a sorry ending to an already sad tale. Lord Tayu's family had been a fine, old house that the emperor had ruined in his own madness. And, Lord Bhima reminded himself grimly, it had been an ugly story that had been repeated in far too many other places on this world.

He stared at the corpse to harden his own resolve. As monstrous as the massacre had been, what the emperor had done to their world had been even more monstrous. Future generations would judge the righteousness of their cause.

Once the sun set, Angira could become bitterly cold. He noticed, however, that the dozen *sinha* made a point of ignoring the cold as they waited for his orders. He studied his young charges and decided that they really thought they were the same stuff as the heroes of the old legends.

They were young, he told himself, and allowed such madnesses. But try as he might, he could not remember a time when he had been quite that mad. Still, they had performed superbly, running through the badlands like so many lean hunting hounds. Even now, despite a night and a day of double-timing, they seemed ready and even eager to push on.

The young lieutenant slipped through the rocks, followed by a second warrior. "I have great news," he announced proudly. "The offworlders are in the valley. And the prince must be posing as their bodyguard."

Lord Bhima stood up, trying to stamp the circulation back into his legs. "How do you know they are down there?"

"We caught a peasant. The fool was supposed to be mounting sentry duty against bandits." The lieutenant gave a contemptuous chuckle. "But we had no trouble sneaking up on him. He almost died of fright."

Lord Bhima frowned. "Did he say what village they were in?"

"Yes"—the lieutenant was a bit slow to add the last word—"Lord. It wasn't his village, but he'd heard it was Guh."

That had been Bibil's old village. Lord Bhima gave a contented grunt. "Then the prince probably is with them, but in disguise. Were the offworlders treated as captives or as guests?"

The lieutenant hesitated as if slightly embarrassed. "I don't know, Lord."

"Didn't you think to ask the peasant?" Lord Bhima glared.

"We were trying to persuade him to tell us that, but he died at that point." The lieutenant drew himself up to attention. "I take full responsibility, Lord."

Lord Bhima drew his heavy eyebrows together angrily. "Just how were you persuading this peasant, Lieutenant? At dagger point?"

The lieutenant looked at Lord Bhima defiantly. "It is against the law for a peasant to take up arms. This whole valley must be a nest of rebels."

"There are bandits all around." Lord Bhima found himself shouting in outrage. "They might just be defending their homes, you fool."

"Lord!" The lieutenant stiffened indignantly.

Lord Bhima curled his fingers around the hilt of his sword. "There are over four thousand peasants down in that valley. If they are only protecting themselves, we do not want to turn that many peaceful, honest folk against us and our cause. That is your first mistake."

The officer swallowed, not liking the look in Lord Bhima's eyes. "Yes, Lord."

Lord Bhima decided with a certain smugness that his skill with a sword was enough to intimidate even a brash young *sinha*. "But even if they are organizing for a rebellion, our prime objective is to capture the prince, not exterminate rebels. That is your second mistake."

"Lord, I will make amends." The young officer started to pull out his dagger to plunge it into himself.

Lord Bhima knew that the lieutenant had been working himself up to this moment. The *sinha* were not only as strong and healthy as fine hunting dogs, but they were also just as predictable. However low the officer might hold Lord Bhima, his sense of duty would drive him on to one final conclusion. And so Lord Bhima's own hand was ready to draw his own sword from its sheath.

It was as simple and fluid a motion as it was deadly. Years of practice had compensated for his loss in youthful reaction time so that no one in all of his years had ever been quite as fast as Lord Bhima.

And yet, despite all those unbeaten years, there had always been a certain doubt tightening his stomach that perhaps this time he would find himself overmatched. It lent a certain fear and excitement to the moment when he reached for his sword.

It was almost as if he was matched not against some real opponent, but the Lord of the Shadows himself in some fleshy disguise. The Lord had come to claim him many times and there had always been that fraction of a second when he had felt his own life balanced on the edge of his sword, ready to tip one way or the other. And his confidence had not been helped any by the ease with which Rahu had knocked him out. Was it a fluke or was Lord Bhima truly slowing down?

But then, when he knew he was going to win again, he had felt an immense relief rushing through him and a sense of release that he had beaten the Shadow Lord once more.

And though the stakes were not nearly as high this time, it was still interesting to watch the young officer's eyes widen in surprise and fear as Lord Bhima whipped out his sword and brought it down in a quick slash, halting the edge just above the lieutenant's wrist.

Lord Bhima was still the swordmaster. The lesson had not been lost on either the lieutenant or his men.

Lord Bhima could not help smiling in satisfaction as he raised his sword. "You will die when I say so. Not before. This is neither the time nor the place for me to find a new second-in-command. That is your third mistake."

The lieutenant bowed his head with genuine respect now. "My life is in your hands, Lord."

Lord Bhima sheathed his sword. "Well, it can't be helped. Make his death look like the work of Lord Tayu's men out for revenge. Strip the corpse and mutilate it. Then we'll move on."

"Lord, we would have no trouble sneaking into the valley," the lieutenant countered. "They're nothing but mud-footed peasants pretending to be warriors."

"Sneaking into the village isn't the problem. The real trouble will come when we try to escape with our prisoners while an entire valley rises up in arms." Lord Bhima smiled patiently. "It will be far less risky if we let the prince and his friends come to us. And I know the perfect place to trap them."

The lieutenant's tone was guarded. "But if they're prisoners, Lord, shouldn't we go after them?"

"The prince may be a fool, but his friends aren't. They managed to get him away from the palace, didn't they?" Lord Bhima reminded the lieutenant. "I don't think it's likely that a bunch of peasants will be able to hold onto him. But in the remote event that they do, we can always come back and carry out your original idea. But for now, let's take the easier course."

The lieutenant nodded obediently. "Yes, Lord."

"So ready the men." Lord Bhima watched with satisfaction as the lieutenant sprang to obey him now. Things, he decided, were shaping up nicely after all.

Chapter Eight

The breath of the animals steamed the air within the stable. And unfortunately for them, the long-haired creatures not only looked like large goats but smelled like them as well. And even after several hours, Sulu had still not gotten used to the smell. As he sat keeping watch, he wondered if he would ever adjust to it. He huddled in his robe, which he and the others had elected to keep wearing because of the cold.

He was about to wake the prince to take over when Sulu heard the thud outside the stable. He touched the sleeping prince and the old man. Then he looked toward Mr. Spock, but Mr. Spock was already awake. He motioned Sulu to move out.

Puga held up a fist as he whispered, "I was fairly good with these when I was a boy."

"Your family's given enough for us," the prince said softly.

"My son wasn't the only fighter." Puga held onto the side of the stall to pull himself erect.

"I wish I had half your heart," the prince said as he helped the old man up.

They were waiting in a semicircle before the doorway as the door opened slowly, but it was Urmi with a pack of food and a water sack on her back. "Hurry. We have to put as much distance as we can between the valley and ourselves."

The prince glanced at the guard sprawled out on the ground. "But what made you change your mind?"

"I never changed it." She shut the door carefully behind her. "I only pretended to go along with the Committee so I could arrange our escape." She added with a sniff, "I think you all might have trusted me a bit more." She included her grandfather in her resentful look.

The prince covered his embarrassment by fussing with his robe. "Well, suspiciousness is as instinctive for an Angiran as breathing."

She opened her cloak and drew three swords from the sash-end of her *soropa*. "I gave a promise to my uncle, after all."

But at first the prince refused to take a sword from her. "I absolve you of that promise."

Urmi swung both the pack and water sack onto the floor. "I had this nice little speech all prepared, so let me finish it. But even if I hadn't promised Uncle Bibil, I think I would have helped you. It's been a short journey but a hard one and I've come to know all of you." She looked from the prince and Sulu to where Mr. Spock still lay. "I've been thinking ever since Mr. Spock took that spear for me. Maybe there's something to what he says after all. And if that's true, maybe there's some use to the prince too with all of his offworld ways."

"You would still be in the minority," the prince said.

She leaned forward urgently. "I've seen what a good heart you have. You risked your life for servants and I can't think of any other claimant who would do that." She nodded to him. "I think even with a short stay, you'll do more good in the castles of Kotah than penned up in some village stable."

The prince examined his own sword. Urmi had bound the ribbons and bells tightly with a rag so that they couldn't make a sound. "But you'll be defying the Committee?"

"They mean well, but they can't see beyond the walls of our valley." Urmi handed a sword to Sulu. "And, anyway, I've a mind of my own."

"You'll be an outcast," he warned.

"Then perhaps I'll learn about the glass cage the prince spoke of." She raised one shoulder and then let it drop. "At any rate, my mind's made up."

"Stubbornness seems to run in your family." The prince nodded his head first to Urmi and then to Puga. "And I'm grateful that it does." He rounded on his heel. "Well, since Urmi wasn't able to steal a cart, we'll have to rig up a stretcher for Mr. Spock."

Mr. Spock raised a hand. "No. You'll travel faster without me."

"Nonsense." The prince tested some of the poles that formed one of the stalls, "I wouldn't think of depriving myself of your company. Whom would I tease?"

Mr. Spock's voice sounded strained. "I will recover faster if I can remain here. Don't be afraid to leave me behind. I'm of far more value as a live hostage than a buried corpse."

"But can we take the chance that they'll be that logical?" Sulu asked.

The corners turned up slightly on Mr. Spock's mouth. "Farmers are far more cautious than princes and romantics."

Sulu swung anxiously around to Urmi. "Would the Committee kill Mr. Spock?"

She shrugged. "Even *they* wouldn't be that foolish."

"Maybe I should stay with you then." Sulu started to hand his sword back to Urmi.

"One of us must survive to report to the *Enterprise*," Mr. Spock managed to rasp. "And the probabilities of success will increase if we separate."

"But—" Sulu began to protest.

"That is an order, Mr. Sulu." Mr. Spock closed his eyes for a moment as if he had to concentrate all his energies on fighting the pain.

"Come, Sulu." The prince picked up the pack and water sack. "I promise you that we'll return at the first opportunity."

"You will return when it is most convenient and not before," Mr. Spock insisted firmly. He pursed his lips for a moment as if he was undecided whether to go on or not. "I do not know what Your Highness's decision will be, but whatever your choice is, it will have important repercussions for Angira. I do not want to be a factor when you make that decision."

"How do you know I'll change my mind?" the prince asked.

Mr. Spock managed a slight smile. "I have frequently observed that people say one thing and then do something quite different."

"I brought these too—though I wasn't sure what they were." She held the communicators out to Sulu.

"Even better," Mr. Spock said approvingly. "Mr. Puga, could you hide one of those so I could get it later?"

Holding one end gingerly between his fingertips, the old man lifted a communicator from Urmi's palm. "Don't worry. I'm used to hiding things from tax collectors. No one will ever find it." He slipped it into his sash-end. "I'll take good care of it and you."

Hitching up his robe, Sulu took the other communicator and attached it to his belt. "You can't stay here. The other villagers might blame you."

Puga gave a merry wheeze. "Bless you, child, and what could they do to me? Take my life? There's little of that left now anyway. At my age, death holds very little terror."

Impulsively, the prince seized the old man's wrist. "You and Urmi are the only two good people that I've met on Angira."

The old man grasped the prince's wrist in return and gave it a fierce squeeze. "We all have our flaws. You're just not seeing the others at their best. They're more scared than we are, that's all. Give them enough food so that their fur grows sleek and golden and they'll follow you anywhere."

"They still couldn't match you and your granddaughter," the prince insisted.

The old man brought his other hand up and patted the prince's arm. "Just make the world safe for all of us."

The prince was silent for a moment, staring helplessly at the old man.

Urmi arched an eyebrow. "My grandfather's waiting for an answer."

"I'm only a shadow lord." The prince tried to turn away, but the old man would not let him.

"Even the smallest shadow can grow," Puga said urgently, "and even the smallest person can match the longest shadow."

"Or even the dream?" the prince asked with a slight smile.

Puga pressed his lips together and nodded his head firmly. "Just so." He let go.

"I'll . . . do what I can," the prince promised lamely.

It was dark outside the stable and the prince took Sulu by the hand to guide him. "Which way, Urmi?" the prince whispered.

"No place," said Mumtas. And torches guttered into life. "I knew you'd overstep yourself if I let you, Urmi."

He stepped out of a nearby house with his ornate spear resting on his shoulder. Four swordsmen with torches fanned out across the street. At the very center of the line was Schami with a spear, along with another spearman.

Urmi dropped her pack and sack to the ground. "Mumtas, it'd be a pleasure to take your head right now; but I'm in a hurry." She drew out her sword. "Just stay out of our way, Schami."

Schami jabbed his spear point at her. "You're the last person I expected to betray us."

Urmi let her right foot slide out in front of her as she got her body into position. "Sometimes people don't know what's really good for them."

Sulu drew out his sword. "You realize that if you kill any of them, you'll never be able to come back here."

"I may not have a choice," Urmi shrugged.

The prince drew out his sword, unwrapping the rag from around the hilt so he could shake out the ribbons. The bells jingled loudly in the silent village. "I wouldn't pose for any monuments quite yet."

"Where did you ever get a sword like that?" Mumtas demanded. He was standing safely behind his guards. "If it's a joke, it's in poor taste."

The prince shook the sword slightly so that it rang again as he took up his stance. "It's no joke. I paid dearly for this."

Mumtas shifted his feet uneasily as if he were no longer feeling quite as confident. "You're a fool if you paid anything for it."

"The price I paid wasn't in coin." The prince was on the militia in three quick strides. Schami thrust his spear point at the prince and lost the blade as well as part of the shaft when the prince chopped them off.

He whirled, twisting his wrist so that he could hack off another spear blade when he brought his sword back up. Another stride brought him right between Schami and the other spearman. The prince's sword sliced through the air, halting only centimeters from Schami's neck. "Would you care to pay the same price for my sword?"

The rest of the militia stood dumbfounded, watching Schami and the prince. Schami glanced down at the sharp edge that was hovering so close. "N-n-no," he stammered.

The prince called out to the other militia. "Would any of the rest of you care to inspect the sword? I'll gladly bring it over to you." The other spearman threw down his now useless shaft and started to back down the street. The others simply dropped their weapons and the torches and ran.

"Halt," Mumtas shouted frantically. "In the name of the people, I order you to stand firm." He snatched at a fleeing militiawoman, but she dodged past him easily, leaving Mumtas's hands clawing at the empty air.

"Go on, Schami." The prince lowered his sword. "My quarrel isn't with you."

"I . . . I . . ." Schami's voice failed him. Twisting around, he started to run after the others.

Mumtas tried to throw himself in front of Schami. "Stop," he yelled. But Schami, who was still clutching the shaft of his spear, swung it at Mumtas. Mumtas brought his spear up so that he blocked the blow with the shaft. And then Schami was beyond him, dashing down the street as fast as his legs would carry him.

For a moment, Mumtas was too full of righteous indignation to remember where he was. "How dare you?" He pointed toward the fleeing Schami. "A blow against me is a blow against the people."

"How convenient." The prince slapped the flat of his blade against his palm. "One could repay so many scores that way."

Mumtas turned sideways so he could look at the prince. "It was only a figure of speech." He smiled anxiously as he took a step down the street. "You shouldn't take me literally."

The prince stretched out his right leg so that it stamped loudly on the ground. With a scream of sheer terror, Mumtas went chasing after his fleeing guards.

Urmi gathered up the pack and sack. "That's probably the most exercise he's had in years." She let out a loud, relieved laugh.

"He can be quite nimble when he has the right incentive." The prince took his pack from Urmi.

"We'll be safe enough now," Puga said from the doorway to the stable. "If Mumtas tries anything, I'll threaten to sic you three on him."

"I'll be back," the prince promised. "And Mumtas won't enjoy it any more than he did this time."

The prince had to take Sulu's hand again when they left the torchlit street. Despite the handicap of having to lead Sulu, they made it to the village wall in just a few minutes. Urmi climbed up on top first with a boost from the prince and Sulu and then, leaning her belly against the top of the wall, she lowered a hand to help them climb up beside her.

They moved downriver, following the path through the silent fields. Urmi led the way and the prince followed, holding onto Sulu to guide him since the prince had better night vision. A half kilometer on, the river began to grow stronger as its bed narrowed and deepened and the rocky walls of the valley closed in so that it was impossible even for the ingenious farmers to grow anything.

Toward sunrise, they reached the northwestern wall of the valley. There, the path began to climb as the river undercut the rock ledges so that there were sudden drops and gaps, and they left it finally as it plunged into a steep gorge. Instead, Urmi took them up a side path paralleling a stream that fell from a small valley. It was pleasant there, with small fruit trees and meadows of grass. Sulu supposed it was a grazing area for the farm animals.

The valley ended in a bowl of rocks and weeds beneath a large crest of sandstone, with folds of red stone like ribs collapsed upon one another. It seemed to gather the starlight as they climbed beneath it, following a path that cut back and forth over the folds of stone. Halfway up, they could look back down the valley as it stretched like a blue-green gash through the stone.

It seemed as if they could see the entire length of the river and its valley with its peaceful orchards and sleepy fields of *amma* surrounding the slender thread of the river. Overhead, small puffs of cloud edged with red were floating gently over the valley.

"This is how I remember your valley," the prince murmured to Urmi. "It's all so peaceful and serene." He stared at the valley as if trying to fix it in his memory. "I wish all Angira could be like this right now."

Urmi slipped in front of him so she could stare at him wonderingly. "Part of you wants to stay, doesn't it?"

"Despite everything that I've seen, yes," the prince sighed. "But it's only a very small part of me that wants to stay."

"Maybe it's the crucial part." Urmi tried to take his arm. "Why don't you bring peace to Angira. You're the one person who could unite the royalists and the common folk against Rahu and the other nobles."

"I have neither the desire nor the training to do so." The prince watched Urmi pass the food pack to Sulu. "I was supposed to advise whichever brother sat upon the throne—a walking library, so to speak. I didn't even want to come back to this crazy place, let alone try to run it. Gram for gram, I don't think there is a world that is lovelier than Angira; but its customs make it such a madhouse that it's difficult for one of its inmates to grasp how much kinder things could be."

She tossed her head back challengingly. "Then

change our customs if you don't like them. Bring that other way of life to Angira."

"I thought you didn't want the prince on the throne?" Sulu slid the pack straps over his shoulders.

"Now that I know him better, I don't think he'd turn the world backward to a time when we had no rights. On the other hand, Rahu would terrorize the people into submission. It would be the torture in the dungeons on a worldwide scale." Urmi's sandals scraped over the rocks as she stepped up to the prince.

"I'd like to, Urmi. I really would. But the task is just way beyond my powers. It's . . . it's like trying to lift Angira all by myself." He backed a step further up the slope. "I'm not a masochist."

Urmi turned sideways so she could motion to the valley. "Who said anything about doing it alone? Don't make your father's mistake. Ask for help and advice from the people."

The prince hesitated, staring into the distance as if he were trying to look beyond Urmi and her valley toward something more remote in space and time. But finally, as if he'd given up, he shook his head doubtfully. "They wouldn't help me. It's like I told you before, Urmi. I'm almost as much of an outsider as Sulu is."

"You might be able to leave Angira," she warned him, "but you'll never be able to escape your memories. They'll haunt you wherever you go." She reached over to a nearby shrub and scrabbled at its roots for a moment so she could hold up a handful of dirt. "Your flesh comes from this, is sustained by this and"—she flung the dirt down—"goes back to this." She looked from Sulu to the prince as if daring either of them to contradict her.

The prince raised a foot and shook off the few bits of

dirt that had landed on it. "Let's not be ghoulish, Urmi. I've spent a good part of my life on other worlds. I don't fit in here anymore." He paused and then added pointedly, "If I ever did."

Sulu was torn for a moment between his obligation to Vikram, the prince, and Vikram, his friend. But in the end, Sulu had seen so much suffering that his conscience would not allow him to remain silent. "Look, you can tell me if I'm out of line, but so far all your complaints have been about the society here, not about Angira itself. I think you'd like to stay here if there was a place for you."

"And Rahu has quite a nice little spot already reserved for me in the cemetery." The prince jabbed the toe of his sandal downward like the blade of a shovel.

Sulu suddenly felt an immense sadness—as if he were burying a loved one. And perhaps he was in a way, as he tried to lay some of his boyhood fantasies to rest. "I learned one thing from this visit: Life isn't simple just because the technology may be. And after all the squalor and trouble I've seen, I think it's time for you to take your world into the twenty-third century."

"You disappoint me, Sulu." The prince looked at him resentfully. "Maybe you're willing to give up on your dreams, but I'm not. I just finished this argument with Urmi."

But some of the things Mr. Spock had said to the prince had struck certain responsive chords in Sulu as well. At any rate, he found it easy to identify with someone who had an entire world to change. "You said you didn't fit into Angira, but you can turn that into an advantage."

"What do you mean?" The prince leaned his head to the side as if he were intrigued by what Sulu said.

"It's like Mr. Spock said: Change begins on the borderline between two cultures." He felt guilty in a way, knowing that he was beginning to speak as much for the fulfillment of his own wishes as for those of the prince. "Your father and his advisers were too involved in Angiran society to correct its flaws objectively. It takes someone with enough emotional distance from the society to see what's wrong."

"Someone like an offworlder?" the prince asked ironically.

"Let me finish." Sulu moved his hand back and forth through the air as if he were polishing something. "It's both in your strength and your weakness that you're unique. You've got an outsider's perspectives and you also know what programs have worked on other worlds. And yet you care enough about Angira to enact those programs with more compassion than any offworlder could."

"But I don't see you taking your own advice," the prince objected.

"I have the *Enterprise,*" Sulu said, "but I suspect you wouldn't be happy with its equivalent."

"You don't have to live in that glass cage if you stay here," Urmi said, warming to the idea.

"You can do even more than that." Sulu thrust his stiffened fingers as if chiseling an invisible block of wood. "You're in a position to carve your own niche for yourself—and change this whole world in the process." And as he spoke, Sulu felt easier in his own heart—almost at rest, in fact. It was as if, after all these years of searching for something, he had finally discovered it.

186

And though he could not claim Angira as his own home, he could take a vicarious pleasure in helping it.

"And not just for yourself," Urmi was quick to elaborate, "but for all of us. And even if you don't keep Rahu from taking the throne, you'll at least show people that there's another alternative. It will be true *panku:* new shoots from old roots."

The prince ran his fingertips over his chin. "At the very least, I could see to it that they kept more of what they grow."

"That would inspire people for sure." Urmi nodded her head.

"A bucolic version of Camelot?" The prince cast an amused glance at Sulu. "But I'm no King Arthur—even on a modest scale."

Sulu leaned his head back and lowered his eyelids slightly. "How do we know the real Arthur wasn't as ragged and dirty as you are now?"

The prince rubbed his palm over the pommel of his sword. "How indeed?" He raised his head like someone who has just been relieved of an immense burden. "You've shrunk the task down to a manageable size. As Mr. Spock says, I can't really help what people make of me. But," he added, "I can help what I make of myself."

"Of course, you can," Urmi encouraged him.

The prince gave an exuberant hitch to the strap of the water sack. "And perhaps it's as Puga said: Heroes begin with simple, average people trying to perform their duties."

"Then you'll stay?" Urmi asked.

The prince pursed his lips for a moment while he considered the matter. "I'm beginning to think that while life in front of a library viewscreen would be an easy enough existence, I could never enjoy it. I would always be feeling guilty about the situation I left on Angira."

Sulu's tone was polite but firm. "One person like you could make a difference on Angira."

"Sulu, you're still a romantic after all." The Prince's laugh almost seemed to bubble out of him. "But I must admit that it's catching."

They traveled for two more days through the badlands, pausing for only a few hours' rest at night. The morning of the third day found them standing on one side of a river gorge very near the "back door" to Kotah, as the prince called it.

Urmi put down her pack and stretched. "It's a pity the sides are so steep or we could use the river to go into Kotah. It's five kilometers by water, ten by land."

Sulu walked over to the edge and looked down. The gorge was some eighty meters wide and some hundred meters deep. Nothing grew on either of the steep, sheer sides.

The prince joined him there. "Beyond that bend in the gorge, this river feeds into a larger one that we call Kotah's moat." The prince swung his arm in an arc to take in the horizon. "Another eight kilometers and we'll be at a small post that guards a drawbridge."

Sulu surveyed the ridgetops. "A few warriors could hold off an army then."

"They can and have," the prince said. "Our province may be counted as backward compared to the plains, but we have never been conquered."

"Though they've given in a few times," Urmi laughed.

"Acquiesced," the prince corrected her with a shrug.

They walked eastward along the gorge until it narrowed to a point only forty meters broad and fifty meters deep. The river, channeled into a deeper, narrower bed, roared and foamed beneath them.

A simple rope bridge spanned the gorge at this point. Two large cables, each as thick as Sulu's arm, hung from posts hammered into the stone on either side of the gorge. From these two cables hung smaller ropes that held a third cable suspended in the air.

"You really don't like visitors coming this way, do you?" Sulu asked.

"This bridge has been cut down when necessary," the prince said.

A hill person like Urmi had no trouble negotiating the bridge, though it rocked alarmingly from side to side. Sulu, however, felt less than enthusiastic when he felt the cables. The spray rolling up the sides of the steep gorge made the ropes slippery.

Behind him, the prince couldn't help teasing, "Come now, Sulu. A fencer such as yourself must have nimble feet."

Sulu stared down at the sheer drop. The river looked very far away. "I'm used to having a floor underneath my feet."

"Just keep your eyes on Urmi's back." The prince laughed and gave him an encouraging pat on the shoulder.

Sulu smiled weakly at the prince. "I think you're enjoying this more than you should."

"And you may laugh at me the next time I try to helm a starship. Please go on, Sulu."

Taking a deep breath, Sulu stepped out onto the

bridge and found his foot sliding off the bottom cable. He gripped the cables tightly and managed to keep his foot on the rope.

"I'm right behind you, Sulu," the prince tried to reassure him.

"And will you be right behind me if I fall?" Sulu tried to joke. He shuffled several steps along the bridge.

"Let's not carry friendship too far." The prince laughed.

But Sulu was already getting the hang of the swaying bridge. So he comforted himself with the thought that while he might not move with Urmi's grace, at least he was getting across.

By now Urmi had made it almost to the end of the bridge. "Come on," she encouraged them. "I can smell the cooking fires over at the guard post. We'll be eating a hot meal soon." She turned around again. "Or not," she added as a half dozen *sinha* rose from behind the rocks in front of her. One of them deliberately stepped up to the foot of the bridge so that the way was blocked.

Sulu and the prince twisted around to try to retreat but saw another half-dozen *sinha* slipping down the rocks to cut them off. Lord Bhima himself straddled the path. "Welcome, Your Highness. I wonder if we could continue that little chat we were having back at the palace."

"Get ready to run when I tell you," the prince whispered under his breath to Sulu, and then he lifted his head to help himself shout better to Lord Bhima. "Indeed? I hope I haven't kept you waiting too long."

Lord Bhima sheathed his sword and started toward them eagerly. "It's never a waste of time when you take in this lovely scenery. Now would you be so kind as to throw your weapons into the river? I promise you that you'll be well treated."

"What makes you think I'd trust you?" The prince adjusted his grip on one of the support ropes.

Lord Bhima paused by one of the posts from which the cables hung. "Because you would have my word. I had nothing to do with the massacre, Your Highness. I was as surprised as you were when it happened."

The prince spread his feet apart. "If that's true, why are you helping Rahu now?"

Lord Bhima slapped his hand unhappily against the post. "I couldn't bring the dead back once the massacre had happened. And I think Rahu happens to be right."

"Then," the prince announced, "your name will be recorded in the history books along with those butchers."

Lord Bhima looked a bit sick, as if the prince had just struck him in the stomach, but he drew himself up shakily. "I might take the cynical view and say that history is written by the winners, not the losers. It's surprising how many euphemisms can be found for 'butchery.' But," he added, and the words came tumbling out of him as if he had repeated them to himself often enough, "in point of fact, it was your father who was the first to act dishonorably."

"It's a lawyer's way to quibble over words rather than deeds." Lifting his hand, the prince waved at Sulu. "Now," he said. When Sulu had started to run, the prince called to Urmi. "Go on, Urmi," he urged her.

Drawing a dagger and her sword, Urmi thrust at the *sinha* barring the way.

"Stop," Lord Bhima shouted desperately—almost as

if he was the one who felt trapped and not the prince. But when Sulu and the prince went on, he gave a surprised shake of his head. "Then you leave me no choice," Lord Bhima yelled reluctantly to them and, after a pause, he instructed his own men. "Either take them prisoner or make sure that they never leave the bridge alive."

A wind suddenly swept into the gorge, making the bridge sway even more. Sulu skidded once as the rope bridge seemed to take an unexpected twist to his left. Desperately he threw his arms around one of the cables as his legs fell through one of the openings.

The prince, though, had a hold of his robe's collar. "Up you go, Sulu." With the prince's help, Sulu got his feet back on the bottom cable.

Sulu nodded his thanks and took a tight hold of one support cable. "We're not going to be able to fight our way off this bridge." Though Urmi had already wounded one *sinha*, two others had taken his place.

The prince glanced over his shoulder as the bridge started to buck and writhe. Two *sinha* were trying to follow. "Well, we can't go forward and we can't go backward and since none of us has wings, we can't go up. That only leaves down."

Though the robe he still wore made it difficult, Sulu managed to draw his sword. "Are you out of your mind? From this height, a dive would kill us."

Bracing his back against one cable, the prince hitched up his robe and slid his sword out. "But if you cut one of the support cables, it should take us much nearer the river."

Keeping one hand on the cable as a kind of guide, Sulu started to move toward Urmi. "Assuming we time

it right and don't get bashed against the gorge itself."
He started on.

"Details are the playthings of lesser minds. Do you have a better suggestion?"

"No, but I sure wish that I did." Sulu slipped twice more on the swaying bridge, but each time he managed to catch himself. When he was about two meters from Urmi, he stopped. "Hold onto the bridge when I tell you," Sulu instructed her.

"What?" Urmi half turned so she could look at them and saw Sulu take a sharp whack at one of the cables with his blade. "Sulu, are you mad?"

"Sulu doesn't like the bridge." The prince raised his sword to engage the *sinha* behind them. "He thinks we should remodel it."

"Not while we're on it." Urmi had to whirl around so her dagger could stop a vicious slice.

"We're going to cut a cable so we won't have as far to dive into the river." Sulu chopped at the cable again and saw the first strands part. The cable was thicker than he thought. "This is almost as bad as a steel cable. What's it made out of?"

"Fibers from the stalk of the *amma* you admired so much." The prince's blade rang as he engaged a *sinha*.

Sulu spread his feet and gripped the cable in one hand to balance himself as best he could while he brought his sword down. But it only severed a few more strands. From in front and behind him, he could hear the clang of Urmi's and the prince's blades as they tried to fight off the *sinha*.

"Tell your clan to use thinner ropes next time." Sulu gave a grunt as he kept on hacking at the cable.

He tried to ignore the scream as one of the prince's

193

opponents fell from the bridge but he could not help
noticing how long it took the man to splash into the
water.

"Sulu, maybe you'd better let us brace our legs to
take the impact," the prince said. "And remember to
let go as the bridge begins to swing back over the center
of the river. Wait too long and you'll go onto the rocks
on either side."

"Great," Sulu grunted as he continued to hack at the
cable.

A fraction of a second later the prince's other
opponent gave a yell as he plummeted toward the river.
Sulu looked behind him and saw the prince standing
alone, his sword still thrust out in the lunge that had
cleared the bridge.

The prince straightened up and turned to help Sulu.
"Well, at least our rear's safe."

But Lord Bhima looked at another young *sinha*.
"You will atone, lieutenant," he said in a loud voice.

And without a moment's hesitation, the young officer drew his sword and started to slide his feet along the
bridge.

"Stop it, you fool." The prince waved his sword at
the *sinha*. "Get back while you can." But the lieutenant
just kept coming. There was only determination in his
face, not fear. "Rahu's turned them into a pack of
fanatics," the prince grumbled, and got ready to meet
him. "They're almost as crazy as we are."

"That takes some doing," Sulu said and then tried to
concentrate on his one task while the fighting went on
both before and behind him.

It seemed like hours—though it was probably only a
few minutes later that the prince asked the officer out of

sheer exasperation, "What's the point of fighting any-more, you fool? Tell your men to get back. Can't you see we're probably going to do your job for you?"

"I must atone to the Lord Bhima," the lieutenant said cryptically, and slashed at the prince's sword wrist.

The prince parried, locking his blade with the other's. And then, before the lieutenant could say or do anything, the prince swung the pommel of his blade up so that it caught the lieutenant on the chin. His head snapped back and his eyes closed as he tumbled after his men.

"The only way to stop them"—the prince got his breath back—"seems to be to kill them."

"We may be joining the dead soon enough." By now, Sulu had chopped through all but the last strands. Wrapping his free arm around the cable, he swung his sword up, ready for the final cut. "Get set," he said.

"Wait," Urmi called. "Let me fight my way onto solid ground."

"Whatever for?" the prince demanded.

"I can't swim." Urmi parried another desperate slash from a *sinha*.

The prince made his way around Sulu so he could be nearer Urmi. "Why didn't you say so before?"

"I didn't think we'd live this long," Urmi said. Despite her best efforts to control her voice, she sounded frightened.

The prince glanced at Sulu. "You can swim, can't you?"

The sword felt heavy in Sulu's hand. "I won't drown, if that's what you mean."

"Good, then between the two of us we should be able to keep Urmi afloat." The prince hooked his arms and legs around the cable so that he looked like a bony sloth. The cable began to sag heavily. "Come on, Urmi."

"I'd rather die with a *sinha* blade sticking in my gut than with water filling my lungs." Urmi made a series of determined lunges but her opponents stood their ground and would not let her off the bridge.

"We either go together, Urmi," the prince insisted, "or we don't go at all."

"Go on. I'm just some dirty peasant, after all." Despite her best efforts, the *sinha* began to press her back.

"Oh, no, you don't. You've helped convince me to stay." The prince started to swing his legs down. "Now you're going to help me change this world. I didn't think you'd be the one to take the easy way out."

"You call this easy?" Urmi grunted as she nearly avoided having her head split in two.

"Simple then. A swordfight is child's play compared to reforming Angira." The prince's feet found the bottom cable. "I'm asking you for help, Urmi. Trust me as I trust you."

Urmi smiled and then pretended to grumble, "Well, I guess I'd better stick around to make sure you don't botch things."

"That's right," the prince agreed cheerfully. "You know my family has a penchant for mishandling Angira." The prince raised his legs to the cable again.

"I'll warn you right now: You'd better be down there to keep me floating, or I'll come back to haunt you. And a wet ghost isn't a pretty sight." Tucking her dagger back into her sash, she swung her sword back and forth in several savage cuts to clear a space between herself and the *sinha* before she retreated two paces. Then, flinging her sword away, she gripped the cables and lifted her legs up around the rope. "All right," she called to Sulu.

"Hold on," he shouted and swung his sword down with all his strength, his face grimacing with the effort. This time the blade sliced through the last strands cleanly.

As they began to fall, Sulu dropped his sword and brought his other hand up to cling to the cable. They whipped through the air toward the river and the spray rose about them so that Sulu had to squint to see. The water looked chillingly blue as it slid by at an alarming rate. And then it seemed like the jagged rocks at the side of the gorge were leaping up to meet them like fangs. Sulu tensed as the rocks grew nearer and nearer. And then they were arcing over the stones; but before Sulu could feel any relief, he found himself rushing toward a new peril as the rocky wall of the gorge loomed before them.

Below him, Urmi and the prince had braced their long, well-muscled legs. And for a moment, it almost seemed as if they were standing still and the stone wall were rushing at them. Sulu was almost sure they were going to smash into it. And suddenly he heard the slapping of the Angirans' sandals and they were swinging away from the wall, back over the rocks on the side of the gorge.

"Now," the prince called.

And Sulu let go.

The water gleamed beneath him and he couldn't be sure if he spotted a shadowy outline underneath the water or not. Was it an animal or some Angiran predator, or just his own imagination? And then he was plunging beneath the water. He almost lost his precious lungful of air at the shock of meeting the icy cold water. But he managed to hold onto his breath somehow.

When he had finally slowed, he could not see anything but the columns of bubbles raised by his own descent. Don't panic, he told himself, and forced himself to wait long enough to watch which way his bubbles were rising. That would help orient him to the surface. The river currents, though, were swift and deep; he could feel them pulling him along even as he tried to angle up to the surface. And his heavy robe, soaked with water, was like a set of weights trying to pull him back down.

A huge rock suddenly loomed in front of him and he slammed into it, almost making him lose his precious supply of air. What if he met more rocks?

And then his head seemed to lift into the drier, warmer air above the water and he was gasping for breath. Three meters to his left, he saw the prince and a spluttering, thrashing Urmi.

"You see, Sulu." The prince had managed to keep hold of his sword and Urmi as he tread water. "It worked out just like I said."

Sulu spit out a mouthful of water. "Your Highness, after having just one of your tours, please don't open up a travel agency."

"But you can't beat my tours for excitement."

"No, I can't." Sulu's arms and legs were already growing numb from the cold. The Angirans' fur seemed to protect them a bit better from the icy temperature of the water. Quickly Sulu shed his boots and robe. "Once is enough," he gasped.

A swirl in the river currents had swept him closer to them and he took Urmi so that the prince could take off his robe. "Well," the prince agreed, "I could use fewer surprises myself."

Lord Bhima watched the dots that were the heads of the prince and his party until a bend in the river finally hid them from view. What excuses should he offer to Lord Rahu?

It certainly hadn't been the fault of the fanatical young lieutenant. He had tried to atone for his mistakes. It was a shame that it had all been wasted.

No, it was the fault of an aging swordmaster who had underestimated his prince. He had thought the prince would surrender easily instead of taking such a desperate course. But apparently the prince was no longer the foppish boy whom Bhima remembered. There was a backbone to him now that had not always been there before. And he either hated or feared Lord Bhima very much now. Perhaps both.

He had failed in his mission. Or had he?

One of the *sinha* worked up enough nerve to ask him, "Lord, do you want us to go after them? We can climb down and dive like they did."

"We've lost enough lives today." He waved his sword over his head to attract the attention of the *sinha* across the gorge. "Come on across again."

"And what are we going to do, Lord?" the *sinha* asked.

Lord Bhima gave a sigh. "There's no choice now. We'll have to sneak into Guh."

"But why, Lord? The prince isn't there."

"There was only one offworlder with them. The other may very well have been left behind in the valley, either as a hostage or because of injuries." Lord Bhima swung away from the river. "I don't intend to go back to Lord Rahu empty-handed."

Chapter Nine

They were swept along for nearly two kilometers by the river's swift currents. By that time, Sulu was chilled to the bone and barely able to move his legs and arms enough to keep himself afloat, let alone help the prince with Urmi. He watched the steep sides of the gorge race by. A scraggly tree stood like a lone, dying sentry. And Sulu wondered if that was the last thing he would see before he drowned.

Suddenly the walls of the gorge fell away—as if the backdrops in a cheap play had suddenly fallen down and the icy mountain water no longer yanked and pulled at him. The river itself had broadened and on the right bank, Sulu could see houses and fences and small, aging wharves. Tied to the wharves were small boats some three meters long, with squared bows and sterns. More boats floated in a semicircle across the river.

"We made it, Sulu," the prince called to him encouragingly.

Urmi gave a shout and sprayed water like an outraged cat. "Hey, help me keep my head above water."

Sulu thrashed his arms clumsily, trying to direct himself toward the shallows by the right riverbank. He was so cold that he could barely speak through his chattering teeth. "I don't know if I'm going to make it."

"Have a look out where you're swimming," an angry voice yelled.

The soaked, heavy ropes of the net felt almost like steel cables when they struck Sulu in the chest, and he went under before he even had a chance to take a breath. Through dazed eyes, he saw the great fishing net billow like a living thing that rose around him to entrap his limbs. Instinctively, he fought to free himself —though the more he struggled, the more the net seemed to wrap itself around him. The air seemed to be forcing its way out of his lungs, though he fought to keep it in.

Dimly, through the roaring in his ears, he heard the prince shouting desperately for the fishermen to raise the nets. And then the net was rising and Sulu with it. He gasped for air as his head broke the surface, and he tried to move his arms and legs but the net held him tightly like a fly in a spider's web. But he could see the dozen boats strung out in a wide arc.

The fishermen, who seemed to be dressed in some odd sort of costume, were simply holding onto the net they had raised as if they didn't know what to do now that they had caught Sulu. In the meantime, though, the prince was shoving Urmi over the stern of the nearest boat—with alarming results for the boat's equilibrium and the owner's own peace of mind.

Though Sulu had thought the cold water had made

his body lose most of its feeling, the ropes constricted around his limbs and the pain was like a goad, driving his mind into a waiting darkness.

"Hold on, Sulu," the prince shouted to him. And then the prince had clambered in after Urmi. He rose to his knees, drawing out his sword.

The fisherman threw himself at the prince. "No, you'll ruin our net."

The prince shoved an elbow into the fisherman's stomach, knocking him down. "I'll buy you twenty nets, man."

As Sulu's eyes closed in both pain and exhaustion, he heard a dull whacking sound. He wondered if that was the prince even as he spun down into the cold darkness.

"As a boy"—Puga pulled his blanket tighter about himself—"I used to sneak into this stable on cold nights. It was always warmer next to the animals. My father was always threatening to make me move into here. He'd have the last laugh now."

Normally Mr. Spock did not encourage other people's reminisences since it only seemed like an excuse to exercise their tongues rather than their minds. But there was something warm and comfortable about Puga—like an old familiar shirt or blanket. And the old man's talk was a natural, soothing sound—like the rattling of tree leaves and the chuckling of a stream.

"Indeed," Mr. Spock murmured drowsily.

The stall boards creaked as Puga settled his back against them. "At any rate, it's not such a hardship for me to live in a stable; but what about you? What if you have to spend the rest of your life here?"

The old man seemed genuinely worried for Mr. Spock's state of mind; and so, for his sake, Mr. Spock forced himself back to wakefulness. "One place," he said philosophically, "is much like another."

Puga shook his head in puzzlement. "How can you say that after all the things you must have seen and done?"

Mr. Spock sat up, holding his blanket against his chest by wrapping an arm around himself. *"You* like it here well enough."

Puga thumped his heel against the dirt. "But I'm an ignorant man. I don't know any better."

McCoy's words came back to Mr. Spock at that moment. "Are you content though?"

Puga pressed his lips together thoughtfully and then nodded his head. "In spite of all the calamities, yes."

"Then you don't need to know any more than that." Mr. Spock lay down again, trying to ease the ache in his side.

The straw crackled as Puga slid in closer. "And you, Mr. Spock? Are you content?"

Mr. Spock had been considering the question ever since McCoy had first asked it. "I have," he said slowly, "achieved many of my goals."

"So does a slime bug when it gets to a leaf of *amma*." The old man flapped a hand in the air as if chasing a moth away. "But there has to be more."

Mr. Spock lay quiet for a long time. *Gaya* breathed softly in the stalls around them and he could feel the warmth of their breath; and for a moment it seemed as if the darkness itself were breathing about him, and he was alone with only the night and himself.

Mr. Spock thought it might be exhaustion or perhaps a touch of fever that made him susceptible to such imaginings; and yet he felt almost as alone as he had when he had chosen to become a Vulcan and taken the

Kahs-wan ordeal. And he was speaking not to the old man but to an earlier, more primitive self that he thought he had abandoned in the harsh Vulcan desert. And that self was now demanding reasons for its fate.

"Contentment," he stated with mild surprise, "was never my desire."

"Nonsense," Puga scolded him as if he were a child. "Everyone wants it."

Mr. Spock frowned at the darkness. "Contentment is not available to everyone; and I, for one, have never desired something I could not have."

That earlier self felt as sad and puzzled as Puga sounded. "But there's always a way to find some sort of happiness."

Calmly, patiently, Mr. Spock tried to explain. "There are some of us who are born on the border between two cultures. We belong neither to one nor the other; and so contentment is a meaningless question for us."

Puga considered the matter for a moment and then patted Mr. Spock's arm solicitously. "Then you take the best from both—like an amphibian that can enjoy the land and the sea."

The spell had been broken by the old man's touch. Mr. Spock shook off that moment of sentimental weakness. "That is a philosophy better suited to the prince than to myself," Mr. Spock insisted. But before he could say anything more, a bright light suddenly filled the cracks between the wall boards of the stable.

Puga struggled to his feet. "What—?"

A man began to scream outside, but his cry was cut short; and suddenly the door burst open and several figures ran into the stable. Their cloaks had been coated in mud so that they were no longer a shining white, but Mr. Spock recognized the cut of a *sinha* cloak.

Lord Bhima pointed his bloody sword at them. "Lord Rahu regrets your hasty departure thwarted his hospitality," he said with a grim smile. "But he now hopes to make it up to you."

Sulu woke up in an airy little room with whitewashed walls. He rolled over onto his side and found he was lying on a pallet of fine yellow fibers. Covering him was a blanket of some wool-like material—probably woven from the long hair of a *gaya*.

"He's up, Your Highness," a middle-aged Angiran said. He was dressed in the same tunic and shorts of dark blue homespun that the fishermen had been wearing. Now that he had a chance to study the costume, Sulu was inclined to think it was some kind of uniform, just from the stiffly starched look of the Angiran's unusual clothing. Yellow stripes on the right sleeve seemed to indicate some kind of rank. And a black leather bandolier with oilcloth pouches crossed his chest at an angle. The severe lines of his uniform seemed abstract—and modern—compared to the many curving folds of the *soropa*.

The man suddenly stood to the side, coming to attention with a straightness that would have gladdened any drill instructor's heart. The prince, wearing a similar uniform, strode into the room. "Sulu, you're finally up, I see."

Sulu sat up groggily. "How long have I been asleep?"

"A night and a day. Since there wasn't a princess convenient to wake our sleeping beauty, we almost left without you. Are you up to traveling again?"

Sulu yawned and stretched luxuriously. "As long as I

206

don't have to go swimming in any more mountain streams."

"Nonsense. Just think. You won't have to take your monthly bath." The prince picked up a pair of shorts and a tunic and flopped them onto Sulu's lap. "Put these on. The uniform is going to be a bit baggy, I'm afraid; but no one was quite your size."

Sulu held the tunic up by the sleeves. "Uniform?"

"Yes." The prince indicated the middle-aged Angiran. "Meet a young subaltern in my father's army. They've quite exceeded my expectations: good discipline, smart drill and all quite professional."

"Subaltern?" Sulu glanced at the middle-aged man.

"My father created an officer staff from the cream of the world's noncommissioned officers and such." The prince squatted down beside Sulu. "In the old army, he never could have risen beyond regimental sergeant-major because he wasn't of noble blood." The prince spread his hands like a child with a new toy. "This is the first of my father's schemes that really seems quite exciting."

Urmi poked her head in through the doorway. "Your Highness, everyone's waiting." She brightened when she saw Sulu sitting up. "It's about time you woke up. You'll never make a farmer."

The prince clapped Sulu on the shoulder. "He's being saved for bigger and better things. Get dressed, Sulu. I'll have them prepare something that you can eat while we walk."

The subaltern was waiting for Sulu in the corridor when he was finished dressing. The walls and ceiling had been formed from rocks carefully and painstakingly fitted together. And centuries of feet had worn grooves into the stone flagging. When they emerged into the weathered courtyard, Sulu saw that they were in an ancient fort. Platoons of pikemen drilled as generations probably had done before them—with pike tips nodding in the air and sandaled feet slapping against the stones.

And then he saw the bandoliered men marching with harquebuses at port arms. He remembered his first day on Angira—it seemed now more like years rather than days—when Lord Bhima had referred so contemptuously to the toys of the army of Kotah. He started excitedly toward the platoon. "Hey, those look like wheel locks."

"Sir." The alarmed subaltern placed himself in between Sulu and the platoon.

"But I just want to take a closer look," Sulu tried to explain.

However, the subaltern refused to budge. "The prince is waiting."

Unfortunately, Sulu's own fascination with guns got the better of discretion. He flung out his arms in frustration. "I thought I was the prince's guest."

"Even guests have responsibilities," the subaltern warned.

The prince and Urmi caught Sulu by the arms and swung him around hurriedly. "Sulu," the prince hissed through clenched teeth, "this is no time to indulge in another one of your hobbies."

"I just wanted to see the mechanism. I don't have anything like that in my collection." Sulu tried to look over his shoulder at the harquebusiers.

"You can do that later," the prince promised. "I'll even chain a gunsmith to your bed so he can answer any questions that might come to you in the middle of the night. But for now, we have more important concerns." And with a nod to Urmi, the two of them frog-marched Sulu away.

An older Angiran with a round, melon-shaped head was hurrying toward them. "Ah, I see your traveling party is complete once again."

The prince stopped and released Sulu. "Colonel, this is Lieutenant Sulu." The prince waved his hand toward the officer. "Sulu, this is Colonel Gelu, the man in charge of my father's regiment of harquebusiers."

The colonel scrutinized Sulu as carefully as politeness would allow. "All of Kotah rejoiced when they heard the news about the prince. You've done us a great service."

The prince folded his arms in amusement. "We owe him at least a pair of pants that fit, don't you think?"

"Without a doubt," the colonel said.

"And Mr. Spock?" Sulu asked.

"The colonel cannot send out a rescue party until I am confirmed by the clan elders as the true heir." The prince was careful to keep his tone neutral—as if he and the colonel had already quarreled about the issue and were trying to patch over their differences now.

"When we heard the news about the assassinations, the Council of Elders assumed control of the province; and my orders from the Council of Elders were very explicit," the colonel said, embarrassed, as if he were expecting to have to defend himself to Sulu. "Under no circumstances am I to leave Kotah's borders. And until they rescind that order or surrender authority to the prince, I can only wait."

"Just keep those men ready," the prince said. "They must march as soon as I send word."

"Not until I'm back to guide them," Urmi said. "I don't want those fools torching the entire village." She held out a sword to him. "Here, this is to replace the one you lost."

Sulu slid the blade from the sheath. There was a design on the blade and ornate lettering. "It's beautiful," he murmured.

"May it keep your enemies from you." The prince gripped the hilt of his sword and Sulu was surprised to notice that he had kept the shadow-catcher.

"You ought to be carrying this." Sulu tried to return the sword.

The prince shoved it back. "I've become rather attached to the one I have."

Urmi laughed. "He thinks it's a good-luck charm. He just doesn't want to admit that he's as superstitious as any peasant."

"We may need all the help we can get," the prince said as he helped Sulu thrust the sheath through his belt. Though the prince's tone was characteristically light, there was still a slight strain to his voice.

Sulu looked up sharply. "What's wrong?"

"I gather that there's some doubt concerning my pedigree. The clan chamberlain has led a deputation of elders to the nearest village to pass judgment." The prince nodded toward a squad of soldiers. "They're as much a guard as an escort."

"It can't be all bad if they've let us have weapons," Sulu tried to argue.

"But how long do we get to keep them?" Urmi asked.

The soldiers, led by the subaltern, marched smartly from the fort. On the ground that sloped gently from the fort to the riverbank, Sulu could see the houses that belonged to the soldiers and their families. And beyond the little village, small boats bobbed up and down on the river as soldiers fished with their giant nets.

The prince pointed out the vegetable garden that sat beside each house. "My father believed in self-sufficiency." He unslung a sack from his shoulder and held it out to Sulu.

"But how much drill time do the soldiers lose?" Sulu asked as he hungrily dipped his hand inside the sack.

"I don't think that much." The prince glanced at the subaltern. "You each take a turn, don't you?"

"Yes, Your Highness," the subaltern answered.

Sulu pulled out a round, flat loaf of bread and sniffed it. It seemed to be glazed with some outer covering of egg white and sugar and within he could smell fruits of some kind. "So how much time do you have to take from your training?"

"I've lost track," the subaltern said curtly.

Urmi glanced at Sulu and raised her eyebrows significantly—as if her own suspicions were being proved correct. Sulu tried a few more questions and received similar, ambiguous answers before he finally gave up.

The subaltern and his squad were strangely reticent as they climbed up through the cloud-covered mountains. It was as if they were under orders to communicate as little as possible with the prince and his party. And more and more, Sulu had the impression that Urmi was right: The squad was more a guard detail than an escort.

Even so, the prince's spirits seemed to lift later in the day as they climbed down out of a mist-filled pass to catch their first real view of Kotah.

They found themselves looking down over a series of

wooded ridgetops that diminished one after another into the jade green plain beyond. And just beneath them was a slender, green gem of a valley. No more than a half-kilometer wide at the top, its sides seemed to slant downward steeply for about two hundred meters.

"I never got to spend much time in Kotah." The prince's eyes seemed to drink in the view. "But I treasure those stays very much." He smiled down at the first valley. "My old nursemaid used to live there. And so did most of her kin."

The path itself swung right so it could parallel a stream. The water was a cheering sound as it dropped downward, a brilliant blue, from rock to rock into the steep-sided valley. The plant life grew richer as they descended, with clusters of small orange globes hanging from vines over the path, and small trees with large roots arched like dancer's legs bore wide green tops filled with oval purple fruit.

The water was channeled off to terraced fields of *amma* and they followed the path, now muddy, underneath the brambles that hung from the surrounding trees. And the path now began to take whimsical turns of its own through the densely packed trees so that they found themselves on the roof of a house of roughly carved cubes of stone broken only by narrow window slits. The door was set a meter inside an arched recess. Their escort did not even hesitate but instead treated the roof as part of the path which seemed to have been created by generations of feet walking the shortest distance from one house to the next.

And as they made their way down to the valley floor, the path seemed to wind carelessly through the houses that perched on the steep valley side. Sometimes they would find themselves crossing beneath someone's upper story, other times across someone's patio of beaten earth where the old people sat, their voices mixing with the gurgling of the water above the deeper bass of the river below. They stared at the party, making comments to one another with a deep satisfaction, as if they had paid royally for just such a spectacle to pass by their front door.

It was only when they reached the narrow valley floor that the stream was led off in deeper stone-paved trenches to parallel rows of pools. Swarms of naked children laughed as they splashed about in the water. "Somewhere, underneath the children, are schools of a fish that is much like your trout," the prince explained to Sulu.

"Everybody seems well fed here," Sulu said, noticing their golden fur.

"The reforms were done more fairly in Kotah," Urmi explained. "You'd hardly expect the emperor to jeopardize his own power base."

"So perhaps there really is hope for the future." The prince jumped back as a group of squealing, wet children pelted across the path in front of them. "It would be nice if all Angira could be this way."

His fingertips just brushed a large branch. "And even nicer if I could have spent more time here rather than stay at the palace."

"The palace is more like a prison than anything else, and this"—Urmi's palm bobbed up and down as if she were weighing something—"this is like paradise."

The subaltern led them toward a tower that dominated the path. A crowd waited underneath the portcullis. A small, round Angiran bustled forward and bowed. "Your Highness, I've prepared rooms for you and your retinue."

"Are the Elders in session?" the prince asked.

The servant paused in mid-bow. "Yes, I believe they are, but—"

"Then I will speak with them directly. We have urgent matters to discuss." The prince brushed past the little servant impatiently.

The little man's hand faltered in the air. "But, Your Highness . . . the trip . . . your clothes . . ."

"They can wait," the prince snapped over his shoulder. He almost rammed into the elderly woman who tottered forward on a cane.

An officious guard grabbed her by the shoulders. "Out of the way, old woman."

"Wait." The prince held up a hand. "Megra, is that you?"

The old woman dimpled. "I didn't know if you'd recognize your old nursemaid after all these years."

"How could I forget you." The prince affectionately traced a small scar on her cheek. "There's the cut I made with the toy sword."

"It was sharp for a toy," she mumbled, pleased that he had remembered.

"Does your brother still live here too?" The laughter seemed to come bubbling out of the prince. "And does he still have those fruit trees?"

"Yes," an old man said. He was leaning forward on his staff. "But throne or not, you're still not allowed to climb them at grafting time."

The prince surveyed the crowd with immense delight. "And these are . . ."

Megra swept her arm in a proud arc to indicate them

all. "My grandchildren and great-grandchildren. I think you might remember some of them."

"You're quite the matriarch." Impulsively, the prince hugged her.

At that spontaneous gesture, the crowd itself surged forward, eager to trade remembrances with the prince. His escort would have tried to keep them back, but the prince seemed surprised and touched by the warmth of his reception and motioned them away.

Left behind by everyone, Urmi turned to Sulu. "At least these people seem to like him well enough."

Sulu stepped out of the way of a group of giggling children coming up to see what the fuss was about. "Well, that may be Megra's doing. I don't think she would let anyone pick on the prince."

Urmi folded her arms across her stomach. "If he could have stayed here more often, maybe he wouldn't have felt so isolated on Angira."

As he watched more people pour from their houses, Sulu said, "I think this is as close as he'll ever come to a real home."

"But will he have a choice about staying or leaving?" Urmi pointed toward the servant scurrying furtively through the crowd and back into the tower—as if he wanted to warn the Elders about what had just occurred. "People have a way of clinging to power—even clan elders. I think there may be some kind of intrigue going on even here. What if the chamberlain came here to put the prince under wraps before he could gather a following."

"If you left it up to these folk"—Sulu nodded to the crowd—"he'd be the emperor."

"Just so," Urmi mused.

The servant returned, pushing and shoving his way

up to the prince. Every now and then they could see the servant speak to the prince urgently; however, the prince seemed reluctant to leave and spent nearly a half hour joking and reminiscing with the others.

Finally, the servant turned to Megra. They could hear him loudly pleading with her. "Please, the chamberlain and the other Elders are waiting."

And it was Megra who stopped everyone and gave the prince a playful push toward the tower. "Go on and greet the politicians. We'll have a nice, long chat tonight. Now let him go everyone. Let him go." And the crowd obediently parted for the prince.

But the prince himself seemed inclined to balk. "I still haven't introduced you to my friends." He beckoned to Sulu and Urmi.

Megra, however, fixed him with a stern eye. "Go on now. When I'm in your palace, you can give me orders, but when you're in my valley, you'll listen to me."

"I know better than to argue." The prince shook his head affectionately. He started to make his way to the tower, exchanging remarks with the rest of Megra's kin.

Skirting the crowd, Sulu and Urmi caught up with the prince just as they entered the tower.

Urmi plucked at the servant's *soropa*. "The prince may not feel tired. But I do. I'm going to use that room for a rest after all."

"Now?" the prince asked. "But I need you, Urmi. For moral support if for nothing else."

"I'll just take a quick nap," Urmi assured him. "You'll probably still be talking when I wake up."

"As you wish," the prince said grudgingly.

The servant immediately pointed to a stairway. "Take those stairs and go up a level. Yours will be the third door on the right." The servant leaned over to the nearest guard and whispered something to him. Then the servant smiled at Urmi. "This man will go along with you to make sure you have everything you want."

"I can take care of myself," Urmi said.

"No doubt," the servant said smoothly, "but you shouldn't have to."

Sulu could not help noticing how closely the escort watched Urmi as he followed her upstairs. The servant himself ushered them into a large, circular room. A dozen elderly Angirans sat on benches set against the walls. In the center of the room was a single footstool which seemed to be for the prince.

The prince didn't hesitate but strode toward the Elders. "Gentlemen, this looks more like a trial than a welcoming ceremony."

"We were a trifle rushed," said a fat Angiran. He had an annoyed, popeyed look—as if he had just sat down on a thumb tack. "So you must forgive the simplicity of the occasion." He bowed his head slightly. "I have the pleasure of being the clan chamberlain."

The prince raised his foot and set it on top of the footstool. "I quite understand. In fact, it rather coincides with my wishes. There is much to do and I would rather not waste time listening to speeches. Do you accept me as the son of the emperor?"

"We must take time to consider such a weighty matter." The chamberlain spread his hands. "It's rather unfortunate that all the credible witnesses perished in the massacre."

"And how many pretenders travel about with an offworlder for a companion?" The prince swept his arm out toward Sulu.

There were murmurs of agreement at that, but the chamberlain stilled the noise with a gesture of his hand. "It has been rumored that you might be an impostor whom the offworlders are trying to foist upon us." He smiled with icy courtesy. "Of course, these are only rumors, which I neither believe nor disbelieve. As the true heir, you can see why we must take our time to dispel these falsehoods so that everyone may follow your banner wholeheartedly."

The prince slid his foot from the top of the stool and lowered it to the floor. "But we can't delay. Even now while we talk, Rahu is out there savaging our world."

The chamberlain pressed his fingertips together patronizingly. "Let the dogs fight among themselves. We're safe enough behind our mountains. And when they're weak and tired, we'll march out"—his palm swiped at the air—"and we'll scoop them all up."

"And how many innocent folk in the cities and the little farming villages will also die in the meantime?" The prince looked around to appeal to the Elders. "The throne isn't our clan's personal property. It means we are responsible for the whole of our world, not just of Kotah." The prince paced forward until he towered over the chamberlain. "Whether we like it or not, Kotah is part of Angira. And Angira is part of an even larger community—a union of sentient beings. We can't turn our backs on suffering."

The chamberlain, however, remained unimpressed. "That sounds all very nice on a plaque for a monument, but it won't put food on a table."

"But we can help one another." The prince slid his fingers together. "And that gives us even greater strength in times of trouble."

The chamberlain reared back on the bench and placed his hands on his knees. "Well, perhaps that all may be true, young man." He was careful to use that term. "At any rate, I don't disbelieve you. If you're an impostor, you're a very good one."

The prince turned to Sulu. "Here's irony for you, isn't it, Sulu? After deciding that I want the throne after all, I can't convince people of my identity."

"I didn't say that, young man," the chamberlain said quickly. "But we mustn't act impetuously. Doubts must be dealt with systematically to prove your identity absolutely."

The prince took several even breaths, as if he were trying to control his temper. "All right," he said quietly. "I will submit to your inquiries; but you must do one thing: You must instruct Colonel Gelu to send a flying column for one of the offworlders. He's being held a prisoner."

The chamberlain chuckled and looked at the others. "Young people are so impetuous." He faced the prince again. "Under no circumstances can they march. We mustn't give Rahu any provocation that will make him decide to neutralize Kotah first. We are to stay hidden so that his attention will be drawn to others."

"I gave my oath," the prince said.

"That," the chamberlain observed, "is hardly our problem." He flicked an index finger toward the subaltern. "Perhaps you should relieve the prince of his weapons." He clicked his tongue. "They are a heavy and unnecessary burden."

"Then I'm a prisoner?"

"Let's call it protective custody," the chamberlain said, "so that you don't do anything rash."

"If I am the true heir," the prince warned, "you are playing a dangerous game."

"If you are the true heir," the chamberlain responded with icy politeness, "you should thank me for my caution."

But at that moment they could hear a commotion outside the door. The prince's hand went to his hilt. The subaltern and his men threw themselves at the door, and for a moment it creaked and groaned on its hinges before it finally burst open under the weight of all the people shoving against it. Guards, servants and valley people all toppled onto the floor.

"What is the meaning of this?" the chamberlain spluttered indignantly.

Megra, with Urmi's help, had managed to keep her feet. "We want our prince." Her voice, though thin, carried loudly enough. The crowd outside the room roared its agreement.

The chamberlain was in such a hurry to scramble to his feet that he knocked over the bench. "My dear people, everything is being well taken care of. We have an authentication process all worked out."

"I've got eyes. I'm satisfied it's Prince Vikram," Megra's brother declared.

The chamberlain stared at the sharp points of the pitchforks and the edges of the hoes. He licked his lips. "Even so, we must move forward, at deliberate speed."

"You'd argue for a month about whether you really had a nose at the front of your face." Megra rapped her cane disgustedly against the floor. "If you want to leave this valley alive, you'll do what you should have done the very first moment you heard the news."

Prince Vikram found himself surrounded by several

young farmers while others sat upon the helpless soldiers. "No," the prince said urgently, "don't harm them."

"Our chief concern is the people of Kotah." The chamberlain carefully edged behind several of the other Elders.

Megra managed to lift her cane long enough to jab at the chamberlain. "And what are we, *gaya?*"

The chamberlain anxiously leaned forward and held a hurried conference with the other Elders. Occasionally, one of them would dart a frightened glance toward the indignant matriarch of the valley and her kin. Megra seemed quite capable of carrying out her threat.

Finally, the chamberlain straightened up and tried to give a dignified tuck to his *soropa*. "If *you* are satisfied that this is the prince," he declared in a shaky voice, "then *we* are satisfied."

Any further words were drowned out in the cheering that followed. The prince was quite literally swept off his feet as he was lifted to the shoulders of several burly farmers, and the crowd surged back through the door. Fortunately, the prince ducked in time or he might have been decapitated prematurely by the doorway.

Urmi, however, still clinging to Megra, had stayed behind. Sulu stepped over to her. "What happened to the guard who was with you?"

"Don't tell the prince this"—she winked—"but I discovered that his soldiers are susceptible to a left hook. It was a simple thing to find Megra and explain my worries to her." She gave Megra a kiss. "My sweetheart here just took over."

Megra gave a snort. "I wasn't going to let them keep the prince from what's rightfully his."

In the meantime, the subaltern and his men were rising from the floor and dusting themselves off in a rather embarrassed way. Urmi indicated the Elders to them. "These gentlemen must be feeling fatigued after all this excitement. Perhaps you'll be so kind as to escort them to their rooms and see that they have a good long rest."

"But we have things to do ourselves," the chamberlain protested.

"Yes, like escaping from the valley and stirring up trouble," Urmi said. She jerked her head toward the subaltern. "Take them."

Still, the subaltern hesitated, glancing between Urmi and the fat man. The chamberlain set his shoulders back pompously. "By the authority of the Council of Elders—"

Urmi's voice cut loudly through his. "You can march with the prince," she said to the subaltern, "or you can listen to the politicians all day. But if you dillydally in this room any longer, you'll feel like a fool."

"There was talk at the fort that you're Bibil's niece," the subaltern said.

"I am," Urmi said. "Did you know him?"

"Only briefly. He saved my hide during a tavern brawl."

"He gave his life for the prince," Urmi said.

"Then that's good enough for me." The subaltern gestured to his men. He added with a sly smile, "Let's place these elder statesmen under a 'protective custody' of their own."

Mr. Spock was awake long before he opened his eyes. A faint smell of smoke still clung to the blanket that covered him. And there was the musky scent of Angirans sweating as they carried him on the makeshift stretcher.

Suddenly there was a scuffling sound off to his right—as if someone had fallen. A sharp whack was followed by a cry of pain. And Mr. Spock's own stretcher jerked to an abrupt halt.

"You'll pay for this," Puga wheezed.

"And who will make me?" a younger Angiran demanded.

"*I* will if you continue," Lord Bhima growled.

"My people have long memories," Puga warned. "They won't forget how you burned the village and killed people. No, don't touch me. I can get up on my own."

Mr. Spock raised his eyelids slightly, glancing to the side. They were among the mesas once again; but where the prince had once fantasized with Sulu, Lord Bhima now stood, watching as Puga struggled to his feet once more. Blood from a small cut on Puga's forehead had matted some of his fur.

"We did what we had to," Lord Bhima said in the patient tone of a parent explaining something to a stubborn child. "You can see how few we are. We needed the distraction."

"Lord." One of the bearers frowned. "You do not have to explain your actions to a peasant."

Lord Bhima rounded on his heel to address the speaker. "If the situations were reversed and he had burned your house and killed a good number of your kin, I think you might want an explanation too."

Puga flexed up and down on his knees as if they were stiff from all the walking they had done. "You seem like a man of honor. How can you support scum like Rahu?"

Lord Bhima signed for the others to begin walking once again. "I won't have our world become a toy for the Federation." He pressed his lips together in a grim, sad smile. "And I am willing to sacrifice my honor and many of our people as long as I can safeguard Angira."

However misguided his methods, Lord Bhima's intentions were good ones. If Mr. Spock could end his fears, there might be some hope yet. He opened his eyes to their fullest. "You shouldn't be afraid, Lord Bhima." He paused as he tried to find his voice, but his throat was dry. "The Federation can tailor a program of modernization for your world that will respect your cultural integrity—as we have done on many other worlds. The emperor lacked experienced advisers who know how to guide worlds through such unsettling times. They could have helped avoid the famines and riots." He added with a trace of irony, "People would have been far more content."

Lord Bhima gave a grunt. "Do you think I care about contentment?"

Mr. Spock stared up at the Angiran who was echoing his own words. He couldn't help speculating just how close this deadly, uncompromising lord was to himself. Was he seeing a similar version of himself who had picked a different path? Or had Lord Bhima chosen those words simply by accident. "Then what do you want?"

"Something you won't find in all of your Federation," Lord Bhima declared with firm conviction. "I want truth. And that is possible only within the Code of the Warrior."

Lord Bhima waited for Mr. Spock's answer, but it took a moment for Mr. Spock to recover from a fit of coughing. In a way he felt like a fool for trying to keep on talking when his throat was so dry; but it was urgent to try and reason with this one Angiran lord—for Mr. Spock's sake as well as Lord Bhima's. "Why do you think you have an exclusive hold upon the truth? Perhaps you'll be able to expand upon what you know."

Lord Bhima regarded him suspiciously. "And what would your Federation gain by all this benevolence?"

"In the long run," Mr. Spock replied calmly, "we all gain from the insights brought by each new member."

Lord Bhima slipped his sword from his sheath. "Don't peddle your hucksters' tales to me. I'm not some gullible boy like Prince Vikram."

Mr. Spock stared unblinking at the sword edge hovering over his neck. "A cause that must rely upon swords to prove its point is a rather weak one."

Lord Bhima nodded his head with grudging respect. "Well, I'll give you this much. You believe what you're saying."

Puga snorted contemptuously. "Lord Bhima and I are different sides of the same coin. I have nothing to lose and he has everything to gain—just by keeping things the way they are."

"Do you really think I care about wealth? I own very little except my weapons." Lord Bhima tapped the side of his head. "I'm talking about foreign ideas and what they can do to a code that's been perfecting itself all these years. What about all the questions you off-worlders have already raised? Already it's as if our young people were born with daggers in their minds.

And the more they think, the more they seem to cut their very souls."

Mr. Spock managed to moisten his throat slightly by swallowing. "It is possible to graft twigs from old trees onto new ones."

"We do it all the time in the orchards." Puga gave an authoritative nod of his head.

"Precisely," Mr. Spock agreed. "Trees may bear fruit for only so long; and then, if they are allowed to linger, they wither and the fruit turns bad. But if you can graft their branches onto new trees, you can renew the orchard."

"Listen to the offworlder," Puga urged Lord Bhima. "He knows more about this sort of thing than we do."

Encouraged by Lord Bhima's thoughtful expression, Mr. Spock went on. "My own people have traditions and a culture far older than Angira's." It was not the most diplomatic thing to say under the circumstances, but Mr. Spock felt compelled to tell the truth. "And yet it was good for them to join the Federation. They . . . I mean, we . . . were a wise and ancient society long before the others; and yet we have learned as much from these younger cultures as we have taught them."

But Lord Bhima had noticed Mr. Spock's slip of the tongue. "And you, offworlder. How does it feel to be one of the new grafts?"

"It is not easy," Mr. Spock said slowly, as if recalling past misunderstandings and slights and even humiliations. "But I have never been afraid of difficulties." He swung his head to look at Lord Bhima. "And I suspect that neither are you."

Lord Bhima laughed lightly as he held his hand out. A *sinha* scurried up with a water skin and unstoppered it before he presented it to Lord Bhima. "No. I've been accused of many sins in my time, but laziness was never one of them." He held out the water skin. "But I don't think our orchards on Angira have become played out yet." He paused and added with a chilling absent-mindedness, "They simply need a little trimming."

Mr. Spock did not answer right away, but instead struggled to raise his head as he opened his mouth. And Lord Bhima expertly sent a stream of water into it. Mr. Spock drank thirstily before he lay back.

"And how many people will die during the pruning?" Mr. Spock asked.

Lord Bhima threw back his head and squirted a stream of water into his mouth. "Do you think it's wise to bait me this way?"

Mr. Spock wiped his fingertips across his lips. "You would not have gone to so much trouble to capture me just to kill me in a fit of anger."

"True enough, but the old man here isn't immune." Lord Bhima rammed the stopper back into the water skin.

But Mr. Spock thought he had Lord Bhima's measure now; and it was with a certain sense of regret that he knew Lord Bhima would continue to serve Rahu. "You aren't one to let someone else do your fighting. I rather suspect that you wouldn't take your vengeance indirectly either."

Lord Bhima handed the water skin to Puga. "No, I'm a warrior, not a politician." He threw back his head and laughed. "That's always been my virtue as well as my vice."

Chapter Ten

Ten days later, Vikram's army had marched out of the pass, scattering a small force of Rahu's scouts who had scampered off almost gleefully as if they could not believe Lord Rahu's good fortune. Apparently the Kotah Elders had not been the only ones expecting a long, protracted campaign to take Kotah. As Urmi had predicted, the Committees of other villages had not been so foolish as her own. With eyes and ears all over the countryside, they knew that Rahu's army was spread over a broad area "foraging"—though, as the prince had said, "Some purists might call it looting."

It had been a simple thing to cut Rahu's supply lines to the palace. They were waiting now at a site the prince had chosen with his commanders. With the household troops of a few minor lords and some village militias, the prince's army numbered some six thousand and his commanders had positioned it with its left flank upon a hill, its right flank on a river, and set a barricade of sharpened stakes in front of it. And at the center were the harquebusiers and pikemen.

But despite all their careful preparations, their army seemed woefully small as Rahu's own army poured onto the field late one afternoon. The prince closed one eye as he squinted through a brass telescope. "Urmi, if we survive this battle, you'll have to compliment your friends. They estimated Rahu's army at thirty thousand and I think they were right."

Urmi watched the army take up positions in neatly ordered ranks. "There doesn't seem to be any end of it."

"But the heart of Rahu's army is the *sinha*." The prince pointed his free hand toward a large, glittering, white-caped rectangle at the rear of the army. "Destroy the *sinha* and you destroy his army. And there are only three thousand *sinha* against a thousand of our harquebusiers. So we can reduce the odds to just three-to-one."

Sulu studied the situation. "But he seems to want to keep them as a reserve. He can throw his other troops at you until he's just worn you down by sheer numbers."

"The strength of the *sinha* is their pride." The prince swept his telescope back and forth. "And a strength can be turned to a weakness." The prince focused the telescope on the horizon where the carts and wagons of Rahu's train were rolling along. "Aren't they going to make camp?"

Urmi placed the edge of her hand at the top of her helmet to shade her eyes against the late afternoon sun. "I think they want to attack while the sun is in your eyes."

"That's rather uncooperative of them." The prince

lowered the telescope as if he were annoyed. "We planned to have the morning sun shine into theirs."

Urmi took the telescope and raised it to her right eye. "They look tired to me. I've had all kinds of reports that they've been making forced marches to collect together and then get here. And they look hungry. I'll bet anything that Rahu hasn't given them much time to eat—if at all."

"Rahu probably wants to catch me before I change my mind and scurry back into Kotah." He gestured toward a blue banner with a golden sun crest that was suddenly unfurled. "There's his symbol now. It's odd how you can hate an object almost as much as you can hate the owner himself."

"But I don't see Mr. Spock or my grandfather." Urmi collapsed the sections of the telescope together in disappointment. Though a rescue column had promptly been dispatched to Urmi's village, they reported that raiders had already been there, burning half the houses and escaping with Puga and Mr. Spock in the confusion.

"Rahu would have them near him, I think. But in order to find them, we'll have to dispose of Rahu's army first." The prince signed to Colonel Gelu. "I think it's time for our little entertainment."

The prince had been cagey about his plans, refusing to divulge them even to Sulu and Urmi, so they were as surprised as everyone else when a *gaya* was led out before the lines so both armies could see it. Covering its back was a large piece of cloth, cut like a *sinha* pelt and embroidered with the golden sun crest of Rahu's clan. Leading it was a soldier who leapt easily onto its back. The startled beast swung around, but the man held a tight hold of its horns.

Loud laughter rolled up and down the prince's lines. "I've cheated a little bit," he confessed to Urmi and Sulu. "The man's a professional clown."

The prince took back the telescope and surveyed the opposite lines. "A noble with an empty stomach is a rather cross creature, and I think our little entertainment has just made them even crosser." He signed to his own banner man who undid the ribbons and unfurled the prince's banner. The large red rectangle of silk flapped in the air for a moment to reveal the prince's mountain crest sewn in gilt thread. And then the wind, which had been blowing stiffly, just as quickly died so that the banner drooped. The prince sighed heavily. "Nature must be a drama critic."

Out in the meadow, the clown had slid from the *gaya* and hit it on the rump. It trotted off some twenty meters, shaking its head as if it could not believe it was free from his maddening presence. Then it halted and began to graze. The clown shouted and waved his arms but the *gaya* stubbornly remained where it was. With an elaborate shrug, the clown turned and pretended to strut in exaggerated triumph back to his own cheering, applauding lines.

Suddenly the front ranks of Rahu's army parted and the *sinha* began to form up before the rest of the army. When they had thrown off their capes, the late afternoon sun gleamed off their ornate, costly armor. Sulu strapped on his helmet. "There's enough gold and silver out there to pay your army for a year."

"Perhaps several years." The prince tapped a finger against his own plain iron cuirass. It made a hollow bonging sound. "But there is a difference between a pageant and a battle."

The prince's own troops had fallen silent now so Sulu could clearly hear the orders that left the front rank of harquebusiers kneeling while the other two ranks rose. Little bells rang here and there among the lines. Many of the soldiers, caught up in the prince's own dark humor, had hung shadow-catching ribbons from their guns.

Rahu's banner dipped once and the cornets began to play quick, commanding notes. And then the drums began to beat. The *gaya* raised its head from the tall grass, but either it was too stubborn or too frightened to leave. Sulu found himself hoping that the *gaya* would come to its senses and run away before it was too late. And then he realized how incongruous it was when so many people were likely to die on this very same field.

Rahu's army gave a great roar, like a giant beast getting ready to spring. The prince's own troops looked at one another uncomfortably. The officers and non-coms could be heard up and down the line as they tried to calm their men. "My pistol," the prince said to an orderly and exchanged the telescope for a wheel-lock pistol.

The *sinha* should have advanced to the steady rhythm of their drums, but in their anger and frustration they simply poured onto the field. They moved with all the eagerness of a pack of hunting hounds, scenting an easy, weak prey. By the time they reached the halfway point, their lines had become ragged. And as they broke into a run, any semblance of a formation dissolved completely.

"Steady," a sergeant murmured to the harquebusiers in front of Sulu. "Hold your fire."

The *sinha* were still a short distance from the stakes

that had been driven into the ground fifty meters from the prince's line. But the *sinha* raised their voices in triumphant cries as if they were already celebrating their victory; and, despite their heavy armor, they ran with a confident stride.

And though the prince's soldiers stirred, not one of them ran. Sulu had to admire their discipline. When the first *sinha* reached the markers, Sulu thought the prince would give the order to fire; but when there was only silence to his left, Sulu looked at the prince to see if he was all right. But the prince was standing there, licking his dry lips and staring intently with eyes narrowed against the sunlight.

The prince was still waiting when the main part of the *sinha*—they were more of a mob than organized units now—had passed the markers.

"Sir?" Colonel Gelu called. The first *sinha* were at the barricades now and the bulk of Rahu's warriors were only forty meters away.

The prince's answer was to raise a wheel-lock pistol over his head and lower it, sighting at the leading *sinha*. He pulled the trigger and the serrated wheel began to turn, striking sparks from a chunk of iron pyrite into the powder pan. When the pistol went off, it seemed as if the prince had missed hitting any of Rahu's men. But the prince's officers lost no time in giving the order. "First rank, fire."

Because of his own interest in antique guns, Sulu had actually drilled with a wheel lock and even practiced firing one; but that had been with a platoon. So nothing had prepared him for the volume of noise from a volley of hundreds of guns. It was a huge crash like gigantic gates toppling from their hinges—a sound that was almost a physical sensation that passed through his body.

A cloud of black smoke rose from the guns, but Sulu could see how the heavy lead balls knocked their victims backward as if they were simply puppets jerked back by invisible strings. The survivors slowed and even halted as if stunned.

But the prince's harquebusiers were like some great threshing machine that could not be stopped once it was set in motion.

"First rank, reload."

"Second rank, fire."

This time Sulu was too deafened by the first volley to be bothered by it, but the black smoke obscured even the field before them so that all Sulu could see was the first rank using small keys to rewind the springs of their wheel locks and the second rank starting to kneel down before they reloaded. And when the third rank fired, the smoke hid even the barricade of stakes.

Behind him, Sulu's deafened ears could just make out the rattle of pikemen getting ready to cover the retreat of the harquebusiers. Columns of pikemen had been spaced at intervals to the rear. The drill had been for the harquebusiers to file through the spaces and have the pikemen form lines and advance while the harquebusiers reloaded in relative safety.

The prince hurriedly handed the empty pistol to his orderly to be reloaded and he drew his sword. But no *sinha* came charging out of the black smoke. And the ranks of harquebusiers kept up a slow but steady fire into the smoke until the prince had the cornets sound the ceasefire.

It took a long time for hearing to return to Sulu's ears

and so he heard the agonized groans only dimly at first, like a flock of crippled birds far away. But the smoke itself did not dissipate until the wind stiffened the prince's banner, raising it from its staff.

Neither Sulu nor anyone else was prepared for the sight of hundreds of bodies piled between the fifty-meter markers and the barricades. Even as he watched, the piles twitched eerily, like strange-limbed monsters coming to life.

"What's happening?" Urmi shouted to Sulu and the prince. "Aren't they dead?" Though she was standing next to him, Sulu could barely make out her words.

"The movement's probably made by wounded men at the bottom of the piles," Sulu yelled back. "They must be struggling to throw off the corpses on top of them."

The prince touched his fingers to head and heart and said something that Sulu missed, but he was clearly shocked by what he saw. Even the officers and harque-busiers looked awed by the efficient and murderous way they had shattered the first attack. Then smoke continued to thin until it drifted up in ghostly pillars and they could see the surviving *sinha* reorganizing before Rahu's startled army.

Without thinking, the prince swung his sword up toward Rahu's banner. "End it now, Rahu. With-draw." The bells at the end of the sword jingled—sounding ominously cheerful over the moans of the wounded. A nearby harquebusier, who had just fin-ished reloading his gun, heard the sound and on some sudden impulse he raised the weapon and shook it carefully so that the bells at the ends of the ribbons rang as well. Another harquebusier raised his gun and imitated the sound. And the ringing passed along the ranks to either flank. There was something both mocking and defiant in the bells—as if a sinister jester were taunting Rahu.

His banner dipped abruptly and the cornets began to blow once more. The prince sheathed his sword guiltily —as if it were to blame. "Here they come again." He took the reloaded pistol from his orderly.

The *sinha* gave a hoarse shout and charged back across the field. Somehow they managed to run faster, harder, their feet pounding against the ground. They were silent now, holding their breaths for the grim race ahead. It was as if they were determined to dart between the lead balls from the wheel locks.

Again, the prince waited until the bulk of the *sinha* had passed the markers before he fired his pistol. The first rank fired almost immediately and the black smoke rose once more; but Sulu could see the front *sinha*. Some of them clutched at their heads or chests, but others charged on—clambering over their dead.

"Second rank, fire."

The guns of the second rank of harquebusiers roared and the *sinha* became mere silhouettes. And even so, a few of Rahu's young warriors managed to reach the barricade. Swords drawn, eager to get at their tormentors, they twisted between the densely hammered stakes.

"Second rank, kneel."

"Third rank, fire."

The words came almost as final as a judge's order of execution. Bodies were almost cut in two at such point-blank range. Some of the *sinha* lay draped over the stakes like odd bundles of rags.

"Third rank, reload."

The first two ranks were reloading feverishly, hands fumbling at the pouches in the bandoliers or using the keys to tighten the springs of the wheel locks. Suddenly a dozen *sinha* appeared at the barricade. Their armor was covered in blood as if they had crawled over the mounds of corpses.

"Good Lord. They'll slaughter our men." The prince pitched his empty pistol to his orderly. "Sound the retreat," the prince ordered his cornets.

The harquebusiers began to withdraw even before the prince's own cornets finished sounding the retreat. The harquebusiers fell back, cradling their guns in their arms, their faces drawn and tense; but they refused to panic as they trotted through the intervals between the columns of pikemen. Except for the bodies littering the ground, Sulu might have thought the withdrawal was only a drill.

From the shouting, it seemed as if there were breakthroughs in other areas as well. The prince pointed his sword as the *sinha* slashed at the backs of the last ranks of harquebusiers. "We have to cover their retreat." With a quick flick of his fingers, he motioned for his banner man to lift the banner.

Licking his dry, cracked lips, Sulu drew his own sword and then they were running past the clinking harquebusiers straight toward the maddened *sinha*. Urmi touched Sulu's arm and pointed to the prince's right while she took up her position on his left. The *sinha* gave a hoarse roar when they saw the prince's banner advancing directly toward them.

And it was all Sulu could do to defend himself as the *sinha* threw themselves at the prince's party. The prince's orderly was the first to fall with a gash across his throat. A second later, the banner man tumbled backward over the orderly's corpse.

"Don't let the banner drop," the prince shouted.

But Sulu was already reaching for it with his free hand. There was no telling how rumors of the prince's death might affect his army and Sulu knew from his military history just how quickly wild rumors could fly through an army on a battlefield.

As he grabbed the staff, he parried a thrust and riposted, forcing his opponent to dance back. But the banner man did not want to surrender it and Sulu had to yank it out of the dying man's grasp. But the distraction of taking the banner had made Sulu take his eye from his opponent.

"Sulu." The prince stepped in and brought up his own sword to knock away a deadly slash. Sulu thrust past the prince, his blade taking the *sinha* in the armpit, which was not covered by the *sinha*'s armor. Then, trying to remember his Angiran anatomy, Sulu twisted the blade slightly to the left and downward into the *sinha*'s heart.

But even as Sulu was trying to free his sword, a *sinha* blade was slashing down toward the prince. "Duck," Sulu shouted, and the prince automatically began to crouch as he brought up his blade. He stopped the *sinha*'s sword, but not before the tip clanged against his helmet. And even as the prince was falling, Urmi killed his attacker.

And then the harquebusiers were all around them, swinging their guns as clubs, and the *sinha* were beaten to the ground. "The prince is dead," one of the harquebusiers cried. His voice had already taken on an alarming higher note as he looked at the prince's bloody face.

Urmi knelt and felt the prince's throat. "No, he's still alive." She tore a patch from her sleeve and pressed it against a cut on the prince's cheek. "This is only a surface cut. It looks a lot worse than it is. The blow just knocked him out for a moment."

The groans seemed even louder now, as if there were more wounded heaped beyond the barricade. But though the thick, black smoke hadn't cleared, Sulu could make out the sound of Rahu's cornets blowing a third charge.

Somewhere in that smoke-filled field, Rahu's warriors were advancing, their gear rattling, their armor blinking. Sulu thrust the banner into the dirt and looked about for Colonel Gelu or any staff officer, but he could only see a mob of harquebusiers around him. Colonel Gelu and the other senior officers were probably busy restoring order in the lines. But unless someone took charge right away, the battle might easily be lost and that left only Sulu.

All of Sulu's reading and fantasizing had not prepared him for this. The musketeers only had to be dashing. They didn't have to make command decisions. And as Sulu stared at the smoke and confusion all about him, he realized that someone was going to have to do something about ending this disorder—and soon. Their survival—and even the fate of a world—depended upon that happening.

And yet Sulu wasn't sure if he was up to the task. It was one thing to risk his own life in a battle and quite another to risk the lives of others. Whether people lived or died would depend upon Sulu giving the correct orders. And until now Captain Kirk or some other officer had always carried that weight.

Sulu raised his sword for a moment so he could stare at the bloody edge and feel its weight. He might be surrounded by the trappings of a musketeer fantasy, but this was the reality. *Elan* had its place in the imagination of a writer and a small boy, but not on a battlefield.

But did Sulu even have the right to take over? Sulu may already have defied the spirit of the Prime Directive, but he certainly would violate the letter if he took control of the prince's army. Then, too, would it do any good? The weapons and tactics were so primitive and the conditions so complicated that Sulu wasn't sure if he was up to handling them.

"Wake up," Urmi was urging the prince.

Sulu looked down at his fallen friend and felt almost as if he were once again fighting for his balance upon the bridge. But this time he was fighting to stay upright within himself. After all, it was Sulu who had a hand in convincing the prince to fight for Angira. Or was he guilty of more than that? Had Sulu been fulfilling his own vicarious fantasies of creating a home world for himself? If so, he bore more than a casual responsibility for what was happening now. He simply couldn't stand here doing nothing because of rules made light-years away.

Besides, if Rahu won, Urmi was right: That madman would spread murder and pillage across the entire world. Sulu sighed. He'd told the prince that one person could make a difference. Well, it was time to take his own advice. Sulu had to assume command even if it meant losing his commission. It was the right thing for Angira—even if it might not be the right thing for Sulu.

He nodded to the young, frightened cornet who was still staring down at the prince. "Give the signal for everyone to take up their old positions." And then he collared the nearest sergeant. "Get your men back in line."

But the sergeant only blinked his eyes stupidly at Sulu as if he was trying to place the strange, alien face. "But the prince—"

"He'd expect you to do your duty," Sulu said in his strongest drill-field voice.

The sergeant reacted as much to his tone as to his words, and he straightened, saluting Sulu awkwardly because Sulu still had a grip on his collar.

Sheepishly, Sulu let go while the sergeant began yelling orders. "Come on. Come on. You heard the woman say that the prince was all right. Get back to your posts." And to Sulu's relief, he could hear the other noncoms and junior officers taking up the command. And cornets up and down the line began picking up the signal from the first cornet.

"You're a good friend to the prince." Urmi unstrapped the prince's helmet. She added, with an apologetic nod of her head, "And to Angira."

Urmi didn't know how much Sulu was risking, but somehow that didn't seem important now.

Sulu squatted down and asked quietly, "Are you sure he's going to be all right?"

Urmi threw the prince's helmet to the side. "How should I know? I'm no healer."

"But I thought you found a pulse," Sulu whispered urgently.

242

Urmi shot a sharp look at him. "I wouldn't know where to find one even if it was marked with a dotted line. But I'm not about to lose this battle." Taking the prince's head upon her knees, she began slapping his uncut cheek. "Wake up, Your Highness."

Sulu bounced back to his feet, looking again for Colonel Gelu; but there still wasn't any sign of him. However, the harquebusiers had formed ragged lines.

Urmi lowered the prince's head to the ground and crawled over to the orderly, snatching the small water skin from his belt. "Do you think they'll have time to reload before Rahu's men come?"

Sulu undid the chinstrap of his helmet and took it off. The air felt cool on his sweaty face. "Maybe. But there are so many variables. Can we assume a certain rate of speed? And did they start as soon as their cornets finished blowing?" He smiled ruefully to himself. What had ever made him think that warfare with swords was simple?

It was a relief to hear the prince spluttering as Urmi splashed water into his face. He would be all right after all. But how soon? Sulu still had to concentrate on the problem at hand.

While the harquebusiers went on with the complicated process of reloading, Sulu tried to work out the problem as calmly as Mr. Spock would have—even though he knew he was a poor substitute for the science officer. And there, in the midst of that primitive battlefield, he found himself wishing desperately for the *Enterprise*'s computers and sensors.

"He's coming around," Urmi said with relief.

Sulu glanced down at the prince, who was shaking his head groggily. It might be minutes or even hours before the prince became fully functional; and they might not even have seconds.

Well, Sulu sighed to himself, he might as well give his court-martial board their money's worth. Throwing his helmet away, he strode forward a dozen paces and turned a startled harquebusier around. "Is your weapon loaded?"

"Yes, but that's my gun," the man protested as Sulu grabbed it.

"Just shout 'bang' at them. They'll never know the difference." And with a determined yank, Sulu took the gun from the man. As he backed up, Sulu checked the gun to make sure it was ready to be fired. At least there was powder in the firing pan.

"You have to wake up," Urmi was saying to the prince.

The clinking sounded very close now. Sulu ought to give the signal soon, but he could see that maybe a fourth of the harquebusiers were still working at reloading their clumsy pieces.

But even if the harquebusiers had all been ready, Sulu still couldn't be sure if he had the right answer. And stopping the charge depended partly on the timing of the volleys. He stared into the smoke, praying for it to clear a little. But he couldn't make out a single figure. He would just have to gamble that he was right.

Raising the harquebus, Sulu fired and was almost knocked down by the heavy weapon. In his hurry, he'd forgotten just what a kick the gun had.

The first rank fired blindly into the smoke, followed by a ragged volley from the second rank. But before the third rank could fire, a man in gilded armor burst through the smoke. Hundreds of grim-faced *sinha* followed him. They ran low, squirming and wriggling their way through the stakes of the barricade.

The third rank fired when ordered, but whether it was nerves or bad luck or simply the fact that more men had forgotten one of the many steps necessary to load their wheel locks, the result was just as unfortunate. This time nearly half of Rahu's men survived.

Some of the more reckless harquebusiers threw down their guns and drew their daggers; but they were no match for trained nobles with swords.

"Sound the retreat," Sulu ordered the cornet and dropped his own wheel lock into the dirt.

"What—?" The prince was sitting up dizzily.

Snatching up the banner, Sulu reached down and grabbed the prince by the left armpit. "Help me get him out of the way," he said to Urmi. She took the prince's right arm and together they managed to hoist the prince to his feet.

The majority of the harquebusiers were withdrawing in reasonably good order. And in a moment, the pikemen would advance; but the prince himself was still in danger. Suddenly a *sinha* in armor with silver inlay charged at them.

"What happened to the prince?" Colonel Gelu and three aides came running up toward them.

"He's been knocked out for a while." Sulu surrendered his position to one of the colonel's aides so he could draw his own sword and meet the new challenge. He was startled to realize that the *sinha* was sobbing as he ran.

"I've had enough of this nonsense." Urmi snatched a wheel-lock pistol from Colonel Gelu's surprised grasp and fired. The noble halted, staring at the person who

245

had shot him; and then, turning slightly on his toes, he dropped onto his back, the sword dropping uselessly out of his hand.

"You may have just written the epitaph for an era," Sulu said as he watched her return the pistol to Colonel Gelu.

"Watch out." Colonel Gelu shouted and the four of them pulled the prince hastily out of the way as the pikemen advanced toward the barricades. Sulu and the others withdrew until they were in front of the reforming harquebusiers. In the meantime, the columns of pikemen had swung to the side to form several long lines.

Frustrated, Rahu's men threw themselves at the pikes, but it was like a thick hedge of long, waving thorns. As the prince's own cornets sounded the advance, a few foolhardy *sinha* tried to stand their ground and were quickly spitted. But the rest of Rahu's warriors backed up, waving their swords and shouting defiance as they made their way through the barricade once again. Still the pikemen moved forward to the steady beat of the drums. And the swordsmen disappeared back into the thick, billowing smoke. Even so, Sulu's numbed ears could make out their challenges. They sounded now like angry, disembodied ghosts. And then even their voices faded away into the distance.

"I don't know whether to thank you or not, Sulu." The prince gingerly felt the edges of his wound. "You've saved the battle; but all the same, it's rather uncomfortable to find out how unnecessary you are."

Sulu handed the banner over to another of Colonel Gelu's aides. "I just did what you would have," Sulu said. But in the back of his mind, he wondered if the court-martial board would see it that way.

The smoke had not yet cleared when the harquebus-iers resumed their positions behind the barricade. The corpses of glittering, richly armored nobles lay with the bodies of the prince's own men on their side of the stakes. And then the wind blew harder so that the prince's banner flapped and snapped at its shaft. But even as the smoke began to drift away, they could hear the angry shouting coming from the direc-tion of Rahu's army.

"It sounds like they're working themselves up for another charge," Sulu said to the prince.

The prince resignedly held out his hand toward his new orderly who had taken the wheel-lock pistol from his predecessor's corpse. "I thought they would have had their fill of this kind of fighting by now. I know I have."

But as the smoke dissipated, they could see Rahu's army beginning to unravel like the threads of a shining tapestry. Frightened soldiers were throwing away their weapons and helmets as they started to stream away. And, with a sudden flutter, Rahu's banner was jerked upward and flowed along with them.

"We've won." Urmi shoved her helmet up over her head and would have thrown it up in the air, but the prince stopped her.

"Not quite. There's still Rahu," the prince said. "Until we hunt down that wild animal, we'll never have any peace." He turned to motion Colonel Gelu to him.

Mr. Spock had never heard the sound before. It was almost as if a giant centipede were trampling past them, but he knew it was only the sound of dozens of feet running through the grass outside the huge wagon in which he lay. The guards called out questions in a confident, easy tone and were answered by a frightened babbling.

Puga, his arms bound behind him, slid on his haunches across the wooden bed of the wagon. "Something's wrong. It almost sounds like a stampede."

The babbling increased in volume—changing to a series of wails. And the animals began to bellow and squeal. Their own wagon gave a kind of lurch and there was a whump as their yokes were thrown to the ground.

Puga stood up with difficulty and then, his chains clinking, he tried to peer through the silk covering the front of the wagon. "The guards have taken the draft *gaya* and ridden away. And now Rahu's warriors are running by. They don't have shields or spears or swords." Puga turned around and his feet did a little thumping dance on the wagon bed. "The prince confounded them all. He's won."

Mr. Spock turned his head to look around the wagon. "Then we must find a place to hide."

"Maybe—" the old man began and then stopped when the wagon shook.

A warrior thrust his head through the slitted opening. His helmet was gone, but sweat had matted his fur into spikes and his eyes were wide with anger and fear. His armor bore the emblem of some noble's house, so he must have been some lord's retainer.

He stared at Mr. Spock as if puzzled for a moment, but then his eyes swept on as if searching for something else. His eyes settled on the trunk at the rear of the wagon. "What's in that trunk over there?" When Puga shrugged, the warrior jumped into the wagon and climbed between Puga and Mr. Spock. Slipping his dagger from his belt, he tried to pry the chest open.

The wagon quivered as someone else climbed up on the front. "I'll look in here," a second man said. This warrior had shed his chest armor but not his leggings so that he looked half-Angiran, half-insect.

The first warrior whirled around, still squatting, and raised his dagger menacingly. "I found this first."

"But you won't get to keep it." The second warrior leapt into the wagon. Puga threw himself across Mr. Spock; but the second warrior ran past them as he pulled out his sword. A moment later, a third man followed him into the wagon.

The first warrior rose from a crouch, springing at the second warrior as his arm swept the dagger toward the intruder. The second warrior tried to bring his sword around, but the first warrior was already on top of him. The two men tumbled backward and the first warrior squatted on the chest of the second, trying to free his dagger.

He didn't even have time to shout as the third warrior's sword took off his head. It went rolling backward toward the trunk and the third man ran after it, leaving the headless corpse to collapse on top of his dead friend.

The old man sat up dazedly. "Why are you looting your own army's wagon train?"

But the warrior was frantically attacking the padlock with his sword as if his life depended on it—and perhaps it did. "You need money to get away. You need even more money to buy a pardon." The padlock broke with a snap and the man used his free hand to raise the lid. His hand dug inside the trunk with a rustling sound. "Papers. Worthless papers." He raised a handful of white squares and flung them away. They showered the wagon like large, ghostly leaves.

He got up abruptly and, with one slash of his sword, slashed a hole in the silk covering the rear of the wagon so he could jump out.

"It's not the most graceful exit," Mr. Spock said.

"It's too late to find some place to hide." Puga slid across the wagon bed toward the broken padlock.

Outside they could hear crashes and snaps and the protesting of metal—as if their wagon had not been the only target of looters.

"Then"—Mr. Spock looked up at the billowing top of the wagon—"we may not live to celebrate the prince's victory."

Puga turned around and his fingers groped across the floor boards until they found the padlock. "As long as Rahu doesn't live much longer."

Mr. Spock smiled slightly. "Will you be content then?"

Puga sat up on his haunches. "Will you?"

With the threat of death facing them now, Mr. Spock was amazed by his own sense of calmness. He didn't have to use his own powers of self-control after all. But part of that was due to the realization he had been wrong to let Puga and McCoy set the terms of the discussion. Lord Bhima had been right to a certain extent. "There are other things besides contentment. There is knowledge."

Puga shook his head. "It seems like a poor thing to settle for. I think Lord Bhima, with all his knowledge of the Warrior's Code, would settle for a swift mount right now."

"Truth has many faces and the seeker must be flexible." Mr. Spock smoothed the blanket that covered him. "To insist on knowing just one face is not to know it at all. And that is because all truth is ultimately about the self."

"Why travel so far then?" Puga asked, puzzled.

"Truth is not a set of statistics or diagrams. It is a process and it can be seen best on a place like the *Enterprise*," Mr. Spock said, and then added with a nod of his head, "or on Angira."

Mr. Spock lifted his head slightly. "The ultimate objective of knowledge is to learn about one's self; and one can learn the most where two cultural identities overlap and where they differ."

"What could you possibly learn here?" Puga wrinkled his forehead as if perplexed.

"Prince Vikram exists on the borderline between two cultures." Mr. Spock turned his face toward the top of the wagon. "It is always instructive to see how a borderer survives and meets challenges—and even triumphs over them."

Puga sighed as if he had finally understood. "And do you plan to do something for your own home world just as the prince has done?"

"I have no such lofty ambitions." Mr. Spock shrugged.

"Then you enjoy seeing someone do something that you can't," Puga said.

"Perhaps," Mr. Spock was willing to concede. He tried to compose himself for whatever might come as he studied the top of the wagon. A sudden breeze made the bright silk billow in shimmering waves of gold. And then, like the edge of a storm racing across the plain, they heard a pattering sound. It swelled gradually until they could distinguish hundreds of booted feet. Men thudded by, panting heavily as if fear drove them on now rather than greed.

Suddenly, the wagon trembled again, but this time a young *sinha* looked inside. He seemed like the only man in Rahu's army glad to see them. "They are still here, Lord," he announced.

Puga rose, the padlock swinging in his right hand. But the *sinha* simply parted the front of the wagon so Rahu could look inside.

Rahu positively beamed when he saw Mr. Spock. "You have no idea how delighted I am to see you." And to the *sinha* he murmured, "Help Lord Bhima find the equipment we need."

Lord Bhima's glowering face appeared behind Rahu's. "I don't like this."

"You don't have to like it." Rahu waved his hand at the swordmaster imperiously. "You just have to help me escape. Now go." And Lord Bhima and the *sinha* disappeared and Mr. Spock heard them jump off the wagon the next moment.

Puga glared at Rahu. "Have you come to take your revenge for losing? Too bad there's only the two of us."

Rahu stepped into the wagon. "On the contrary. I hope for all of us to get away from here with our skins and heads intact."

Mr. Spock rolled onto his side, stretching out his arm despite the pain. He caught Rahu's ankle, tumbling him forward, and the old man swung his padlock. But it was an awkward swing, catching Rahu on the shoulder rather than the head and the next moment Rahu had his sword point at the old man's throat.

Reluctantly Mr. Spock released Rahu's ankle.

Rahu settled back. "Though I must admit it will give me some satisfaction to see you two suffer."

Chapter Eleven

It took a moment to arrange the pursuit; and even longer to cross the bloody field. The *sinha* lay not only heaped before the barricade but throughout the trampled meadow—as if many of the wounded had crawled away to die. Swords, spears and other weapons littered the ground where Rahu's army had once stood; and a good many nobles, perhaps leading their own household troops, had left behind their expensive armor as well.

About a quarter of a kilometer beyond lay Rahu's baggage train. The many cumbersome wagons sat where they had been left in an oval.

The prince glanced over his shoulder at the company of harquebusiers who followed them. "Maybe I'd better detail a platoon to prevent looting."

Urmi clutched at his arm. "Wait, there's someone there by that big wagon."

The prince took his telescope from his orderly and

had a look. "It's Rahu, and he's just sitting there as if he were out for a picnic." He lowered the telescope suspiciously. "And I thought we'd be up all night tracking him down."

"He's up to something," Urmi said with fierce conviction.

The prince handed his telescope back to his new orderly. "Yes, well, we'll never find out standing here. Shall we go see what he's up to?"

Though Rahu was still in full armor, he was sitting calmly on a fold-out stool next to a giant wagon. The wagon bed was covered by bright, shiny cloth and Sulu was startled to realize it was all of the finest flame silk. "That wagon top must have cost a fortune."

"It's like Rahu to live like an emperor before he is one." And the prince signaled to the company of harquebusiers to form a circle around the wagon.

As the prince advanced, Rahu himself had remained on the stool with a confident air—as if he and not Vikram were in control of the situation. "Thank you for coming to me, Vikram. It saved me the trouble of looking for you."

The prince took off his helmet. "Rahu, your family always had a penchant for staging last stands. Why don't you try to be different."

"Perhaps I will, Vikram." And then he called to the wagon, "Lord Bhima, we have visitors."

A flap was thrown back from the front of the wagon top to reveal Mr. Spock in a chair. A huge bandage swathed his chest. But even so, he managed to hold his head up weakly. A bruised Puga stood beside him, leaning with one hand on the back of the chair for support. Lord Bhima stood next to the chair as he held his sword against Mr. Spock's throat. A *sinha* with a dagger did the same to Puga. "I thought that I might buy our safe passage with this exotic pair of pets."

The prince spun round anxiously on his heel to Sulu and Urmi. "This is a rather ugly turn of events. I have the obligations of a host to Mr. Spock and those of a guest to Puga; and yet I don't dare let Rahu loose to raise another army. I may not win the next battle against him."

"No, you might not," Sulu admitted reluctantly. "But maybe you could negotiate a better deal with Rahu."

The prince nodded his head toward the setting sun. "No, any delay plays into Rahu's hands. It's going to be dark soon. I can't risk letting Rahu break through my lines and make his escape."

Urmi fingered the pommel to her sword irritatedly. "If you can't attack and you can't wait, what are you going to do?"

"As our Vulcan friend says, there are always other possibilities." Lifting his head, the prince called to Rahu, "You know very well that I couldn't let you go even if you were holding my own father hostage. But I have a counterproposal. We will fight a duel. If I win, you will be my prisoner. If you win, I will be yours and my men will let you go. In either case, Mr. Spock and Puga are to go free."

Suddenly alarmed, Urmi jerked him around to face her. "But you can't trust oathbreakers like them to keep their word."

"I'm not going to them unarmed." The prince pulled free of her hand. "If they do break their oath, I should be able to hold them off long enough for you to come to

256

my rescue. And whatever else happens, I'll at least know that I tried."

"But if you lose," Urmi hissed, "Rahu will be on the loose anyway."

"I won't lose." The prince shrugged. "I feel lucky today."

Urmi raised her hands and shook them in exasperation. "You're wagering your life, not money."

"One life could end the war and all this suffering," the prince reminded her gently. "Surely those are worthwhile stakes."

For his part, Rahu had stood up to hold an equally brief but earnest discussion with Lord Bhima before he looked back at the Prince. "I like my proposal better," Rahu said. "However, I'll agree to a duel—but only on one condition."

"And what's that?" the prince asked suspiciously.

Rahu swept his palm toward the wagon; but though he did his best to appear relaxed, there was still a certain anxiousness to his movements. "Lord Bhima must be my champion."

Urmi sucked in her breath. "That tears it. You can't go against the likes of him."

The prince narrowed his eyes as he studied the swordmaster. "He's much older than when he taught me."

"His reflexes may be a bit slower, but he knows too much," Urmi argued. "And how often have you been able to practice while you've been gone? That man trains every day. He's married to his sword."

The prince glanced sideways toward Sulu. "To paraphrase someone else, this may still be a time when one must survive by one's wits as well as one's sword."

"This is more witless than wit," Urmi blurted out. She paused and then added a bit more contritely, "I didn't really mean that. It's just that . . . that I've grown rather fond of you."

The prince smiled as if pleased. "And I'm rather fond of you too. That's why I'm doing this."

"Can't we discuss this first?" Urmi said meaningfully. "The glass cage doesn't have to fit just one, you know."

But Rahu wouldn't give them the time. "What's your decision, Vikram?" Puga was jerked straight by the knife that now hung beneath his throat.

The prince shrugged apologetically. "I'm sorry, Urmi. You see how things are."

"Honestly, sometimes I think you're bound and determined to become a ghost before your time." She nuzzled him quickly on one cheek and then stood back, embarrassed and defiant.

"I promise not to haunt you as you threatened to do to me." The prince took his pistol from his sash and handed it to her before he looked toward Rahu. "No tournament rules?"

"It would be beneath me to fight that way," Lord Bhima scowled.

The prince gave a tense laugh. "But it's not beneath you to defend an assassin and usurper?"

The swordmaster sheathed his sword abruptly and stepped away from Mr. Spock. "I suppose it really doesn't matter how you die."

Rahu clapped his hands together as if he could not quite believe his luck. "Then it's agreed?"

"Yes," the prince shouted and then held up his arms. "Help me off with this armor," he said to his orderly. "I have to be able to move fast."

Sulu shook his head in amazement as he finally

258

realized what the prince was up to. "That quick draw was only a movie stunt. You can't risk your life on that."

The prince stood stiffly while his orderly undid the straps to his cuirass. "Of all the people here, Sulu, I thought you would at least understand me. I'm tired of letting other people die for me. I refuse to let that happen again. And if I'm a romantic fool for feeling that way, then so be it."

Sulu was torn between logic and his own natural impulses; but in the end, he decided that the least he owed his friend was some kind of encouragement. "Well, you'll only be a fool if the trick doesn't work."

"Your Highness—" Mr. Spock started to say.

"There's no need to thank me, Mr. Spock." The prince removed the armor plate from his left thigh while his orderly removed the plate on his right. "So you might as well save your breath."

"I can't see any reason to thank you, when you're behaving like some irresponsible schoolboy." Though Mr. Spock's voice was high and thin, the disapproval was plain.

"Mr. Spock, you are as charming as ever. But the only choices that you have are whether to walk or to be carried to safety." The prince looked at his rival. "Rahu, I will start forward at the same time as Puga and Mr. Spock—if he can walk."

"I can walk," Mr. Spock said in a dignified voice. "But slowly." He reached a hand up to Puga's shoulder and rose carefully.

"Then I will stroll just as leisurely." The bells attached to the ribbons rang faintly as the prince set his right foot in front of him.

Lord Bhima helped lower Mr. Spock to the ground

and then helped Puga climb down before he jumped down himself with the *sinha*.

Leaning on Puga, Mr. Spock took short, measured steps, his face a blank mask as if he were doing his best to conceal the pain he felt. The *sinha* kept pace with them, dagger still drawn.

The prince walked calmly into the light of the sun, his shadow sliding backward over the trampled grass as if it now had a life of its own. And as it stretched itself across the field, the dark silhouette no longer seemed to belong to the prince but to some giant instead.

As they neared one another, Puga croaked, "I knew you had it in you, lad. You'll make a good emperor."

"If he lives that long." Mr. Spock frowned.

"Yes, it should be interesting," the prince agreed cheerfully as he waited at the halfway point. Once Mr. Spock and Puga were past, he followed the *sinha* back to Rahu.

Lord Bhima had never been a person to give an advantage to anyone and so he was waiting with his back to the sun. Still clad in his armor, he was turned sideways, his legs already spread, the knees slightly bent, his back and head erect in a straight line. He looked as if he had sunk invisible roots within the ground so that the prince seemed to be walking across the shadow of a giant tree rather than a man. "So you think you can beat your old master, do you?"

The prince did his best to control his own mounting excitement. "I certainly intend to try."

Lord Bhima shook his head. "I think you've counted too much on your luck." He lowered his hands so that they were clenched near his sides.

The prince had to squint into the last of the sunlight.

He said nothing, but slowly slid his left foot back and let his body slip into its own rhythmic pattern. He was aware of the weight of the sword in its sheath and his left hand hovered slightly behind him. But he concentrated his attention on Lord Bhima's eyes—as his former instructor himself had taught him to do.

It was silent in that one spot, though in the distance they could hear occasional shouts as the prince's army continued its pursuit. The sides of the wagon boomed and flapped in a sudden breeze like some pompous politician getting ready to speak; and the sun, setting in the gun smoke, began to turn a bright red, hanging like a raw, bloody wound in the sky.

And still they watched one another and waited for some break in the other's attention, some slight surrender to impatience that would give the other the edge.

And in the end—perhaps because he was a little more tired, or a bit overconfident, it was Lord Bhima who gave in. His right hand darted across his stomach and his fingers closed round the hilt and then the sword was sliding with a hiss out of its sheath in that old familiar motion.

And for once he was glad that an opponent was going to die. The young fool with his peasants and his guns and his bells had made a mockery of the Code of the Warrior. His army had met the *sinha,* not like warriors, but like factory hands processing so many *gaya* for the slaughter. Lord Bhima was killing not just to save his own life; he was fighting for an age and for all the ancient and true ways of doing things.

His sword seemed to leap out of the sheath like a living thing. He had never felt so much a part of his sword before. It was almost as if his sword were part of

261

him now, or he was part of the sword. His left hand was drawn to the hilt almost by magic and the blade whipped over his head and then down all in one smooth motion.

He had expected to see the prince's eyes widening in fear the way all the others had and see the desperate, fumbling attempt to draw the sword out faster or, if by some slight chance the sword was already drawn, to see the prince trying frantically to bring the blade around for a parry or to step back away from the slash.

In all these years of battles and tournaments and challenges and countless practices, Lord Bhima had seen only variations on those two basic reactions.

So he was a bit surprised to see the prince lunge forward from such a low angle. His face seemed to be at about the level of Lord Bhima's chest. And the surprise changed to fear when he heard the ringing of the bells but could not see the sword rising above the prince's head.

And he was the one who panicked and tried to stop. But it was already too late to stop his body, which was stepping in for its usually deadly blow. He felt the prince's blade bite into his stomach beneath the cuirass; and then the prince thrust the sword point inward. Lord Bhima did not feel the pain right away. It was more like a pinching sensation.

So this is how the others felt, Lord Bhima thought to himself, as he sank to his knees, his sword dropping with a clink against the dirt. Fool, he said to himself idly, the blade will get nicked. And then he realized with a start that it really didn't matter. "That draw is new."

The ground itself seemed to be dissolving into a blur of red with the twilit air; but he forced himself to look up. The prince's disembodied head seemed to float above him. "It's an offworld trick."

A fire began to burn in his body and the flames seemed to eat at his heart and lungs so that he could barely gasp, "So you didn't waste your time then."

"No," the prince said quietly, "I didn't."

And it seemed to Lord Bhima that the prince's features darkened until his face was a familiar, shadowy mask. Lord Bhima forced himself to stay erect, refusing to bow to the Lord of the Underworld. "So it was you, after all," he whispered inaudibly. "But it took you a long time before you beat me."

The prince turned away, looking angrily at Rahu as the cause of it all. "Come, Rahu," the prince said, "your sword. I'll deal with you far more fairly than you would have dealt with me."

Rahu twisted sideways. "You didn't really think I'd give up so easily, did you?"

He signed to the wagon and the *sinha* emerged with a tensed bow, the arrow pointed unerringly at the prince. "I may have lost my swordmaster, but I have certainly upped the quality of my hostages."

Dully, through a darkening haze, Lord Bhima heard the conversation. "You gave your word," Lord Bhima called and was surprised at the pain that it cost him to speak.

"Then you were as naïve as the prince. I don't intend to let our world go to perdition just on the result of a single duel." Lord Rahu held his hand out toward the prince. "I'll take that musical instrument you call a sword."

Lord Bhima could feel the shadows clutching at him, trying to draw his soul into the ground. "Not yet," he told them. "Not yet." There had been very little honor in this whole affair; but there was still one small thing he could do—and perhaps redeem a small fraction of his former reputation. Somehow from deep inside himself, he gathered up the last bit of energy left in his body and lurched forward. But he could not see Lord Rahu. He could only flail at the air in a blind rage. "I warned you that I wouldn't let you use and then discard me."

Lord Rahu easily managed to dance backward before the arrow hissed through the air. Lord Bhima's body jerked as the arrow hit and he fell face forward.

"Down," Urmi shouted.

And the prince threw himself face forward into the dirt as harquebuses fired with sharp, ugly cracking noises. Lord Rahu was knocked off his feet, arms flung out like a rag doll. More lead balls tore vicious holes in the wagon and the *sinha*.

The prince raised his head cautiously, but Rahu lay as still as Bhima. Spitting out a mouthful of dirt, he sat up. Urmi and Sulu were the first to come to him.

"So the guns decided things after all," the prince said, sounding sad and puzzled.

Sulu had done his best to be cheerful during the victory banquet, but as soon as he could, he made his excuses and left. He walked slowly through the palace —past groups of servants busy scrubbing away the last signs of the massacre—until he came to the stairs leading to the observatory.

When Sulu entered, Mr. Spock looked up from the scroll that he was reading by the light of a lamp. "I thought you would still be celebrating, Mr. Sulu."

Sulu hesitated. Mr. Spock was perhaps the last person Sulu would have picked for a heartfelt conversation; but there was no one else. "Sir, I suppose you've heard about the battle."

Mr. Spock rested the scroll on his stomach. "Why do you ask questions for which you already know the answers?"

Sulu felt uncomfortable staring down at Mr. Spock as he lay on his pallet, but Sulu would have felt equally uneasy if he had sat down in the nearby chair. "I took control of the prince's army, sir, in direct violation of the Prime Directive."

"It would seem so, Lieutenant. May I ask why?"

Sulu might have been talking to one of the statues within the chapel for all the expression on Mr. Spock's face. "I couldn't allow the prince to lose."

"It isn't our place to play favorites." Mr. Spock began to roll up the scroll.

"But it was more than the prince, sir." Sulu spread out his hands. "This whole world could have become a bloodbath."

"Though probabilities of violence were high, we cannot be sure." Mr. Spock added the scroll to a pyramid of scrolls beside him. "Nor can we be sure that Rahu would not have become a good emperor—or that some stronger, better form of union might have emerged from the chaos."

Sulu felt like slumping in a chair, but he forced himself to stand. "And what are the probabilities of the latter two events, sir?"

"Low," Mr. Spock admitted. "But even so, we are not allowed to influence events or shape worlds to suit our own purposes—however high-minded they may be."

"Sir, isn't choosing not to act an action in itself?"

"Yes, but that choice has been made for us." Mr.

Spock folded his two hands together over his chest. "And by joining Star Fleet you have agreed to that choice."

Sulu swallowed. Whatever contact they'd made between them—however small—now seemed to be gone. "Yes, sir."

Mr. Spock picked up another scroll and began to unroll it. "The *Enterprise* will be back within communication range in a few days. I suggest you let me do the talking."

Sulu licked his lips nervously. "And what will you say, sir?"

Mr. Spock raised his eyebrows. "What I need to, Lieutenant." And, raising the scroll so that it hid his face, he began to read. "Now I suggest you turn in. We have a great deal of work to do and I want to begin the first thing tomorrow morning."

Though Sulu desperately wanted to discuss the matter more, he knew there was no use arguing with Mr. Spock. "Yes, sir," he said and, pivoting on his heel, he left the observatory.

EPILOGUE

As Sulu sat at a table in the palace observatory and listened to the sounds of the palace below, the Federation with all of its rules and court-martial boards seemed far away. The mythic figures after whom the Angiran constellations had been named were carved into the marble walls and the floor was an intricate arabesque created from the signs that formed the Angiran zodiac. The ornate brass telescope stood on its pedestal, looking more like a cannon than an astronomical instrument.

But then Captain Kirk's voice came loudly over Mr. Spock's communicator. "McCoy and I are beaming down now, Mr. Spock, so don't go running off."

"I wasn't planning on doing so, Captain." Mr. Spock lay flat on his back upon a pallet on the floor of the observatory. Sulu had to admire his fellow officer's calmness, but then he had done nothing as drastic as Sulu had.

With an uneasy feeling in his heart, Sulu stood and

came to attention as twin columns of sparkling light filled the room and he heard the familiar crystalline shimmering sound. McCoy gave a little jump when he saw how close he was to the telescope. "Good Lord. What's gotten into Scotty? I could have materialized right in the middle of the thing."

Kirk glanced at the telescope. "Well, you would have made an interesting centerpiece for the mess table then."

"If I have to zap my atoms around through space, I expect a little sympathy at least," McCoy grumbled.

"You are always welcome to walk," Mr. Spock observed from his pallet.

Holding his medical kit in front of him like a shield, McCoy strolled over to Mr. Spock. "Somehow I don't think this is quite what the captain had in mind when he left you two behind. You were supposed to keep the door open, not kick it down."

Sulu guiltily slid the cylindrical cap over the writing brush. He was sure that Mr. Spock had detailed his crimes when they had first opened communication with the *Enterprise* several days ago. "I realize that, Doctor."

Kirk shoved the telescope experimentally. It swung easily a few degrees before he stopped it. "And do you also realize that diplomacy does not mean getting involved in the middle of a civil war—let alone stop a charging army?"

Every visible centimeter of Sulu colored. "Yes, sir. But—"

"But what, Mr. Sulu?" Kirk demanded.

Sulu knew that there could be no excuses for his actions. "Nothing, sir."

"Tell me, Mr. Sulu." Kirk balanced an arm on the

telescope's pedestal. "Doesn't the academy still require a study on xenopolitics?"

"It still does, sir," Sulu admitted. It was, in fact, one of the tougher courses at the academy.

Kirk laced his fingers together. "And among other things, didn't your instructor cover the rules governing intervention within another planet's internal affairs?"

"Yes, sir." Sulu felt as if he were being rehearsed for his court-martial.

"And you passed the course?"

"You know he did, Jim." McCoy removed the bandage from Spock's wound. "Otherwise, he wouldn't be here."

"I'll put my explanation into my report." Or, Sulu thought to himself, into his letter of resignation.

Mr. Spock looked up from the wax tablet on which he was making his calculations. "Captain, it isn't like you to discipline someone after this much badgering. I must therefore conclude that the issue is now non-existent."

"Have you taken up mind reading at a distance?" McCoy reached for his tricorder.

Mr. Spock resumed writing on the wax tablet. "When the captain must bite someone, he bites quickly. He doesn't bark a lot before he does it."

Sulu stared in surprise when Kirk broke into one of his broad smiles. "Sir?"

Kirk straightened. He had been as startled as anyone to hear about his two crewmen's troubles—and also perhaps a little guilty. It had been a big burden to place upon the young helmsman's shoulders. And it was as much relief as anything else that had made him pretend to give Sulu a hard time. "I just wanted to make you sweat a little so that you'd think twice before you go off and rescue the next prince and his planet. You may not have Mr. Spock to help you talk your way out of trouble."

Mr. Spock finished the calculations and laid the tablet near Sulu's foot so he could pick it up. "Am I to assume that Star Fleet command accepted my interpretation of matters?"

McCoy turned on his tricorder and began to examine the wound. "We just fed it into a computer to translate it into bureaucratese, and they answered in the same language. As far as we can make out, they've accepted your actions."

"I simply applied logic to the situation—and referred them to a few of Professor Farsalia's more abstruse works on the process of social change." Spock reached toward the stack of blank wax tablets. "I'm glad that they saw reason." Mr. Spock frowned as the doctor's tricorder blocked his view of the tablet. "Doctor, I am trying to work."

"And so am I, Spock," McCoy snapped. "I'm the one who has to patch everyone up after they go barging around on some adventure."

Mr. Spock began to work on the new tablet. "Somehow I don't think a medical excuse would have made the bandits leave me alone."

"But what did you say, Mr. Spock?" Sulu asked. He was still a little dazed at finding himself off the hook.

Mr. Spock spoke absently, almost in a monotone, as his mind concentrated on the next problem. "I simply explained to the captain that we happened to be with the legitimate head of the government. And"—Mr. Spock paused for a moment before he finished an equation—"I seriously questioned whether Rahu could be taken as a genuine rebel."

"He sure did a good imitation of one," Sulu said. Apparently Mr. Spock hadn't abandoned him after all.

"True political rebels do not act as if they were conducting a blood feud." Mr. Spock fingered his stylus while he considered the next equation. "I made inquiries while I was his prisoner and as far as I could ascertain his chief policy was for revenge."

McCoy snapped off his tricorder. "I think you're splitting hairs, Mr. Spock."

Mr. Spock wrote down the final part of the equation. "Mr. Sulu simply did what the prince would have done had he been conscious. In fact, I have been rather impressed by the energy the prince has thrown into creating a program of reforms." Mr. Spock paused long enough to eye the doctor. "He has done remarkably well, don't you think?"

"Are you hinting in your not-so-subtle Vulcan way that you were right and I was wrong about the prince?" McCoy examined the poultice on Mr. Spock with a professional curiosity.

Mr. Spock twisted his head so that he could consult an Angiran star map nailed to the wall. "The thought had crossed my mind, Doctor—as it has on so many other occasions."

"I'll just bet it has." McCoy reached for his medical kit. "You're only programmed to find out what's right and what's wrong."

Mr. Spock's eyes studied the star map critically. "Grant me a certain flexibility at least. Unlike a certain Lord Bhima, I do not insist that my way is the only one."

"Well, you certainly do make a big noise about using your powers of logic." McCoy selected an antibiotic suitable for Mr. Spock's physiology.

271

Mr. Spock looked back to his tablet. "I merely *suggest* to people that logic is the best strategy for dealing with life. But I am willing to acknowledge that there are other methods—even if they *are* less efficient."

McCoy slipped the vial of antibiotic into the hypospray. "That's right. We're so inefficient because we spend all that time looking for happiness when we could be pondering such weighty problems as how many angels can dance on the head of a pin."

Mr. Spock lowered the tablet abruptly. It was as if he had been setting up the doctor for this moment. "Even happiness may be relative, Doctor. My contentment comes with knowledge and the ultimate objective of knowledge is to learn about one's self."

McCoy made an adjustment to the dial of the hypospray. "Well, wouldn't you be happier among fellow seekers?"

"No, Doctor. One can learn the most where two cultures overlap and where they differ. Such knowledge becomes clearest when there is a definite contrast—as light with dark, as a human with an ape, or"—Mr. Spock raised his tablet again—"as myself with you."

Kirk crossed his calves. "I think you've just been insulted, Doctor."

"I *know* I have." McCoy set the hypospray against Spock's leg and sent the antibiotic into Spock with a soft, serpentine hiss. "Well, that poultice actually seems to have kept away any infection, but this is just a precaution."

"It's rather fascinating how easy it was to replace you, Doctor." Mr. Spock's stylus began to scratch thin, spidery lines into the wax. "I simply headed for the nearest village and found a little old man who knew a few herbal cures. A pity he went home to rebuild his village, or he might have been able to teach you something."

McCoy removed the poultice and put it into a sample bag for later analysis. "He shouldn't take any credit. Everyone knows how hard it is to kill Vulcans. All the little gears in their heads keep on turning mechanically even when their bodies have been dead for days." But despite his harsh words, McCoy conscientiously began to clean the wound.

Chuckling to himself, Kirk motioned for Sulu to resume his seat. "I don't know how Mr. Spock was, but Dr. McCoy's been almost unbearable. He's had all these psychological barbs growing into spines because no one else has a hide tough enough to take them."

Sulu slid the cap from the writing brush and once again began transcribing the calculations from a wax tablet to a sheet of parchment. "I guess we had other channels for our aggressions, sir."

The captain plucked at Sulu's sleeve. "Even so, I don't think it's any excuse to be out of uniform." Both Sulu and Mr. Spock were in the tunics, shorts and sandals of the prince's army.

"It was either wear these outfits or wear rags, Captain. And since we didn't want the Angirans to think Federation officers were underpaid, we let the prince's tailor provide these." On a separate piece of parchment, Sulu made a note for a series of lectures he would deliver to the Angiran astronomers.

Since the observatory door was open, Urmi knocked at the doorframe. "They were offered commissions in the imperial army, Captain, but they refused." She strode into the room and they could see that she was wearing a plain iron cuirass. "I don't know why. They would have had their own tent and all the *amma* they could eat." She smiled down at Mr. Spock. "Won't you reconsider, Mr. Spock? Who will teach me about moons and planets?"

"Mr. Sulu and I are leaving behind more than enough material for you to study." Mr. Spock lay the old tablet down on his stomach and reached a hand to the side, groping blindly for a fresh one.

Urmi picked up a new wax tablet and placed it in his hand. "But a piece of dry parchment won't have half your charm."

"Oh, I don't know about that." McCoy applied the new bandage over Spock's wound.

The prince leaned against the doorway. Like Urmi, he wore a cuirass. "I rather suspect, Urmi, that Mr. Spock has had his fill of campaigning in the dirt and smoke." He came over to Mr. Spock's pallet. "Nonetheless, I wish you would stay longer."

As if he were embarrassed by all this attention and wanted to hide it, Mr. Spock nodded his head to the prince and began to make new calculations. "The *Enterprise* is assigning a number of advisers to help you. And the Federation will be sending more. They will all be quite capable."

"But will they have your sensitivity or insight?" The prince bowed his head first to Mr. Spock and then to the doctor.

McCoy dipped his head in an Angiran farewell. "Sensitivity and insight from Mr. Spock? Don't tell me there's a side to him that he keeps hidden on board the ship."

"Perhaps he's like Dr. Jekyll and Mr. Hyde," the prince suggested as he turned.

Captain Kirk folded his arms over his chest. "And what brings out the Mr. Hyde in him?"

"I think it's more like *who,* Captain." The prince inclined his head to Kirk.

The captain lowered his head in return and then flipped the back of his fingers toward the prince's armor. "Surely, things aren't so bad in this room that you had to come here with protection."

The prince tapped his finger against the metal cuirass. "We're off to end the last pockets of resistance, Captain, so I thought we'd better say good-bye."

Urmi peered at McCoy curiously. "Are you McCoy?"

McCoy gave a little bow. "At your service."

"You see, my dear." The prince waved his hand at the doctor. "He can be just as courtly as Sulu."

Urmi leaned forward so she could stare at the doctor's smiling face. "Maybe, but I at least thought he'd have fangs." She sounded a little disappointed.

The prince pulled Urmi back with a laugh. "Perhaps he filed them down especially for the occasion." He nodded apologetically to the doctor. "I'm afraid your reputation has preceded you, Doctor."

McCoy glanced down at Mr. Spock. "Aw-oh. I think I'd better consult a lawyer." He rubbed his hands together. "With a little luck, I might be able to attach the next ten years of Mr. Spock's pay for the libel he's done."

"Mr. Spock isn't good at gossip," the prince protested. "He has no head for the delicious sorts of details that set apart good gossip from bad." He glanced over his shoulder at Mr. Sulu. "It was Sulu who described life on board the *Enterprise.*"

"Indeed, Mr. Sulu." Kirk regarded Mr. Sulu with new interest.

Sulu cleared his throat nervously, wondering if he had gotten off of one hook, only to impale himself on top of another. "It was for the sake of art, sir. The court poet wanted details for the epic he's going to write."

The doctor twisted one corner of his mouth up in a sardonic grin. "About you and Spock?"

The prince pretended to measure Spock. "Heroic trimeter will suit Spock, I think."

Urmi squatted down. "They'll be singing your praises for generations, Spock."

"Pity the future," McCoy mumbled.

Spock shifted on the pallet as if he were growing increasingly uncomfortable. "I was simply performing my duties."

"Admirable, admirable," the prince murmured. "I'll have to remember that line. It will make a nice sort of refrain, don't you think?" The prince wagged a finger at Spock. "Oh, and I was supposed to get your full name."

"It wouldn't do you any good," McCoy said. "Your poet would tear his throat apart trying to pronounce it. Vulcans have a lot of little winning ways just like that one."

"Spock should be sufficient," Mr. Spock said firmly, "for poetry or otherwise."

"But I want to do right by you," Urmi insisted, "especially after I misjudged you so badly."

Spock brought the tablet in closer to his face to shut out the others. "I merely followed where you led."

"Now, now, no false modesty, Mr. Spock." The

prince wagged a finger at him. "Or I shall write Professor Farsalia to send a field team to study you. You offer some interesting insights into the role of the Outsider, after all."

"That I'd like to see," McCoy declared with wicked glee. "A whole generation of anthropologists studying Spock in his native habitat."

"I think Professor Farsalia would agree that Mr. Sulu and I were simply catalysts." Mr. Spock faced the star map on the wall. "And now if you'll forgive me, Your Highness. My excursion with you has put me far behind my work schedule."

The prince held out his hand to Urmi and helped her to her feet. "Come, my dear. I recognize an imperial dismissal when I hear one." The two Angirans rose and joined Captain Kirk by the window where he was enjoying the view.

"I regret that we haven't the time to show you the delights of our world," the prince said. "There are more aesthetic and calmer tours than the one I conducted for Sulu and Mr. Spock."

"I understand your sense of urgency, but don't you even have time for a meal aboard the *Enterprise?*" Kirk turned to Urmi. "Or perhaps Urmi would like a short tour."

"I can't trust this great lout out of my sight." Urmi hooked her arm affectionately through the prince's. "I never know when he might get it into his head to fight another duel."

"But I gave you my word that I wouldn't challenge anyone else." The prince pretended to be offended. "After all, I'm losing my swordmaster here."

Sulu could feel his cheeks reddening once again. "I'd

really be just so much spare baggage. You need people who can help you set up a modern constitutional monarchy."

"They can advise me in the complexities of government, but not in the intricacies of the heart." The prince reached a hand into the sash-end of his *soropa* and took out a wheel-lock pistol. "But, at any rate, here is the pistol I used during the battle." He and Urmi strolled over to Sulu. "Keep this so you can remember how you and it changed the destiny of a world."

Sulu took the pistol, letting it rest in his palms like a precious treasure. "I'll put it in the most prominent place in my collection."

Urmi used her free hand to point out the engraving on the pistol that proclaimed it as a gift of friendship from the two Angirans. "Be sure to do more than that. Come back to us soon so you can see the new Angira that's being born."

The prince clapped a hand on Sulu's shoulder. "The poets and storytellers have already started polishing our story. If you wait too long to return, you won't be able to recognize yourself."

Sulu set the gun down on the table. "Just let me know when they start carving the monuments. I want to be there to pose."

"It will be an imperial summons." The prince's hand gave Sulu's shoulder a squeeze and then let go.

"Don't forget that you have roots here now," Urmi reminded him. "If they don't treat you right on that ship of yours, you come right back here." Her arm made a snaking motion through the air. "People need home burrows—even if they never use them."

The prince wriggled a hand in the air as if parrying

cuts and thrusts from invisible swords. "And forgive us if Angira loses some of the flavor of the seventeenth century."

"That doesn't seem so important anymore." Sulu grinned. "After having nearly been stabbed, drowned and eaten, I don't think the seventeenth century is all that it's cracked up to be."

Captain Kirk twisted one corner of his mouth as he looked at Sulu. "So you'll be able to go back to pushing buttons again even if it isn't quite so dashing?"

"Captain, the seventeenth century is something better to be imagined than experienced." And Sulu began to inspect the pistol, delighting in the fine craftsmanship of its wood and metal.

AFTERWORD

I would like to take the time here to thank Ruth Kwitko Lym who was kind enough to help with some details. I'd also like to express my gratitude to Elizabeth Lynn who helped me with the swordfight from *Sanjuro* and to Quinn Yarbro on swordfighting in general. I should add that any mistakes are my own exclusive property.